C000148958

Forged By Iron

Forged By Iron

Olaf's Saga Book I

Eric Schumacher

Copyright (C) 2020 Eric Schumacher
Layout design and Copyright (C) 2020 by Next Chapter
Published 2020 by Legionary – A Next Chapter Imprint
All rights reserved. No part of this book may be reproduced or transmitted in
any form or by any means, electronic or mechanical, including photocopying,
recording, or by any information storage and retrieval system, without the
author's permission.

To my family and friends, for your love, patience, and continued support.

Acknowledgements

There are many people to thank for the creation of this novel. First and foremost, I want to thank you, my readers, for your continued support, your nudges, your reviews of my work, your comments on social media, and for so much more. I again want to thank Marg Gilks and Lori Weathers, whose keen eyes and attention to detail hone my words and my poor use of commas into the story you are about to read. With each book, I endeavor to present a cover that helps set the tone and vision for the story. Thankfully, I have masters like David Brzozowski for layout and Andrew Dodor for imagery, to transform my ideas into a work of art. Thank you, gents. And last but certainly not least, to my publisher, Next Chapter, I thank you for working so hard to get my books into the hands of readers around the world. It is to you all, and to the countless others who have accompanied me on this journey, that I owe a huge debt of gratitude.

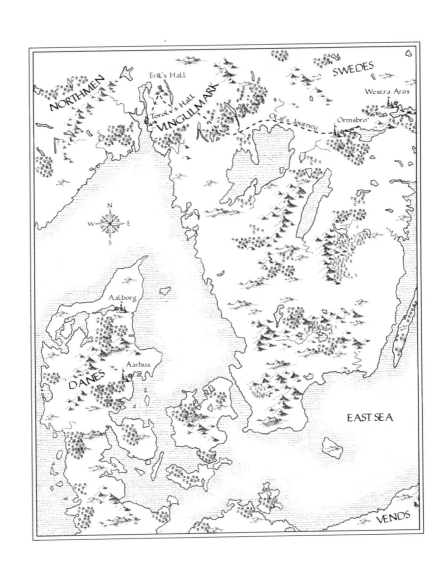

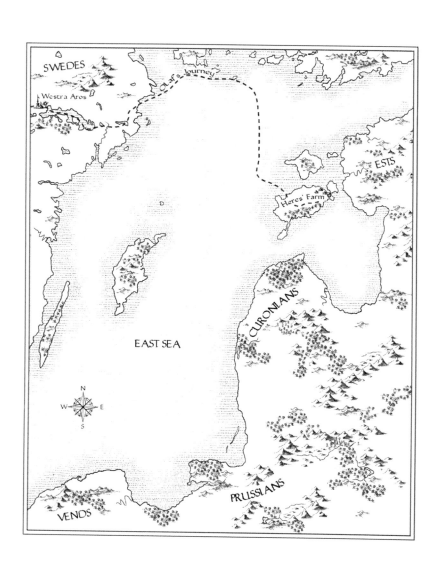

SWEDES

Westra Aros

Olaf's Journey

ESTS

Here's Farm

D

CURONIANS

EAST SEA

N
W   E
S

PRUSSIANS

VENDS

Glossary

Aesir – One of the main tribes of deities venerated by the pre-Christian Norse. Old Norse: Æsir.

Aldeigjuborg – the Old Norse name for a trading post located on the Volkhov River near Lake Ladoga. It was a prosperous outpost in the 8th and 9th centuries. Staraya Lagoda is the Old East Slavic name for the trading post.

bonder – Free men (farmers, craftsmen, etc.) who enjoyed rights such as the use of weapons and the right to attend law-things. They constituted the middle class. Old Norse: baendr.

borg – A fortified settlement.

byrnie – A (usually short-sleeved) chain mail shirt that hung to the upper thigh. Old Norse: brynja.

dragon – A larger class of Viking warship. Old Norse: Dreki.

East Sea – Baltic Sea.

ell – A former measure of length equivalent to roughly forty-five inches.

Estland – One of the Scandinavian names for what is today Estonia. Other names for the area include Eistland and Esthland.

Eysysla – The Old Scandinavian name for the island of Saaremaa.

Frey – Brother to the goddess Freya. He is often associated with virility and prosperity, with sunshine and fair weather. Old Norse: Freyr.

Freya – Sister to god Frey. She is often associated with love, sex, beauty, fertility, gold, magic, war, and death. Old Norse: Freyja.

Frigga – She is the highest-ranking of the Aesir goddesses. She's the wife of Odin, the leader of the gods, and the mother of the god Baldur. She is often confused with Freya. Old Norse: Frigg.

fylke (pl. fylker) – Old Norse for "folkland," which has come to mean "county" or "district" in modern use.

Gardariki – The states controlled by the Scandinavians who settled in that part of ancient Russia and Ukraine.

godi – A heathen priest or chieftain. Old Norse: goði.

Hel – A giantess and/or goddess who rules over the underworld (also named Hel) where many of the dead dwell.

hird – A personal retinue of armed companions who formed the nucleus of a household guard. Hird means "household." Old Norse: hirð.

hirdman (pl. hirdmen) – A member or members of the hird. Old Norse: hirðman.

hlaut – The blood of sacrificed animals.

Hnefatafl – An ancient Norse board game.

Holmgard – Norse name for Novgorod. Old Norse: Holmgarðr.

Irland – Ireland.

jarl – Old Norse for "earl."

jarldom – The area of land that a jarl ruled.

Jel Island – An island off the coast of Vingulmark.

Jormungand – A snake or dragon who lives in the ocean that surrounds Midgard, the visible world. Old Norse: Jörmungandr.

Kattegat – The sea between the Northlands and the Danish lands.

kaupang – Old Norse for "marketplace." It is also the name of the main market town in Norway that existed around AD 800–950.

knarr – A type of merchant ship. Old Norse: knǫrr.

Midgard – The Norse name for Earth and the place inhabited by humans. Old Norse: Miðgarðr.

Night Mare – The Night Mare is an evil spirit that rides on people's chests while they sleep, bringing bad dreams. Old Norse: Mara.

Njord – A god associated with sea, seafaring, wind, fishing, wealth, and crop fertility. Old Norse: Njörðr.

Norns – The three female divine beings who influence the course of a man's destiny by weaving their fates. Their names are Urd (Old Norse: Urðr, "What Once Was"), Verdandi (Old Norse: Verðandi, "What Is Coming into Being"), and Skuld (Old Norse: Skuld, "What Shall Be").

Odin – Husband to Frigga. The god associated with healing, death, royalty, knowledge, battle, and sorcery. He oversees Valhall, the Hall of the Slain. Old Norse: Óðinn.

Orkneyjar – The Orkney Islands.

Prussia – A historical region in Europe, stretching from Gdansk Bay to the end of Curonian Spit on the southeastern coast of the Baltic Sea, and extending inland as far as Masuria. Around AD 800 to 900, the tribes were named Old Prussians.

Rus – According to the *Russian Primary Chronicle* (ca. AD 1040-1118), the Rus were a group of "Varangians," likely of Swedish origin. *Rus* appears to be derived from the Finnish word for Sweden, *Rotsi* (later *Ruotsi*), which in turn comes from Old Swedish *rother*, a word associated with rowing or ships. Russia derives its name from "Rus."

seax – A knife or short sword. Also known as scramaseax, or wounding knife.

sel – A summer cottage typically found on a seter.

seter – An area, typically in the mountains, with a barn where farmers (bonders) brought their livestock (cattle, goats, and sheep) to be milked after a day of grazing in the mountain pastures.

skald – A poet. Old Norse: skald or skáld.

shield wall – A shield wall was a "wall of shields" formed by warriors standing in formation shoulder to shoulder, holding their shields so they abut or overlap. Old Norse: skjaldborg.

steer board – A rudder affixed to the right stern of a ship. The origin of the word "starboard." Old Norse: stýri (rudder) and borð (side of the ship).

skeid – A midsize class of Viking warship.

sköl – A toast to others when drinking. Old Norse: skál.

skyr – Skyr is a fresh sour milk-cheese, but yet consumed like a yogurt.

The Lake – Lake Malaren. During the Viking Age, it was known as *Lǫgrinn*, which means "The Lake."

thing – Also known as law-thing, it is governing assembly of a Viking society or region, made up of the free people of the community and presided over by lawspeakers. Old Norse: þing.

Thor – A hammer-wielding god associated with thunder, lightning, storms, oak trees, strength, and the protection of mankind. Old Norse: Þórr.

thrall – A slave.

Valhall (also Valhalla) – The hall of the slain presided over by Odin. It is where brave warriors chosen by valkyries go when they die. Old Norse: Valhöll.

valkyrie – A female helping spirit of Odin that transports his favorites among those slain in battle to Valhall, where they will fight by his side during the battle at the end of time, Ragnarok. Old Norse: valkyrja (pl. valkyrjur).

Vendland – A name used for the regions east of Lübeck by the Scandinavian peoples since at least before the turn of the tenth century.

Vidar – A little-known Norse god sometimes associated with revenge. During Ragnarok, the god Odin was devoured by the wolf Fenrir. Vidar, a son of Odin by the giantess Gríðr, immediately killed the wolf to avenge his father's death. Old Norse: Víðarr.

Vingulmark – A district on the northeastern side of the waterway the Vikings called the Vik.

Westra Aros – Modern-day Västerås, which is one of the oldest cities in Sweden. The name originates from *Västra Aros* (West Aros). The area has been populated since the Viking Age.

Yngling – Refers to the Fairhair dynasty that descended from the kings of Uplands, Norway, and that traces its lineage back to the god Frey.

Yule – A pagan midwinter festival lasting roughly twelve days. It later became associated with Christmas. Old Norse: Jōl

Part I

There he stood as one who dreamed;
And the red light glanced and gleamed
On the armor that he wore;
And he shouted, as the rifted
Streamers o'er him shook and shifted,
"I accept thy challenge, Thor!"

The Saga of King Olaf

Chapter 1

Vingulmark, Ostfold, Summer, AD 960

I stood on a bluff, peering first at the sea far below, then over at Prince Olaf, the son of King Trygvi. Beneath the amber bangs that danced on his forehead, Olaf's blue eyes were alight and his cheeks round from his smile. I knew why he looked so; I had seen him thus several times before. It was the twinkle of mischief that Olaf got when he was about to embark on some adventure. I hated that look, for it usually involved me, and more oft than not, it landed me in trouble. This adventure was no different, and my stomach roiled with misgivings. For Olaf was only eight winters old, and I only twelve, and the drop to the sea was farther than I remembered it being.

My name is Torgil, son of Torolv, the lord of an island called Jel, an island on the coastline of Vingulmark in the Ostfold, which my father had earned in his service to the king. Men called Torolv "Loose-beard" on account of his wild beard and his violence in battle, but also in jest, for he was known to let his words loose when he lost his temper, which was often and mostly aided by ale. I suppose I inherited that temper, though I needed no ale to stoke it.

3

My father once told me that he had known little peace in his life, and I believed it. He spoke little of it to me, but I heard many of the stories in our hall when other men came to visit. Decades before my birth, my father had joined Jarl Trygvi's men in helping the good King Hakon drive Erik Bloodaxe from the land. He had been no more than a boy then. While Erik's removal had brought some peace to the realm, there was never truly any rest from the fighting. Incursions from the land-hungry Danes and marauding sea kings kept the men of Vingulmark in a constant state of battle, which I suppose had much to do with my father's temper.

When I was seven winters old, the sons of Erik Bloodaxe returned to the North with vengeance in their hearts and a will to see it through. After many battles and with the help of the Danes, they finally killed King Hakon and took the High Seat for their own. Not a fortnight after Hakon's loss, my own mother, a raven-haired, green-eyed woman from a land far to the west, took ill and died. King Hakon had been a good and just king, and my mother a wise and gentle partner, and their loss struck as deep as any well-swung blade against soft flesh could. I still remember the tears that flowed from my father's eyes and the copious amounts of ale he drank to dry them. I remember too the sadness and loneliness and fear that defined my days and nights during that time, for my father's temper was as capricious as the uneasy peace that had settled on the realm. Had it not been for my father's maidservant, Helga, I know not how I would have survived.

Not two summers after my mother's death, Harald Eriksson, the oldest remaining son of the Bloodaxe brood, brought death to Hakon's loyal friend and kinsman, Sigurd, jarl of Lade. I was nine winters old by then and remember clearly how my father raged at that news and how he began the work to protect our people from a similar fate. Knowing that King Harald would come for us next, my father built a new hall on a hill that lay on the southernmost tip — and most strategic point — of the island he ruled. The hill he chose was heavily forested and we spent long days felling trees and clearing the hilltop until we could see the Vik stretching southward before us. On clear days, I could even see the dark line of Vestfold to the west.

A beautiful place, that hilltop borg. But more importantly, a protected place that would be hard to take, should Harald Eriksson come for us. It was my first taste of hard work and it left calluses on my hands as thick as gloves. But at the end of it, my father was well pleased with the fort and palisade and hall that we had built from Jel's stout timber.

It was at that time that Jarl Trygvi elevated his title to "king", for he would not be known in the land as inferior in rank to Harald Eriksson. It was also during that time that the new King Trygvi began to visit us. Whereas my father used to go to him, now he, his family, his hird, and many of his nobles came to us, for our lands lay at the midpoint of Vingulmark and could be reached by sail or wagon. Each spring our household scrambled to prepare space and food for them all, and each summer they arrived by the dozens with their entourages to plan and prepare. My father grumbled at the burden, but deep down I think he enjoyed the activity and the honor of hosting the king. Though he still fought by the king's side when called, he had long since stepped aside as one of his household warriors, and I think he missed that prestige. In some small way, these visits replaced that absence.

I also think my father enjoyed seeing Queen Astrid, whom he and my mother, before her death, had fostered in her youth. It had been my father who had introduced the girl to King Trygvi, a bond that had further solidified my father's standing with the king and with her father, a nobleman who lived in the north of Vingulmark. But equally important, my father was fond of Astrid. Though he would never admit to it, I think she filled part of the hole left by the loss of my mother.

Which brings me back to the present and why I was there with the son of King Trygvi and Queen Astrid, about to make a witless leap into the cold sea. About us stood a dozen other boys, all of them older and the sons of my father's men and other nobles, all of them calling for us to get on with it and jump. I knew them well, though I cannot say I liked them much, especially at that moment. Many had done this jump before, and I did not like how they hounded us.

The actual jump did not concern me. I was small for my age, but I was agile too. I was confident I could leap and land correctly. My concern was for Prince Olaf, who was my charge each summer when the king visited. Should something ill befall him, I would not only feel the wound of worry for the boy, but also the sting of my father's lash for my failure, and the scorn of the king. Of the three, it was my father's lash and disapproval I feared the most.

It only made matters worse that Olaf had not been invited on this adventure. I had wanted to make the jump alone to prove myself to the older boys. But Olaf had heard me boasting to the others and so had begged to come along. I had tried to refuse him because the jump was dangerous and my father had put Olaf under my protection, but my protests went unheeded by the others. They wanted to see the king's son leap into the sea. Olaf, they argued, had the right to come, despite its danger. Inside, I knew that they did not care what an injury to him might mean to me — should something go wrong, they were not to blame — and I cursed them for that. And so instead of jumping alone, Olaf stood beside me, smiling, and I prayed to any god who would listen to keep Olaf safe from harm.

"You jump here," said a freckle-faced blond boy named Ulf, pointing at a spot on the bluff where a small stone jutted from the earth. He was the son of a landholder on Jel Island whose farm, Thordruga, lay close to my father's hall. The farm's name meant "compost heap," so naturally, as children will do in their cruelty, we called Ulf, "Dung Heap."

"I know where I am to jump, Dung Heap," I hissed as I removed my shoes and cloak and stepped to the edge of the bluff. Far below, the murky sea rolled toward the coast and crashed onto the stony beach. It would be cold, I knew, but the chill would not rival the pain of landing poorly. "I will go first," I said to Olaf, who stood behind me. "If it is safe, then I will call to you to come after me."

The smile on Olaf's pudgy face stretched. I knew that look and lifted my hands. "Olaf! No!"

Olaf ran forward. "See you at the bottom," he hollered as he sprinted for the ledge and leaped into the air. The boys yelled their delight at Olaf's zeal, drowning out my own holler of dismay, for I had seen his foot slip as he vaulted from the ledge.

Olaf never had a chance. From the moment he flew from the cliff, he struggled to keep his balance. His arms flailed. His feet pumped as if trying to run on the wind. But there was no stopping his body's momentum and its inexorable tilt. His whoop turned to a shriek as his frame inched ever more sideways. I watched hopelessly, unable to right his fall or help him. He hit the water with a smack of such awkward force that it echoed off the bluff and up to our awaiting ears.

Without another thought, I leaped, my eyes focused on the spot where Olaf had vanished beneath the ocean's surface in a fountain of white spray. My stomach lurched and my arms flailed as I flew downward, struggling to stay upright and to keep my feet beneath me. I could feel my clothes rippling and my dark ponytail flying up behind me. The water that moments before had looked so far away rushed at me with alarming speed. As I hit it, I felt first the sting of the ocean's surface as it smacked my open palm. The cold water then embraced me and my body shot downward through the grayness. My bare feet landed on something slick and slimy, and I imagined the giant sea monster Jormungand lurking in the depths. I recoiled and struggled to rise, kicking and floundering until my head broke the ocean's surface.

Ten paces away, the water churned where Olaf had entered. He had yet to surface and I swam to the spot, then dove into the grayness, my eyes stinging from the salt and the chill as I scanned the murk. Nothing. Panicked, I dove deeper, craning my neck in every direction to locate my friend. It was then that I glimpsed something white far beneath me. I dove even deeper and grabbed for Olaf's body. My fingers clutched something — a tunic, mayhap — and I pulled and kicked for the surface. But I had not expected the weight of Olaf's body, which moved upward with my yanks, but not quickly enough. My lungs burned as I kicked and heaved. My limbs tingled.

Above, beyond the ocean's surface, the sky beckoned like a portal to a different world. So close, and yet, with Olaf weighing me down, beyond my reach. I redoubled my efforts but made little progress. We would both perish if I did not release my grip. And yet, I could not. I would die with my charge before letting him go.

More arms suddenly reached out for us. Other boys had come to our rescue and now pulled Olaf upward. To air. To safety. Relieved of my burden, I kicked violently to rise and gasped for breath as soon as my mouth broke the water's plane. It was a foolish thing to do, for no sooner had I opened my mouth than I swallowed a mouthful of seawater and coughed violently. Beside me, the other boys began pulling Olaf's unconscious body shoreward, his young face pointed toward the bleak sky. I did my best to follow with my tingling limbs and my racing heart.

"Get him on his side," said Ulf as soon as the boys had pulled his body beyond the crashing surf and laid him on the pebbled beach. Olaf moaned as the boys turned his body. Then, suddenly, he spewed his belly's contents onto the rocks. Ulf patted his back, and Olaf lurched again, his bile and recently chewed food mixing with the gray water on the stones.

"He will live," Ulf said with obvious relief.

"Thank the gods," replied another.

I sat back with my rump on the pebbles and wiped the moisture from my face. It was then, in the aftermath of the leap, that my emotions washed over me. That Olaf had stolen my moment before the others, and come so close to death in doing so, infuriated me, and it took every fiber of my young body to keep from beating the little turd further. Beside me, the prince vomited again and all my angry mind could think was that it served him right. At that moment, I hoped he vomited a dozen times. I spat seawater from my mouth and turned my eyes to the sea, away from the boys fawning over the prince.

And that is when I spied the ship.

Chapter 2

The ship sat low in the water, its sweeps dipping and pulling, propelling it through the undulating sea like a graceful serpent. A warship.

Ulf rose.

"Who are they?" I asked as I stood with the others. No sail hung from its mast, so the ship was hard to identify.

"Holger Einarsson," responded Ulf.

Holger was a noble who lived to the south, on the border with the Danes who had recently overwhelmed the Swedes in that area. I knew little about him save that he was loyal to King Trygvi and that he had married a Danish woman in order to keep the peace in his lands. I supposed he had come at the request of the king, just as the others had, and so I thought little of his appearance save that he was a friend and not a foe.

"Come," said Ulf. "Let us go see what news he brings from the south."

I kicked my friend who still moaned on the ground. "Get up."

"Leave him be, Torgil," Ulf spat, eyeing me malignantly. This was a king's son, his gaze said to me, and I had no business kicking him. His look only incensed me more. As is oft the case with me, even now, I was having trouble containing my ire and cared little for his thoughts. He pulled Olaf to his feet. "Come, Olaf. Before Torgil hurts you more."

The journey back to King Trygvi's hall was slow and unpleasant, at least for me. It was not far from the bluff to the hall, but it was uphill, and Olaf was weak and needed the support of the others. I too was weak, not to mention cold and wet, but I refused to have the others help me, which only magnified my torment. I was too proud, I suppose. And too angry. So instead of walking with the others and engaging in their excited banter about Olaf's exploits, I plodded along behind, my thoughts locked on the misadventure like a falcon's talons. I had known Olaf for much of my life, and I knew — I knew! — that he would rob me of my glory. That is why I had not wanted him there and why his near drowning, and now the attention the others gave him, angered me so.

Funny, but I do not recall worrying at the time how close he — or I — had come to death. My father often talked with his comrades by the hearth about the blade-thin gap between life and death. How the lucky shift of a head in the shield wall, or the decision to go right rather than left meant life for one and death for another. And how the Norns, those weavers of a man's fate, wielded the blades that cut the threads of a man's life for simply taking a wrong step. None of those thoughts came to me then. I suppose they should have, but I was young, and my mind saw things more simply.

"What happened today stays among us," I grumbled as the group drew nearer to the walls surrounding our borg. "If any of our parents hear of it, it will be punishment for us all."

Ulf laughed. "A beating for you, mayhap. Not for me. And not for the others. You alone are Olaf's keeper, are you not? Yet it was we who pulled Olaf from the sea."

The others laughed at that, stoking my rage further. "Damn the lot of you," I cursed them, but they only laughed louder.

I have said this before: my father's borg stood on the crest of a hill from which one could see in every direction. It sloped down in the east to a large bay and, across it, the heavily forested mainland of Vingulmark. Holger's ship had arrived and was now tied to my father's dock, where my father, King Trygvi, and Queen Astrid, stood to welcome the newcomers. A larger group of onlookers stood on the strand, barely glancing in our direction as we descended through the fort to join them. As the greetings concluded, King Trygvi draped his burly arm over Holger's smaller shoulders and, with my father and Queen Astrid trailing, marched back through the palisades and up into the massive hall that lorded over the landscape.

We boys waited until the other guests had departed, then headed for the doors of the now crowded hall. Inside, a fire crackled in the long hearth that ran down the center of the cavernous space, bathing the interior in a soft, warm light that danced on the guests and shield-bedecked walls. My father's thralls wove through the mingling crowd, doing their best to deliver drinks and platters of food to the eating boards where the guests were beginning to take their seats.

"Please, sit," boomed my father's voice. The hall was his. Therefore it was he — not the king — who presided.

Olaf and I kept to the shadows near the hall's entrance. "Put on your hood," I commanded him icily. "It will hide your swollen face." Olaf nodded and followed my direction. "Come." I made my way to a table where Ulf and some of the other boys huddled around two of my father's young hirdmen.

The older of the two hirdmen was a newly sworn warrior named Ubbi, who was Ulf's older brother. Not long before, Ubbi had been like so many of us: just a son of a local bonder looking for adventure and awaiting his chance to prove himself. My father had honored him and his family the previous summer by elevating him to his hird, for during those times, my father needed as many warriors as he could afford. Ubbi normally sat at the table with my father's other hirdmen, but this night, he was among the boys. Beside him Ingvar, his lifelong friend and another of the newly anointed hirdmen, sat nodding and grinning at something Ubbi was saying. Olaf and I slid onto the bench near them.

"They are going a-viking and want us to join them," Ubbi was saying in a hushed voice. It was clear he was speaking of Holger Einarsson and his men.

"When?" asked Ulf with barely contained excitement.

"Soon, little brother," said Ubbi, scuffing Ulf's red hair.

This response had us looking at each other, then back at Ubbi. I stole a piece of lamb from my neighbor's trencher and popped it into my mouth. "What did King Trygvi say to that?" I asked between chews.

Ubbi shrugged. "He has not said anything yet."

"I would be surprised if King Trygvi decides to go," offered Ingvar.

"Why?" responded Olaf defensively. "My father loves to fight."

Ingvar smiled at the prince. "Aye, he does. But Erik's sons are not to be trusted, which is why he has not raided, the past two summers. They could come while Trygvi and his army are away and steal you," Ingvar said with a wolfish grin before poking the lad in the ribs. Olaf jerked and giggled.

"I am sure he is considering Holger's offer," added Ubbi. "I, for one, yearn to go."

My gaze shifted to the dais at the far end of the hall, where King Trygvi was taking a seat behind the eating table. He was a bear of a man whose frame filled his chair and whose ruddy face was encircled by a mane of brown streaked with strands of gray. An elegant blue cloak draped over his broad shoulders, partially covering his white tunic. Silver bands encircled his wrists. Gold rings adorned his fingers. A thin gold band lay cockeyed around the crown of his head. To his left, the young Queen Astrid sat upright and alert, her curvaceous frame lost in the folds and shine of her finery. To King Trygvi's right, in the place of honor, sat an empty chair. It was intended for my father, but he usually preferred to move about the hall during a feast so that he could mingle with the guests.

Holger Einarsson had settled with the local nobles at the table nearest the dais. He was not the largest of men, but size is not always an indicator of skill. Men oft spoke of his quickness and cunning. Like an adder with his sword, they said, though it was hard to say whether that was truth or merely the gushing words of a gold-starved skald. The adder part of the description was at least fitting, for he resembled a snake, with a tanned toughness to his skin and a serpentine darkness to his eyes. His black hair fell in greasy waves to his shoulders, framing a gaunt face that was half concealed by the long, black braids of his beard.

I turned to the nearest serving girl, whose name was Turid. She was the daughter of Queen Astrid's favored maidservant, the widow Sigrunn. The two of them attended the queen wherever she went, though Turid liked it little, I could tell. When time permitted, she was oft out playing with the boys, a preoccupation that vexed her mother mightily. She was not much older than me, just as tall, as thin as a twig, and as graceful as a deer when she ran. Her braided hair was the color of the hearth fire, her eyes like a spring sky, and her pale skin was dotted with orange freckles. When our paths crossed — which was not as frequently as I would have liked — I wanted nothing more than to impress her, though I usually embarrassed myself miserably in my attempts.

I grabbed a wooden cup from her tray as she passed.

Her blue eyes widened. "It is ale, master Torgil."

I was about to reply when my father appeared behind the girl and my eyes shifted to his looming figure. He was a boulder of a man, with broad shoulders and a thick chest over which he wore a rich, woolen cloak fastened at his left shoulder by a copper brooch. His pronounced forehead fell like a stone wall to two bushy brows under which his dark eyes regarded me closely. A broken nose attested to a life that had seen its fair share of battles and struggles. Hair the color of sun-kissed wheat cascaded down his back in a neat braid, though he was mostly known for his bushy beard. In truth, he was a frightening figure to behold, which is why, upon seeing him, Turid ducked her head and moved on to the next table.

I sat with my mouth agape. My father plucked the ale cup from my hand and sniffed at it. A crease formed between his brows. "You are too young to drink ale."

"I did not know it was ale when I grabbed the cup, Father. I seek only water and food."

He motioned to me with the cup. "You are wet."

"We were swimming, Father." I motioned to my now silent comrades, who knew of his fiery temper and knew too that one misspoken word might ignite it.

"Warm yourself by the hearth before the chill sets in."

I was about to thank him for his advice when King Trygvi's resonant voice silenced the crowd. "Ah," he called. "My son has returned with his host." At his words, all eyes turned to us boys, and my stomach lurched. "Come, Olaf. Pay your respects to Holger Einarsson." King Trygvi gestured toward the newly arrived guest.

Holger studied Olaf intently as the boy rose from our table and approached. Olaf nodded to the man from beneath his hood. "Welcome, Holger Einarsson," he squeaked. "It is an honor to see you again."

Holger nodded his thanks and pointed with his knife at Olaf. "You grow quickly, Prince Olaf. Sooner than you think, you will be in the shield wall with us, eh? Your father should bring you along on the adventure I just presented to him."

King Trygvi smiled politely to acknowledge Holger's words but waved the guest silent. "In due time, Holger. In due time." His brows suddenly bent over his eyes. "Why do you hide in your hood, Olaf? Show yourself to us."

Olaf hesitantly removed his hood. The conversation stilled.

King Trygvi leaned forward in his chair. "Is that a bruise on your face?"

My father glanced at me, and in that mere glance, I could see the storm clouds forming. I tensed.

"Yes, Father," Olaf answered. To his credit, he withstood the king's withering gaze. Olaf may have been a young fool, but he did not lack for courage.

The king's eyes scanned the hall, then came to rest again on his son. "How came you by this bruise?" There was a growing edge in his tone. "Did someone do this to you?"

Queen Astrid's blue eyes found me. My father noticed her look and placed a restraining hand on my shoulder.

Olaf ran his hand over his cheek. "I jumped from the bluff, Father," Olaf explained, his voice clear in the now hushed hall, "and landed poorly."

The king studied his son for a long time. I held my breath as my father's grip tightened on my shoulder. The other guests waited too. Only the crackle of the flames in the hearth could be heard. Then, suddenly, the king burst into laughter. "By the gods, Olaf, that is a long fall. It is no wonder you are bruised."

The guests chuckled hesitantly. All, that is, save my father and the queen. Queen Astrid's call pierced the laughter. "Torgil Torolvson. Come here."

I swallowed hard and stepped forward as the laughter died and the eyes of every guest turned upon me. Most looked concerned, though Holger seemed amused by my discomfiture. My former foster sister leaned forward in her chair as I bowed to her and to the king in turn. She had grown from an awkward, pimple-faced adolescent into a beautiful young woman, tall and fair, with golden hair that rested in waves on her buxom chest. As a youth, she had been a happy child, carefree in nature, but much of that temperament was gone now, lost to the pressures of her stature as a queen. As I stood before her now, her face took on a stony countenance, her freckles vanishing behind the heat in her cheeks. "Is it not your duty to protect my son? Why did you allow him to do this?"

"I —"

"He did not allow me," Olaf blurted. "I went with Torgil and the other boys to see them jump. When I got to the bluff, my excitement took hold of me and I jumped before Torgil or the others could stop me. In truth, I tripped as I jumped, which is why I landed so poorly. It was foolish."

I glanced up into the queen's narrowing blue eyes, then turned my own eyes to the rush-covered floor. My knees felt weak, my stomach sick. Olaf's intentions had been good. He had tried to put himself at fault, but my ears, like the queen's, had heard a different tale — a tale that pointed to my own failure to protect him. "I am sorry I did not do more to protect Olaf," I mumbled.

The king and queen sat back in their chairs. There was mirth in the king's eyes, and something else besides. Pride, perchance? But not so with Astrid, who was still frowning. "We will talk of this later, Torgil," she said. "Now, both of you, leave us." She excused us with a backhand wave. We dutifully turned away.

"That went well." Olaf grinned.

I did not share his delight, for my father waited in the back of the hall, his powerful arms folded over his chest, his eyes boring into me. All I felt was a distinct sinking in the pit of my stomach. "You should have kept your lips tight," I hissed.

Olaf gawked at me. "I protected you."

"You made matters worse."

"Wiggled your way out of another one, eh, Olaf?" joked Ubbi as we returned to our table. The others grinned at Ubbi's words. A frown pulled my face downward, which did not escape Ubbi's keen eye. "Worry not, Torgil. A few good lashings and this whole matter will be behind you." The group laughed. Olaf now frowned, though I was certain he still did not understand what he had done.

I glanced at my father and swallowed hard at the thunder I saw in his features. I knew that look all too well, and knew too that I would need to avoid him this night. If the ale took hold of him and his eyes landed on me, I had no doubt he would beat me.

That cruel thought had just settled on my mind when King Trygvi stood at the dais and hoisted his cup. "My warriors. My oath-sworn. Lend me an ear." The hall fell silent. "In the coming days, Holger Einarsson will raid in the land of the Vends," he announced with a sweep of his paw toward his guest. "He has invited us to partake in his adventure. I, for one, would like to feast my eyes on the open sea again. It has been too long."

"And feed your blade on Vendish blood!" called a boisterous warrior named Tofi from one of the tables.

King Trygvi laughed and pointed his cup at the man. "Aye, that too, Tofi!" He turned back to the room. "Fear not, ladies, it will be but a quick raid. We can ill afford to be gone too long, with Harald Eriksson and his brothers so anxious to take our lands. For that reason, I am leaving Lord Torolv and half of my men here to guard Jel, and to protect my family as well."

The guests exchanged glances, though it was hard for me to interpret their expressions in the hall's gloom.

Before I could ponder on this longer, King Trygvi stepped from the dais and began walking among the guests. "If I tap your shoulder, you shall accompany me to Vendland."

Time has faded the names of those chosen by the king, but it was clear as the men stood that King Trygvi valued age over experience in his choosing for this adventure. Ubbi and Ingvar were chosen, as were many of the other younger warriors, while many of the older men who had followed Trygvi on countless exploits remained seated. The casual onlooker could not have sensed my father's displeasure, but I knew him well and could see his jaw working beneath his beard. I thought he might challenge the king's decision, but instead, he guzzled his ale and held his tongue.

I turned back to my companions and joined in a toast to Ubbi and Ingvar, though I found it difficult to quell my misgivings. My father was a perceptive man and an experienced warrior, and though he was possessed of a violent temper, that temper was rarely ill-placed.

Holger and his men left the following morning with King Trygvi's oath to join him in five days' time. They were to meet just east of Sotanes near Veggir, which was but a two-day sail south of our borg on a fair wind. My father did not go to see Holger off, or to join the king after Holger's departure. He stayed inside and smoldered like one of the logs on his hearth fire, for he did not like the arrangement that had been struck between the king and his nobleman and needed time to cool his ire before attending the king.

"He tempts the Norns," grumbled my father as he watched Holger's ship slip past Jel's southern tip from the doorway of our guest hall. I sat at the eating board, watching him. Between us crackled a small fire, which spewed a cloud of white smoke that twisted upward toward the hole in the roof, smelling of pine. As Northern hospitality demanded, we ate in the guest hall so that the king and queen and their retinue could enjoy more space in the main hall.

My father turned from the doorway and strode back to the eating board, sitting heavily on the bench across from me. "Going a-viking with a ship full of boys is witless," he mumbled, then shoveled some porridge into his mouth. Some of it caught on his thick beard and he wiped it away with his sleeve.

"They are not all boys. Does he not take Tofi and a few other men from his hird?" I asked quietly as I picked a piece of ash from my porridge. "Surely it will help to have them along. And Holger and his men too?"

My father regarded me silently as he chewed. "I do not trust Holger," he admitted quietly. "He who resides so close to the Danes."

"Why not?" I asked.

My father scowled. "Things are changing, Torgil. We have an enemy for a king and no more support from the Tronds now that Jarl Sigurd is dead. The Vestfold and Ostfold, including Vingulmark, are by themselves now, our alliances with other districts tenuous. If Holger senses a weakened King Trygvi, he might throw in his lot with the Danes to whom he is connected through marriage. Or mayhap with King Harald, if he feels there is more to be gained from that relationship."

It seemed so clear to my father, but I was still confused, and so I asked my next question more delicately. "Does not this journey prove Holger is loyal? By asking the king to accompany him, I mean?"

My father snorted derisively. He shoveled more porridge into his mouth, then mumbled around his mouthful, "Who benefits more from this adventure? Holger or the king?"

I thought on that riddle for a moment. "They both benefit," I replied, to which my father responded by smacking his spoon against my head. I winced.

"Mind your temper, Torolv," said my father's maidservant, Helga, who knelt beside the fire, adding cutlets of pork to the pot. She was a portly, elderly woman who had served Torolv since he was a child; she was the only person who could speak to my father so. After my mother died, it was she who raised me when my father left home. Truth be told, I loved her like a mother, though she could easily have been my grandmother by age. She was steadfast in her care for us, and rarely said a harsh word to me, except, of course, when I deserved it. As I have mentioned already, I have a temper like my father, but her well-placed spoon on my rear usually cured me of my tantrums.

"Of course they both benefit, Torgil," my father was saying. "But who more? A king who has everything and little need for this adventure, or a noble who has less and needs a king's men to help him collect more?"

I nodded as comprehension dawned on me. "Then why does King Trygvi support Holger?"

My father shrugged his large shoulders. "A noble name will never die, if good renown one gets," he said, quoting some ancient proverb. He liked his proverbs. "Chasing fame is the way of kings, and our king is more ambitious than most in this regard, which is one reason why he agrees to this folly. But there is much more to it than that. I think he sees this as a way to keep his men both busy and happy, which is important. If they find booty, it is also a way to pay for his men. And it is a way to keep Holger happy, which is equally important, since Holger lives so close to the Danes. On top of that, it is a good opportunity to test his young warriors. It is an adventure that seemingly has little risk, though why he takes so many youngsters is hard for me to fathom. That is what troubles me. I think he could achieve all of these things in a different manner, but he will not change his mind. He pledged to Holger and has chosen his warriors, and a man's word is like the hardest steel. Once made, it cannot be broken. Remember that, eh? And so he will go, for better or for worse."

"The lads are good fighters. King Trygvi might tempt the Norns, but I think he will be fine. You will see," I said.

My father grunted. "Even so, I will be training the lads from morning to night, starting today."

I perked up. "Can Olaf and I join?"

"When you are done with your chores, you may watch. I do not want you two getting under our feet."

I frowned but accepted my father's command. I had learned in my twelve summers that his mind, once made, was as immovable as a boulder.

Chapter 3

The days leading up to King Trygvi's departure were a maelstrom of activity. One ship would accompany the king's dragon on his southward journey, which meant that two ships total needed to be prepared and outfitted for the nearly one hundred men who would ride within them.

As the older men saw to the ships and the women prepared the provisions, the younger men readied their gear and themselves for what lay ahead. The air rang with the grating of whetstones on blades and the pounding of hammers on metal in the smithy. The blacksmith's forge burned hot from morning until late at night, enveloping the borg in the stench of iron and wood smoke and sweat. I loved it, for I could almost smell the excitement that hung over our estate.

"Tighten up! No gaps!" my father yelled at the two shield walls of young men advancing on each other with their practice swords. "Work together. Trust your neighbor."

Wanting desperately to be part of it, Olaf and I loitered near the practice fields, watching our kinsmen and friends hack and parry, block and thrust. King Trygvi and my father wove between the young men, stopping the action to offer instruction or to challenge their mistakes. The challenges were never without reason, though in my father's case, a growl of criticism was usually accompanied by the smack of a stick or whatever instrument of pain he happened to be carrying. I pitied the poor warrior who made the same mistake twice.

On the second day of training, Olaf noticed Turid lingering nearby. A basket of the queen's wet clothes rested on her thin hip. He called out to her to come and join us. She smiled, shook her head briefly, then moved away. I watched her go, wondering if she wanted to join the action or if she fancied a boy among the group. A twinge of jealousy coursed through me at that second thought.

I suppose I stared too long at her departing form, for Olaf suddenly elbowed me. "You like her," he said with unconcealed surprise and a smile on his face.

"I do not," I protested.

"Torgil likes Turid," he sang. I pushed the young prince so that he stumbled away with a laugh. "Torgil likes Turid," he repeated, louder now so that the older boys could hear. Aware of their glances, I scowled and tried to cover Olaf's mouth with my palm. He laughed and scurried from my reach. I followed, angry now and intent on silencing his taunts with my fist.

"Olaf! Torgil!" my father called to us. "Stop distracting the lads and come make yourselves useful."

Thankful to be rid of Olaf's teasing, I stopped pursuing the loudmouthed wretch and pushed my way through the milling boys to my father. Olaf followed on my heels. My father eyed us cantankerously and handed each of us a hand axe. He then called the young warriors to form a semicircle around us. I knew not what he intended, but it was clear he wished to make an example of us. My heart pounded at the thought.

"In several days," my father called to the crowd of young warriors, "you lads will raid the land of the Vends. What do you suppose you will find? Hardened warriors? Farmers?"

"Farmers!" the group yelled, then laughed at their shared disregard for the enemy.

My father frowned as he played with his beard. "Why do you find that amusing?"

An unsettled hush fell on the young warriors.

"Why?" my father called to them, more sharply this time. "Cannot a farmer kill if he is protecting his family or his flock?" My father turned to me. "Torgil. Throw your axe at that pole." He pointed to a pole the warriors used to practice their sword strokes. It stood some ten paces away to my left.

Without a word, I turned, hefted the axe my father had handed me, and tossed it. The axe spun from my hand and lodged an inch into the pole at about the height of a man's forehead, just as my father had trained me.

My father then pointed at Olaf. "Toss."

Understanding the lesson my father was teaching, Olaf buried his axe blade into the pole a hand's length below mine. Then he yanked his day knife from his belt and buried it into the wood next to his axe. Day knives could kill when wielded properly, but to see them tossed effectively was highly uncommon for they were unbalanced blades and not meant for fighting. To see a boy of eight winters do so was even more impressive. Even my father stared at the prince before recovering and gazing at the stunned crowd around him. "Those," my father said, pointing to us, "are boys with simple weapons. Yet even they can kill. Never underestimate your enemy, lads."

The young warriors mumbled their understanding and made to start their sparring again when my father lifted his hand to stop them. "Wait! I have not dismissed you."

The boys turned back to him.

"What other lesson has the tossing of those axes shown you?"

The boys looked at each other. I, of course, knew the answer because my father had told me many times over, but these boys did not. I watched them chew on the question.

"I will help you," my father said. He pointed to Olaf and me. "Where are the boys standing?"

The warriors pointed to us.

"And where are their weapons?"

The lads pointed to the pole.

"Precisely. The boys have tossed their only weapons. They are now defenseless and can easily be cut down. So what is the lesson?"

"Do not toss your weapon," called Ubbi.

My father lifted a finger as if to make a point. "Do not toss your *only* weapon. Ever. Is that clear?"

The boys mumbled their understanding and moved in to congratulate us —- or more accurately, Olaf. I frowned, for the young warriors all but shoved me aside in their efforts to shower the prince with their bootlicking praise for his knife throw. I do admit that it was an impressive feat, especially for a boy so young, but my vexation was greater. I muttered a curse at their disregard for me and pushed myself clear of the obsequious crowd.

On the climb back to my father's hall, I stopped to wash my face in a barrel of water. After dipping my head into the cool liquid, I flipped my hair back so that my wet mop fell on my neck and not in my eyes. A sudden screech behind me made me turn. My jaw dropped, for there stood Turid, her overdress and a basket of clothes dotted with the spray from my sopping mane.

"I am sorry," I sputtered as I sleeved the excess water from my forehead. "I did not see you there."

Her gaze moved to my head and she giggled. I reached up and felt the spikes of my hair standing on end. Grinning, I tamed the wet strands with my fingers, feeling my cheeks warm with embarrassment as I did so. She motioned with her narrow chin to the practice field. "I saw you and Olaf on the practice field. I wish my mother would let me do those things."

Farther up on the hill, her mother, Sigrunn, stood with her hands on her hips, calling to her daughter.

"One moment, mother!" she called over her shoulder.

I did not understand her mother's reasoning. It was not uncommon for women to know how to wield a weapon. Mayhap a field of warriors was not the place to learn, but there was no reason to forbid it outright. "Why will Sigrunn not permit it?"

"Because my father —-" she started, then stopped. Her red brows furrowed. "Because he died fighting." She shrugged. "I suppose she fears I have more of him in me than her."

Her father had served in the hird of Astrid's father but had died in battle when Turid was little. "Is she right in that?" I asked, somehow intrigued by the notion.

She grinned at me as her freckled cheeks blushed. "Aye. She is. When I was young, before he died, he used to teach me how to shoot a bow and how to sharpen his blades. I liked it."

"Turid!" her mother called again, more sharply now. "Come at once — there is work to be done! The queen awaits."

Turid rolled her eyes comically and I grinned. "Coming!" she called to her mother. "I must go," she said to me, then started to move away. After several steps, she stopped and glanced back at me. "Mayhap one day you can train me."

I was so surprised by the statement, I knew not how to respond, and so I just nodded lamely.

Turid's grin stretched, then she turned and ran back to her mother. I wiped the moisture from my face, suddenly aware of how forcefully my heart thumped in my chest.

The following morning, King Trygvi and his men departed. The men moved sluggishly, for the previous evening they had feasted on the stew of a sacrificial horse and my father's strongest ale. Their laughter and shouts and boasts had rung out long into the night, but rising early had robbed them of their cheer. Now they gathered quietly near the water with their family and friends as my father's godar slaughtered yet another animal — a bleating goat this time — and splashed its blood onto the hull of Trygvi's ship and into the lapping waves of the bay. The horse had been for Odin and Thor and Tyr, the gods of war. This new sacrifice was for Njord, the god of the sea, who would carry the army successfully across the whale road to their foe.

When the ceremony ended, a drum called the king's warriors to his ships. As the others said their farewells, the king came to my father and clasped his wrist. "I will see you soon, Torolv Loose-beard. Do not forget the oath you made to me."

My father nodded. "I shall not forget. Your family is safe with me."

The king embraced my father roughly, then turned to me and knelt so that his face was close to mine. "My son's welfare is in your hands, Torgil, son of Torolv. Promise me that you will help your father in keeping him safe."

I had always been Olaf's keeper when he came to our estate, but the request had always come from my father. To have this famous Viking not only put his faith in me, but do so to my face, was intoxicating. How could I refuse that request? "I promise, my king," I vowed. King Trygvi nodded firmly to me, then turned and strode to Queen Astrid, who stood nearby.

"Oaths are like iron, Torgil," whispered my father as we watched the king embrace my former foster sister. "You cannot break them. To do so is to bring shame to you and your name. See that you keep it."

I did not respond, nor did I think too much about my father's lofty words. Rather, I turned my head back to the ships and the men and wondered when it would be my turn to sail the whale road to battle.

Chapter 4

The blast of a horn echoed in the distance. Groggily, my mind registered the sound, then sleep took hold of me yet again.

"Rise!" my father roared.

I shot upright, and my eyes found my father in the dimly lit hall. He was shrugging into his byrnie and scowling at me. "What is it?" I asked as I struggled from my fur bedding and wiped the sleep from my eyes.

"Did you not hear the warning?" he thundered as he tightened his sword belt around his mail shirt, then hefted his shield from where it rested against a wall. "Dress yourself and grab your seax and spear!"

The horn came again, louder now in my sudden wakefulness. I had no idea what time it was. I knew only that something was amiss. With rising panic, I scrambled into my trousers and shoes, then grabbed my cloak. My father was at the door of our hall, peering out into the darkness. Men's shouts came clearly to my ears. My father cursed and my panic transformed to abject fear.

"Helga!" my father called to our maidservant, who had come to see what the matter was. "Gather what food and clothes you can carry and make for the north gate. We will meet you at Thordruga," which was Ulf and Ubbi's farm. Of all the neighboring farms, it was closest. "Quickly!"

She knew better than to ask questions and scurried away into the kitchen.

I had fastened my seax to my belt and grabbed my spear. My father's eyes shifted to me. "Grab your practice shield too."

I did as commanded and joined my father at the door. The sun was rising in the east, and in that morning light, I saw the outline of four warships sliding onto the beach below our borg. The silhouettes of many men filled each ship. I could not make out whether they were friend or foe, but judging from the shouts of our own warriors, they did not seem friendly.

My father slid his helmet onto his head. "Come," he commanded and headed out into the pale morning.

I followed, trying my best to stay close to him as we ran for the main hall. Around us, chaos ruled. Women carried babies or dragged their crying children. Warriors hastened to the east gate, where our sentries shouted and pointed toward the ships. Below them, those who had been sleeping beyond our walls streamed through the open gates into the safety of my father's borg. Everyone seemed to be running in opposite directions.

My father grabbed a passing warrior. Ulf! He carried a spear in his hand and a shield on his arm, and I wondered as I looked at him whether my own face showed as much fear as his. "Get a message to the sentries," my father commanded as he pointed to the eastern gate. "Tell them to wait as long as they can before barring the gates. More of our people come and we must let them in." Ulf nodded and ran off, his oversized helmet bobbing comically on his head.

Then my father turned to me and grabbed my shoulders. "I make for the gate. Head to the main hall. Tell Queen Astrid that she must prepare to leave. If the enemy breaches the palisade, take her and Olaf to Thordruga. I will meet you there. Do you understand?"

I nodded.

"Go!"

I ran for the main hall, which loomed on the hill before me. Queen Astrid stood in the doorway, her tall frame backlit by the hearth fire within as she struggled to keep Olaf by her side.

"Let me go!" Olaf screeched as I stopped before them. His face was red with exertion and anger. He held a knife in his hand, and I knew the young fool wished to leap headlong into the fray.

"Calm yourself!" Queen Astrid hissed at her son.

Olaf's struggles boiled my own blood. Did he really think he could help our men on the wall? The little bugger would be cut down before his eating knife pricked a foeman's leg. But that was Olaf. Looking before he leaped. Only this time, his tantrum was distracting everyone from focusing on what mattered most: the attack. "Shut your lips and be calm!" I growled at him. "My father has commanded us to watch your mother and so we must."

"Who are they?" asked Queen Astrid as Olaf continued to struggle.

"I know not, my lady," I answered truthfully, then turned again to peer at the scene below. Of the four ships that had landed, one was King Trygvi's dragon. Even in the half light, I could tell its lines from the others, though I did not understand why his men were scrambling across the beach with torches and blades in their hands and fiendish screams on their lips. None of it made sense, and yet, there could be no mistaking their intentions.

"Close the gate!" I heard a voice roar and men scrambled to bar it from within.

In the eerie light of the attackers' torch flames, I could see our warriors casting spears from the palisades or shooting their bows. In answer, torches twirled over the walls in search of something to ignite.

I will never forget that scene, for even in the chaos of that moment, there was a strange symmetry to the attack that made sense to me. Enemy warriors moved north and south with their flames while directly down the hill from us, the eastern gate splintered from the blow of a battering ram. It did not take much to see that the eastern gate was merely a distraction. The main force made for the other gates to encircle us so that we could not escape. My father had not the men to defend such an attack, and if I tarried much longer, we would all be trapped. It was to the west gate we now had to flee or we were doomed.

"We must move," I said and looked up into the queen's alarmed face. "Now, my lady!"

"But the walls are holding," she protested half-heartedly.

"Let me go!" Olaf shouted.

"Enough!" Astrid screeched and backhanded her son from behind. The blow knocked Olaf's head so hard, his legs wobbled. I took advantage of that blow to pull the blade from his grip.

Before he recovered, I turned back to Queen Astrid. "My father has commanded it, my lady. We must hurry." I sought the face of her maidservant, Sigrunn, hoping for some support there, but found only a mask of terror as she attempted to shield her daughter, Turid, from the door. "Please," I begged.

Queen Astrid gazed out at the battle. "I do not understand. That is my husband's ship. He must be here," she whispered.

I did not know why King Trygvi's ship was in the harbor, but I did know that men were here to kill us and that we must seek safety. "We cannot wait," I urged. "Gather clothes and what food you can carry," I said, repeating the command my father had given to Helga. "Quickly. We must make for the west gate. Olaf." I turned to my friend, whose tantrum had finally dissolved. "Stay by your mother's side. Do not leave her." He nodded.

More cries filled the air; these to the south of us, where a new flame licked at the palisade. My heart skipped as I ushered Queen Astrid and Olaf back into the hall. "Get your things!" I yelled at them, no longer caring for their rank. Slowly at first, and then with increased urgency, they rushed to do my bidding as I kept my eyes on the battle.

Below me, the east gate cracked open and some of my father's warriors rushed to stop the enemy from streaming in. One of them was Ulf; I knew him from the way he moved. I watched in shock as an enemy spear ripped through his young torso and erupted from his back. I tore my eyes away, to left and right, where flames danced upon the palisade even as men fought to defend it.

"We must go!" I grabbed Turid and pushed her toward the kitchen door where there was a side entrance. Sigrunn came close behind. Queen Astrid pulled one of my father's old swords from its place on his wall as Olaf tugged at her arm.

"Run!" a voice bellowed from the hall's entrance just as I ushered the queen into the kitchen.

I turned to see my father. Blood smeared his face and the sword he carried. Relief washed over me, followed instantly by renewed terror as he sprinted across the hall and joined our group. Together, we stumbled out of the hall's kitchen and gathered in the shadow of the high gable. The group stared at my father.

He broke the spell with a sharp command. "This way!"

We wove through the structures of our estate, running as fast as our feet could carry us through air thick with smoke and ash and floating embers. As I suspected, we headed for the west gate, for it seemed the one exit not yet under siege. My father led, with the women and Olaf not far behind. I guarded the rear of our group, not because I was slow, but because my father had commanded me to do so. Behind me, the morning reverberated with the cries of the dying and the wounded, the clang of battle-steel, the roar and shriek of combatants.

At the west gate, my father waved us over into the shadow of the palisade. Just as we reached it, the gate burst open and a throng of warriors rushed through. They carried axes and spears and shields and did not stop to investigate their surroundings. Instead, they ran for the action and for their share of the plunder. When they were a stone's throw from us, my father inched to the open gate and peered out, then he waved us forward.

We sprinted for the forest, fifty paces distant from the west palisade. I heard a shout behind me, but it was impossible to tell whether the yell was for us or another. We pounded into the woods, following a track that led us west, then north, wrapping around the hill toward the farm Thordruga. Toward safety.

We ran until our lungs burned, but still my father pushed us onward. Eventually, we reached a small rise that looked down into the valley where Thordruga lay. Sweat dripped from my hair and into my eyes, stinging them as I studied the quiet farm below. Thordruga was no more than a farmhouse, a scattering of smaller structures, and a pen for sheep and pigs. Rectangular fields of half-grown barley lay beyond. Within the hall, cows lowed for their morning meal, while from the hall's chimney hole whirled a thin trickle of smoke.

The farm belonged to Ulf's father, Oddi, who had been at my father's estate with his wife and sons, attending the king. I had seen one of the sons die. If Oddi and his wife were not here, it seemed likely they had suffered a similar fate. That sudden knowledge turned my mind to another. "Did Helga make it here?" I whispered to my father.

"We will soon find out," he answered grimly. "Stay here with the others. I will go to the gate."

As we watched, my father crept down the path to Oddi's farm to be greeted by the warning barks of the farmer's hounds. My father hopped the gate and crouched to conceal himself. A man appeared at the door of the hall and, recognizing my father, came to him. I could see them conversing, my father motioning in the direction of our borg as he did so. Oddi's man shook his head, then rushed back into the hall. I could hear him calling out commands but could not make sense of his words. Then, suddenly, he reappeared with a bag in his hand, which he proffered to my father. My father nodded to him in thanks, then, crouching, sprinted back to us.

"We go," he said through his panting when he reached us.

"Where?" asked Queen Astrid.

"East," was all he said.

"What about them?" the queen asked, meaning the residents of Thordruga. "Are they not also in peril?"

My father regarded Queen Astrid with his stern eyes and blood-bathed face. "My oath to your husband was to see to your safety, and so I shall. Oddi's servants will only slow us down and make my task harder. They know they are in peril and will hide. That is all we can do."

The queen frowned. "Who were those men?"

My father took a swig from his waterskin, then poured a measure into his hands and rubbed at the blood still caking his face. The water softened the filth but did not dislodge it —- the gore now dripped from his cheeks into his beard and made him look like some creature from the underworld. "It was Holger, my queen," he answered as he proffered his waterskin to her.

"Holger?" she asked, astonished, as she lifted the skin to her lips.

"Your husband was betrayed. I know not how, but I saw Holger in the darkness, urging his men forward. He was calling for them to find you."

"But I saw my husband's ship. Was he not there?"

My father shook his head. "No, my queen. I believe it was a ruse to get past the sentries at Jel's southern tip."

As the gravity of my father's words settled on us, Queen Astrid's eyes moistened. She looked away and wiped at her cheeks, refusing to let us witness her grief.

"I will kill Holger," pledged Olaf in a vicious hiss.

My father scowled, his dark eyes squinting yet ablaze, the creases between his brows more pronounced by the grime on his face. It was a look I had seen many times, and a look that had melted the resolve of many men. But not Olaf. He met the gaze as only a confident son of a king might do. "Be careful boy, for the gods are listening. If you make a pledge like that, you must keep it."

"I will," he said.

My father nodded, unimpressed.

"What is east?" Sigrunn asked, interrupting the moment. She, like her daughter, was tall and slender, though I had noticed in our escape that she lacked the grace with which Turid had been blessed. She lacked the stamina, too, for she sat on her rump, huffing mightily and sucking thirstily at the waterskin.

"A place to hide until the danger passes."

"Do you think they will search for us?" asked Sigrunn.

"Will they come for us?" my father repeated with a callous laugh. "They are here for us — for them!" He pointed at Queen Astrid and Olaf. "They will most certainly come for us, and if they catch us, they will kill us. Or worse, enslave us. But not before they are done ravaging you and your daughter and the queen. Now up on your feet — we must move." My father turned to go.

"What of Helga?" I asked as we descended the hill.

"She did not arrive," he responded coldly.

I raced after my father. "Mayhap she got lost? We could wait."

My father rounded on me. "She knows the way to Thordruga as well as any. If she is not here, then she is hiding or —-" He stopped himself. "Pray that she lives," he growled. "That is the best we can do for her now."

I imagined Helga's portly body lying dead on the ground in our borg and my heart broke. For several winters she had been my only mother, and her presence filled most of my memories. Now she was simply gone. Ripped from my life by a faceless enemy on a dark morning. It seemed unreal to me, and yet more emotionally painful than anything I had ever experienced. My eyes misted and I wiped at a tear.

My father saw the gesture and scowled at my weakness. "Come," he commanded.

I followed wordlessly with the others close behind, the weight of despair crushing my chest.

The morning was just beginning to warm when we reached the rocky beach that separated Jel Island from the mainland of Vingulmark. You see, Jel Island was not really an island; it only appeared to be. It was shaped like a bent elbow with the forearm stretching north. The actual elbow was connected to the mainland of Vingulmark by a thin, rocky strip of beach just north of my father's borg. A small stream bisected that strip of beach, flowing lazily through the stones and pebbles from a bay to the north of us to the bay that flowed below my father's fort.

We halted in the trees and gazed out at that beach. "Wait here," said my father, who then ventured forward from the tree line, his head swiveling as he approached the stream. Finding no trouble, he came back to us and knelt. "Work your way north through the water. It will throw any pursuers from our trail, at least for a time. When you have gone fifty paces, head for the tree line on the far side. Torgil, you lead."

"What about you?" I asked him.

"I will follow. Now go," he hissed.

I pulled my seax from its sheath and hurried to the stream, where I stepped into the cold water and picked my way over slick stones, heading north, away from the smoke that now rose above the borg. I could hear the others behind me but did not dare look back, for fear of slipping. Even so, twice I stumbled. Sigrunn fell and Turid helped her up.

When I had gone fifty paces, I motioned for our group to head for the trees on our right, then I followed. My father loped up the stream then, dodging loose rocks and hidden potholes, surprisingly agile for his size. As he came, he waved for me to follow the others, but I could not. For in the distance to the south, a ship had just appeared. It hugged the western coastline, and just as my gaze fixed on it, the prowman saw us. His yells were lost to the wind, but I could see him urging his men forward.

My father grabbed my arm and yanked me toward the woods, tearing me from my trance. As he did, he ventured a glance at the ship and cursed. It was close to the shore — mayhap two long flights of an arrow distant — and coming fast.

The others were waiting for us in the tree line, sharing a water-skin. They had not seen the ship and so were shocked when my father grabbed the skin from Turid's hands and said, "Follow me. Quickly."

"Should we not rest —" Sigrunn tried to ask, but my father was already sprinting past the group. We ran after him.

We soon came to a cart path that headed north and south through the forest. I knew this to be the trade route that took goods north to the fylke of Akershus, but I had never seen it. My entire life up to that point had been spent on Jel Island. My father crossed the path and headed east, deeper into the woods. Here there were no tracks or roads, only trees and mud and branches that tore at our clothes and sucked at our shoes. Sigrunn stumbled on an exposed root, and I pulled her onward, wondering all the while why my father had chosen the forest with its shadows and obstacles. Later, I would understand that my father was fit, but the rest of us were women and children, and our stamina was not nearly as great as his. Had we taken the cart path, we would have been overrun in no time. Here among the trees, we had a chance.

Behind me, I could hear Sigrunn's rasping breath and Astrid's pleas to Olaf to hurry. Turid had fallen behind me now, too. She was a graceful runner, but as I said, none of us were warriors like my father, who, ten paces ahead, dodged and wove his way through the trees. I did my best to follow his path, though I too was tiring. Somewhere ahead of us was a lake, I knew, but how far it was and what would happen when we reached it was a mystery and a concern. How would we cross the lake? Would we swim? Was there a boat or a place to hide? All these thoughts tore at me like the branches of the trees and feet-grabbing roots we tried to evade.

I could hear them behind us, our pursuers. In my mind, their blades flashed as their iron-clad bodies ducked and danced and crashed through the trees. Stealth meant nothing to a man eager for a notable kill, and notable we were. A queen, a prince, and a chieftain would earn a man no end to boasting and a reputation that would last for generations. I did not want to be part of that killer's story.

Down into a gulley we sprinted, and then up the other side, my father urging us onward. We were panting and red-faced now, sweat pouring from our brows. Sigrunn was grunting and slipped more than once as she climbed, for the rise was higher and steeper than we expected. Queen Astrid and Turid grabbed her arms and pulled her forward.

"Leave me," she huffed. "I can go no farther and will only slow you down."

I cursed her weakness and the danger it put us in, but Queen Astrid was not so easily discouraged. "If you stay, I stay," she said, and that seemed to get Sigrunn's feet moving again, albeit more slowly than before.

We now stood at the crest of a low hill and from our position, we could see back into the forest through which we had come. There, glimpses of steel flitted in the shadows. The warriors were closer now, their yells louder too. We turned to run again, but my toe clipped a root and I stumbled. A hand grabbed my cloak and righted me. I ran on.

The tree line ended halfway down the other side of the hill and suddenly we burst into light and a sloping field of tall grass still wet with morning dew. My father was in the lead. The rest of us trailed behind in haphazard fashion. Before us was a small cabin and beyond it, a sun-kissed river. Three roughly clad men stood beside the cabin, facing us. The oldest — a graybeard — had a sword in his hand. The others held hand axes. All looked capable of killing and probably had.

"Run!" my father bellowed at them, startling a paddling of ducks who took flight at his shout.

Their scowls evaporated as their eyes moved past us to the figures emerging from the tree line. I did not dare look back, though I could hear their shouts even closer now. My lungs burned, but I knew that to stop was to die. As if in answer to that thought, a spear struck the turf before me. I evaded it and ran on.

Ahead of us, the three men had turned and scurried to a partially beached raft. It was a flat affair made of rope-bound logs, large enough for mayhap ten grown men standing shoulder to shoulder. Two men pushed the craft into the water, while the other climbed aboard and grabbed a taut rope that was tied to a pole near the shore on our side of the river and a tree on the far shore. He started to pull.

"Wait!" my father roared, but the men did not heed my father's words. Instead, the two in the water scrambled onto the raft.

My father splashed into the water and grabbed the raft. One of the men turned and tried to kick him off. "Piss off!" he yelled.

In one motion, my father blocked the kick and pulled the man into the river. In the next motion, he unsheathed his seax and brought it to the man's neck. "Take us or this man dies," my father called up to the ferrymen.

The old man called for his helper to stop pulling, then motioned for us to come. Our group had now reached the river's edge and we splashed into the cold water. My father held the raft as Queen Astrid hauled Olaf aboard, then pulled herself up. I followed, then turned to help Turid, who was behind me. My father climbed aboard and held fast to the line to ensure the other men did not pull. I reached out to Sigrunn, who was wading into the water and reaching for my outstretched hand. Our pursuers were now some thirty paces from us and coming fast.

"Leave her!" one of the ferrymen called.

But I would not leave her. I had lost too much already that grim morning, and I refused to lose Sigrunn too. I kept my arms out-stretched and Sigrunn leaped. Our fingers locked and I clenched her hands in mine.

"Pull!" my father roared, and the raft lurched forward.

Turid scrambled down beside me and grabbed her mother's other hand, and together we hauled her onto the moving raft.

The enemy warriors sprinted to the water's edge. At their head was Holger, his greasy black hair whipping his face as he yelled at his men to kill us. Some had spears and one had a bow, and these they used as we pulled ourselves farther from the shore. Most of those missiles splashed harmlessly into the river, but some fell among us. A spear struck the raft beside Olaf's leg. Another narrowly missed Turid. An arrow struck one of the ferrymen in his thigh. As the man grabbed at it, another arrow struck his neck and he collapsed into the water.

And then we were mid-river and the missiles could not reach us with any accuracy, and Holger called off the pursuit with a sharp slice of his hand. One of his men pulled his sword and raised it to cut the rope, but Holger stopped him. I could not hear their conversation but I assumed Holger wanted to preserve the rope, should he need to use it. I can think of no other reason, for had he sliced it, we would have floundered in the river's current like a fish on a string.

"I will kill you, Torolv Loose-beard!" he called across the water. "You, your queen, and her whelp! Do you hear?"

My father did not reply. I am sure he heard those words, as did we all, but he did not break from his pulling.

I lay back on the wet raft, thinking now that we were finally safe. That we had escaped danger. I did not know how short-sighted that truly was. What I could not know then was that the Norns had only just begun to weave our wicked fate and that nothing would be the same again.

For no man can escape his fate.

Chapter 5

My father struck as soon as the ferrymen dragged the raft from the shallows to the shore. The graybeard had just turned to say something to our group when my father's sword took his head. So true and powerful was his stroke that the head merely rolled to the left as his body crumpled to the ground. I am not sure he even knew that he was dead, for the corpse's leg twitched as if he was still trying to walk.

His companion turned and, seeing the older man fall, fumbled for his seax, but my father's sword reached him first. I will never forget the look of surprise on that man's face, nor his squeal as the blade slid through his gut and exploded from his back.

I knew my father was a hard man and that he had killed in battle, but I had never seen him kill, and the sight of it shook me to my very core. I knew not whether to cry or run or curl up into a ball, and so I did none of those things. I just stood and gaped. Beside me, the ladies gasped. Olaf flinched. Though none of us could turn our eyes from the ghastly scene.

"Torgil!" my father growled, tearing me from my stupor. "Grab their weapons and what possessions and food you can find."

I did my father's bidding, picking with shaking hands through the pouches of those lifeless corpses, for though I had seen them die, I expected those dead men to grab my arm at any moment for the sheer injustice of their death and the callousness of being robbed. As I struggled at my task, Queen Astrid berated my father for killing innocent men. My father ignored her. Instead, he grabbed the items I was able to find — a few silver coins, an old sword, a semi-sharp seax — then hurried us into the woods.

"Will you not answer me?" Queen Astrid hissed, her voice as sharp as my father's blade. Her cheeks were red beneath blue eyes that had turned fierce. "Why did you kill those men?"

My father spun and lowered his face so that it was close to the queen's. His fist clenched on the hilt of his sword, and I knew he was on the verge of one of his black tempers. When he spoke, the words came through gritted teeth. "If you wish to live — if you wish your son to live — then no one can know where we travel. No one."

I held my breath for the queen's response, willing her to keep her mouth shut so that my father did not fly into one of his rages. Whether she sensed how close my father was to his edge or she accepted the necessity of my father's violence, I know not. All I know is that she acquiesced with a sharp nod before stepping away and marching up the path that led north through the trees. My father's dark gaze turned on the rest of us, and in that look, I understood that his words to the queen were meant for us all. *No one could know where we traveled.* Without a word, he tossed the extra sword to me, threw the seax at Turid's feet, then turned and followed the queen.

"What about Holger?" Turid called to my father as she slid the seax from its scabbard to check its blade. "Will he stop pursuing us now?"

"He will come," he answered flatly. "Once they find a way across the river."

Emboldened by her question, I joined the chorus. "How long will that be?"

My father did not answer, only skewered me with a look that told me just how foolish my question was. Embarrassed, I slowed my pace and chided myself for my stupidity, then turned my anger on Sigrunn, who was falling behind once again. If she did not keep up, she would be the death of us and I made sure she knew it.

"Keep your lips tight, Torgil," the queen barked in defense of her maidservant. "It is not for you to chastise my servant."

My father stopped then and took a deep breath. We stopped with him and waited. When he spoke, he did not look at us, but it was clear he was struggling to keep calm. "We head for the home of Astrid's father in Oppegard. It is a full day's hike from here. Since no one can know where we are or where we fare, we cannot be heard or seen. That means no talking. Do you all understand?" He did not wait for a response. "I will lead. If you see me stop and motion you into the woods, follow my command." My father's eyes found my face. "Torgil. Take up the rear. If you hear men approaching, alert us quickly with a whistle. Is that clear?"

I nodded, though I was not certain I could do that with my mouth as dry as it was.

"Good. Now let us move."

We walked on through the woods, our footfalls muted by the wet ground and the blanket of leaves that clung to our shoes. My stomach grumbled and I wondered what time it was, for the trees in Vingulmark grew thick and the canopy of leaves and branches cast us in a dark shade that veiled us from the sun's path. I listened to the forest sounds, trying to discern man from animal, my head on a swivel as I peered behind me, to the right, and to the left. Birdsong and the scurrying of forest animals in the underbrush accompanied us as we walked, though my young mind conjured more frightful images. Of warriors and their shuffling feet. Of hushed conversations instead of babbling brooks. Of the sudden flash of an arrowhead instead of the dart and dash of a bird.

Though I cursed my own fear, I took some consolation in seeing the others casting their eyes about too. Surely they felt the same ever-present stir of unease in their guts as I did? Only Olaf, who walked directly ahead of me, seemed oblivious to the danger. His eyes followed the butterflies and the birds that joined us, and I had a mind to cuff him for it.

Later, we came to a clearing where a small settlement basked in the sunshine of high day. To the west, I could see the sparkling ocean, and beyond it, the green rise of Jel Island's northern tip. The trees surrounding the clearing stretched east to a rocky hill before turning north again.

"Kambo," my father whispered, answering the question that was on my mind. "We will work our way east through the trees and skirt it."

"We need a rest," Queen Astrid responded.

My father frowned, but a quick glance at our faces made him acquiesce. "Come."

He led us through the trees until we reached the rocky hill. There, in the shade of some tall gray slabs, we sat and ate in silence. In the distance, I could hear the lowing of cattle and hammering on wood. Queen Astrid looked in that direction and frowned. She wanted to warn them, I could tell, but knew she could not.

"They will be fine," came my father's whispered assurance. "If they have seen nothing, they have nothing to tell."

Queen Astrid's frown deepened. "Still, Holger and his men will try to extract information of our whereabouts..."

She left the rest unsaid, and the sadness in her tone left a lump in my own throat that robbed me of my appetite. The others, too, cast miserable eyes on their food. Olaf, of course, had not detected the doleful tone of his mother and continued to contently chew his bread. I wondered sometimes whether it was merely his youth or if he was just a distracted child. I mostly hated that distraction, but at times like this, I yearned to possess it also.

With fuller bellies, we climbed a path that wove through the rocks, then turned north again as the hill leveled out. Down through the trees, we could see men and women going about their chores. It was strange to think of the impending danger they might be in and that that danger was due to us. We were the harbingers of an unseen storm — a storm to which they remained blissfully unaware. I prayed to the gods that the storm might miss them, then I averted my eyes and walked on.

Our path veered westward for a time. Here and there along the way, we encountered halls and smaller settlements and these we avoided as we had Kambo. By afternoon, my father informed us that we were in the fylke of Akershus. He knew this because we now followed a stream in a gulley that curved away from the ocean and headed northeast. The path eventually turned from the main stream, weaving through several tree-blanketed hills before leveling out on a flat, forested area crisscrossed with shallow waterways.

It was as we were crossing one of those waterways that my father stopped and motioned us off the path. We followed his lead and scurried into the underbrush on the far shore. I lay flat behind a fern with Olaf to my right and Turid behind us. I could hear the jangling of metal, the creak of wood, and the low mumble of voices, but long, tense moments passed before the party showed itself.

It was a trading party, led by a bear of a man who clung to a lead rope that encircled the neck of an ox pulling a cart stacked high with pelts. Two more men walked beside it. Four goats trailed the cart, each on a lead rope. A boy not much older than me prodded them along with a cane. All were armed, and though they conversed and chuckled with each other, their eyes scanned the forest. I knew we were in no danger so long as we stayed quiet, yet my heart still thumped in my chest. Should these men see us, they would wonder why we hid and we would have no explanation. It would force my father to make a hard decision, and I did not know whether we could fight three armed men at once.

The party crossed the stream we had just crossed and disappeared from sight. Their sounds eventually faded to nothing and my father rose. "We are about halfway to your father's hall, my lady," he said. "We should rest now and travel the remainder of the way by night."

We found a small depression some fifty paces from the path, and there we took our rest. All of us were dirt-streaked and travel-weary. My feet ached and my belly grumbled. My wet trousers clung annoyingly to my legs. To make matters worse, it was getting darker and colder, yet we could light no fire. All we could do was wrap ourselves in our cloaks and try to fill our stomachs.

"What will become of us now?" asked Turid suddenly. In our flight, her red hair had fallen from its braid and now hung in tangles about her thin, freckled face. She wiped aside a loose curl and peered at the queen.

Astrid had no response for Turid save a sad gaze. Seeing this, Sigrunn rubbed her daughter's shoulder. "We will be fine, Turid. You will see."

I turned my eyes to the shadowy frame of my father, standing watch near our little camp, and wondered if he knew what our fates might be, or whether he too pondered that very question.

A gray summer evening descended, and we ventured on. As before, we stayed well clear of the halls and settlements we saw, though the warmth they promised and the smells emanating from those places were maddeningly enticing. We walked in the woods, where we knew no sane man would wander at night. Several times, we heard the howl of wolves in the distance. My father told us that they would not attack a group such as ours, but I was not so sure and walked with my new sword drawn and in my hand. Even when my arm tired from its weight, I clung to it, as much to spare me from the wolves as to protect me from the shadows lurking in those night woods. My young imagination convinced me that some foul creature might creep from them, like the undead draugar who at night wreaked havoc on the living. We would have been easy prey for them, I think, but by the luck of the gods, they spared us.

The shadows receded with the dawn, and it was then that we reached Oppegard, the main farm owned by Queen Astrid's father, Erik Karasson. The land in that place was fertile and flat, though in the midst of it rose a small hill upon which sat Erik's hall and its outlying structures. The hall was every bit as large as my father's own borg. And like ours, a tall palisade surrounded it. A sign of the times in which we lived, I suppose. Circumventing the hill on the west side was the road we had been following — the main trade route in the Ostfold.

I had met Erik Karasson once before and remembered him for his baldness and his fitting byname, Bjodaskalli —- the bald man of Bjodar. For Erik had originally come from a farm of that name in distant Hordaland, far to the west. He had joined King Hakon in his fight against the Danes and, for his service and loyalty, had been gifted Oppegard as a gift. My father had long been his friend, which is how he had come to foster Erik's daughter, Astrid, and how King Trygvi had discovered the beautiful girl. But King Trygvi was now dead and Astrid was queen in name alone, and so we sat in the cold, overcast morning, eyeing Oppegard from a copse of trees.

Queen Astrid stepped from the shadows, but my father grabbed her arm. "No. We wait," he said, pulling her back.

Her brows bent in confusion. "Why? Erik is my father. Surely we are safe here."

"Lord. We must get Olaf some proper rest," whispered Sigrunn, motioning to Olaf, who rested in her arms. He grinned stupidly at the mention of his name even as his eyes drooped. "The lad is asleep on his feet."

My father scowled. "We cannot just walk out into the open and endanger everyone on your father's farm, or ourselves. It is best that only a few people know of us. We must find someone we trust. They can get word to your father and perchance find a place for us to rest, away from curious eyes."

Queen Astrid gazed out at the farm before her but nodded. Sigrunn stroked Olaf's head, and he closed his eyes contentedly. Turid had propped herself against a tree and now rubbed her face. I gazed longingly at the distant farm with my stinging eyes, wanting so badly just to lay my head on a pillow and sleep.

"There is someone," Queen Astrid said softly. "Come."

And so we headed east into the woods and away from the promise of warmth and food and sleep that had been so close.

"Where are we headed?" asked my father as we snaked through the trees on a narrow track.

"To our seter," called Astrid over her shoulder as the track began to ascend.

"Is it far?" I asked.

"It is at the top of the hill we are climbing," Astrid answered. "Not far now."

We walked in silence until the path broke into a large field that climbed to a hilltop. Just under the crest, on a flat stretch of ground, sat what looked to be a cottage and a barn. A rope hung between the two structures upon which several garments flapped lazily in the breeze. Cows and sheep grazed in the tall grass and lay in the shadows, out of the warming sun. Between the two structures, near the clothesline, an older man was chopping wood, the crack of his blade echoing off the hillside and down to our ears. The tranquility of the scene was marred only by the man himself, who swung the ax with his right arm, for he was missing half of his left.

Astrid pulled her disheveled hair back into a simple bun, then straightened her dress and squared her shoulders.

My father frowned at her. "What are you doing?" he asked.

"I am going to greet my family's cowherd," she said.

"I will go with you."

"No," she said firmly and stayed my father with a hand. Before he could say more, she stepped from the shade of the trees and marched upward through the tall grass toward the axe man.

Chapter 6

As Astrid neared, the cowherd set down his axe and dropped to a knee. Astrid closed the distance to him and helped him rise, then spoke to him. I could see her hands moving and pointing to the south. The man stroked his beard with his one hand as she spoke, listening thoughtfully. Finally, Astrid turned and beckoned us to join her.

"This," she said as we neared, "is Gunnar, my father's cowherd."

The man made a frightening sight. His clothes were grimy and his skin leathered and weather-worn. He was missing his left forearm, as I have said, but that bothered me less than the scar that traveled from his upper left cheek, near his nose, to his upper lip, removing his left nostril and leaving a channel in his mustache where hair should have grown. The scar pulled his left lip up into a perpetual grimace. His dark eyes regarded us warily until he recognized Sigrunn and Turid, at which point the left side of his mouth bent up further, giving him the appearance of a growling hound. It took me a moment to realize that he was actually grinning.

"He is a man of few words," Astrid told us as she patted his shoulder, "but he is one of my father's most loyal men. He will tell my father of our arrival."

Sigrunn and Turid did not seem bothered by Gunnar's frightful appearance. Whereas I stood back from the man, they went to him and greeted him warmly. At first, their display of affection startled me, but then I remembered that they must know each other from Astrid's many visits to her father's farm.

The door to the cottage creaked open and my father swung toward it, his hand moving to the handle of his sword. Out peered the round face of an older woman and my father relaxed. The woman stepped outside and bowed to Astrid. "My lady," she said in greeting.

Astrid smiled and returned the bow. "It is good to see you again, Gunhild."

I guessed that she was roughly the age of Gunnar, though shorter and rounder. Strands of gray and red escaped from the knotted kerchief she wore on her head. Freckles dotted her fair-skinned cheeks. As she approached, I detected a strong scent of cheese and knew she must be the milkmaid. A soiled apron hung from her neck, and she wiped her meaty hands on it before taking Sigrunn and Turid into an embrace.

"To what do we owe this honor?" Gunhild asked as she let the two women go. It was a kind question, even if asked with a suspicious hesitancy.

"I will tell all shortly," said Gunnar. His voice was low and gritty. "Get them inside, Gunhild, and make them comfortable."

As we moved to the cottage door, I realized I had lost track of Olaf. He had wandered off from our group to pet the sheep. I called to him to come inside. He, of course, ignored my call and moved only when his mother's urging reached his ears. I grumbled and moved with the others to the cottage.

It was a rustic affair, that cottage. Small and warm and sparsely furnished. But what struck me most was the smell. As soon as we entered, the sour aroma of cheese encased us. I was not particularly fond of cheese, but my empty stomach growled nevertheless.

Gunhild must have heard that faint rumble in my belly, for she suddenly looked at me. "You poor dears must be famished. Come. Sit." She pointed to the table and some benches. We dropped our sacks and sat without a word. Gunhild vanished into a side room and returned with a bowl of soft cheese, a platter of bread, and a jug of water.

Sigrunn made to rise as Gunhild began to serve us. "Let me help."

Gunhild waved her back to her seat. "You are under my roof, Sigrunn. When I come to your dwelling, then you may serve me, eh?"

The mention of Sigrunn's dwelling had us casting looks at each other, then down at the food. I do not know what was on the others' minds, but my mind turned to the borg that was no longer ours. Which brought my thoughts to my father and what he must be thinking. Everything he had built, and everything he had planned to give to me, was now gone. We were homeless. Landless. Worthless. And with that thought, I lost my appetite.

Gunnar sensed our discomfiture, for he knew our story and why we were here. "Mind your words, Gunhild." He grabbed a travel bag and a cloak. "I will return before nightfall," he announced, then he stepped from the room and left us to our meal.

Gunnar returned just as the sun began its descent in the west. He led an ox up the hill, which in turn pulled a small cart that was loaded with goods. Beside it strode four other men. All were armed and armored, though it was clear from his brooch and the silver at his neck that the older, balder man was a lord. I realized as Astrid greeted this man with a formal bow, that this must be her father, Erik Bjodaskalli. The bald man of Bjodar. It was a fitting name, for his skull looked like the bottom of an egg sitting in a nest of wild orange hair. That hair dropped into a thick beard of the same color, complementing the ruddiness of his cheeks. He was a short, portly fellow but his eyes were a keen blue, and it was those eyes that studied his daughter's face now. He touched her cheek in greeting, then moved to my father. My father dwarfed the fellow, but the difference in size did not seem to bother Erik, who said some words to him before turning his eyes on us.

"Come," I heard him say to my father. "We have much to discuss. But first, let us eat. I have brought food and fresh clothing for you all."

Erik walked toward Olaf and me, and I prepared to receive his greeting. In my periphery, I could see Olaf plucking some hay from his tunic. I kicked his ankle to ensure he was ready for his grandfather, but it was for naught. Erik stopped several paces from us and merely studied Olaf with his icy eyes, his expression unreadable. Then he strode into the cottage. We followed. The three men who had come with Erik remained outside.

The adults sat at the table. Olaf and I sat on stools with our backs to the wall. Now rested, Sigrunn and Turid joined Gunhild in bringing food from the cart to the table for Astrid and the men.

"Tell me all," Erik said when the food had been served and he had slaked his thirst with ale.

My father obliged his friend, telling him of Holger's visit and invitation to raid, of King Trygvi's acceptance and foolishness in taking mostly the younger men, of Holger's night raid and our subsequent flight. Erik nodded or grunted as my father wove the tale for him. Nearby sat Gunnar, his face grave. Though he ran a whetstone along the edge of a pair of shears, I could tell he was listening.

"It is a foul deed that has been done," said Erik around a mouthful of cheese and bread when my father had finished his tale. "I am sorry for your loss, my friend, but I thank you for bringing my daughter and my grandson safely to me. And I thank you for bringing this grave news to us." He drained his cup of ale and called for more. "I am afraid it is not altogether surprising, though. We have known for some time that the brood of Bloodaxe was not content to sit in the west; that those bastards would come for us just as they came for Jarl Sigurd. And now it is all coming to pass. You may not have heard but King Trygvi is not the only king to have fallen."

My father's brows bent downward. Beside him, Astrid went still as a stone. Olaf was playing with the tie-strings on his trousers, but I leaned in to hear what news Erik had to tell.

"We have heard that King Gudrod has also fallen near Kaupang. From the sounds of it, the attacks happened at roughly the same time. We just learned those ill tidings this morning. And now this..."

My father's head fell as Astrid gasped. King Gudrod was cousin and foster brother to King Trygvi, and the two were close friends and staunch allies to each other. And now both were gone, and with them, all remnants of the peace and political order that had existed since King Hakon began his rule in the days of my father's youth.

"They will come for you and for all of the lords loyal to King Trygvi," my father said when he had regained his composure.

"Aye, they will," said Erik. "But I have survived such upheavals before. I do not worry for myself."

Astrid frowned. "You would support Harald and his brothers, the killers of my husband?" Her voice had risen with her incredulity, as had the color in her fair cheeks.

"If I must," responded Erik calmly. "If the lords do not mobilize to fight them, then what choice have I?"

"Have you dispatched messengers to the other lords?" This question came from my father and I wondered if his idea was to take part in the fight, should they gather to resist their new overlords.

"I have, but it is too early to know where they stand on this." Erik grabbed another piece of bread and bit into it. "Still," he began again with his mouth full, "whether we choose to fight or bend our knees to our new king does not remove the threat to you, Astrid, or to your boy. He is heir to the High Seat of Vingulmark through his father's line, and Harald will want him removed to make room for his own sons. From what Torolv has said, he has already tried."

"What are you saying, exactly?" Astrid asked.

"I am saying that you cannot stay here any longer than is necessary."

Astrid's mouth fell open. "Will you not protect us?" My father placed a calming hand on her arm but she shrugged it off and glared at her father. "You would put me and my child out?"

"Calm yourself, my daughter. I am not putting you out." Erik kept his voice low, but I could hear the warning in his tone. "I am saving you and your child. If you remain here, you will be found and you will be killed. And so will your child. And so might your entire family for harboring you."

"Who is to be killed?" Olaf asked, suddenly alert to the conversation.

The adults turned their heads to him and Erik scowled. "This conversation is not for your ears, boy. Wait outside." He pointed to the door.

Olaf's cheeks flushed and I saw on his face that familiar mischievous expression. His hand was on the handle of his seax. Erik's brows folded downward at Olaf's implied threat.

"Olaf," I said as calmly as possible. "Come. Let the adults have their conversation."

He kept his eyes on his grandfather but nodded at my suggestion. I gently grabbed his arm and pulled him up. "Come, Olaf."

"You too, Turid," I heard Sigrunn call to her daughter as the adults turned back to the table.

The three of us exited the hall and left talk of killing to the adults, even though it would be all of our throats who would feel the bite of the blade, should Harald's men find us.

I rounded on my charge when we had gone a fair distance from the cottage. "That is your grandfather, Olaf. You do not threaten him as you just did."

"What would you know, Torgil? My grandfather cares naught for me. He never has. He cares only for his sons and their sons. It has always been so. One day, I will change that."

I remembered Erik's less-than-friendly greeting to the two of us and suddenly understood that there was more to the story of Olaf and his grandfather than I previously thought. "I did not know it was so bad between you. Still, you should not threaten the man who gives us a roof to sleep under and food on our table."

Olaf huffed. "He does so for my mother. Not for me. He thinks me a fool." He marched off down the hill and I turned to Turid, who was looking at him with a slightly shocked expression on her gaunt face.

"I am frightened, Torgil," she said softly as her eyes trailed Olaf.

And so was I, but I was too proud to admit it to her, and so I held my tongue.

We learned our fate soon enough. As we sat about the table that night, Astrid and my father explained to Olaf and me that we could stay at Erik's seter until trouble appeared. And when it came — which my father was certain it would — we were to head east, to the land of the Swedes and a friend of Erik's named Haakon the Old. That would get us one step closer to Holmgard in the land of the Rus, where Astrid's brother, Sigurd, served a prince named Sviatoslav. Haakon the Old, they explained, would take us in when the time came, though why they believed this was unclear to me. In the meantime, Gunnar and Gunhild would see to our welfare and in return, we would help them on the seter. It was a fair enough arrangement and one for which I was grateful.

Still, questions persisted, and these I asked when my father and Astrid finished unveiling the plan. "What of our home?" I asked.

My father leveled his eyes on me but took a long moment to answer. "We have no home now, Torgil. At least, not for a time."

"So what is to become of us?"

My father twirled his cup of ale in his fingers. "Whoever looks not forward to learn his fate, unburdened will his heart be."

"What does that mean?" I snarled, needing practical responses at that moment instead of one of my father's stupid sayings.

My father frowned at my tone. "It means that only the Norns know our fates, Torgil. And our fates are woven together with theirs now." He motioned with his bushy chin to Astrid.

I looked at the queen, then at Olaf, suddenly resenting them and the oath we had made to protect them. Yet I knew, too, that to break that oath was to bring shame to our family's name that would pass down through the ages, and that was a fate worse than death.

My father interrupted my thoughts. "Torgil? Have you heard my words?"

"Aye," I mumbled.

"And you, Olaf?" asked Astrid. "Do you understand what Torolv Loose-beard is saying to you?"

He looked up from picking at a wood splinter on the table. "I understand," he said, though I doubted he was truly paying attention.

"Good," she said. "No more sulking now. That includes you too, Sigrunn and Turid. We know not what the future holds, so let us not be burdened by it. Let us make the most of our misfortune and prove our worth when we rise each day. And let us pray that the opportunity will soon come for us to retake what was taken from us."

And so began our new life as fugitives.

Chapter 7

It took several days, but life on the seter soon fell into a predictable rhythm that helped mask memories of the previous days. We rose each day before dawn to the lowing of cows and the bleating of sheep. With the sun's first pink glow to our left, Olaf and I hiked to the stream that flowed through a steep gulley on the opposite side of the hill from the cottage. There, we filled the buckets we carried and struggled back to the seter, trying and failing to keep the water from splashing on us and the path. By then the adults were gathering the animals and driving them to the barn for milking.

At midmorning, we all gathered in the cottage to break our fast on warm bread, porridge or skyr, and wild strawberries, which Gunhild, Sigrunn, and Turid had prepared for us. We moved to our individual tasks after the meal. Gunhild coached the women in all manner of dairy production. They made butter and buttermilk, the pungent brown cheese known as Gamalost, whey and skyr, sour milk, and even a fermented milk beverage that the adults enjoyed at night. The domain of the men was outside, cutting and stacking wood, gathering water and hay, sharpening tools, or keeping the animals from venturing too far afield.

Weapons training with my father began in the afternoon. This I enjoyed immensely, for however strict his instruction — and it could be strict indeed — it afforded me time to step into the world of men and to interact with my father in ways I had not known when he was lord of his estate and too busy to instruct me personally. We trained mainly with wooden swords that Gunnar had crafted for us, though also with our one spear, our two shields, and our seaxes. Gunnar often joined my father in these sessions and showed us as much mercy as my father, which was none. Many was the time Olaf and I ended our training on our backsides, with fresh welts and bruises to add to the ones from the previous day.

While I excelled in martial skills, I noticed with increasing jealousy that even at his young age, Olaf was god-gifted, with keen coordination in either hand — a rare gift that I could not emulate. It was my envy of Olaf that led to my roughness with him in our training, and the harsh rebukes I would receive from my father because of that roughness. That, in turn, only made me more bitter.

Late afternoons were spent on repairs. The weather was not easy on structures in the North, and it seemed that something always needed fixing, whether the wood plank of the barn, a section of daub on the wall, a portion of thatch, a tool, or a rope. One-handed Gunnar proved a capable carpenter and craftsman and taught me much about woodwork and the maintenance of a farm. Olaf held himself aloof from those tasks, preferring to spend his time fighting imaginary enemies with his seax, at least until a sharp rebuke from my father brought him back to his senses.

I cannot entirely blame Olaf for his lack of attention, though, for I too was guilty of such infractions, especially when Turid appeared. It did not help that she tarried a little longer when she saw us training. At first, my inattentiveness amused my father, but that soon grew to frustration and a swift smack to the head when it required him to repeat an instruction.

At night, with the meal finished and the chores done, Olaf and I compared our wounds, taking pride in their size and color and recalling just how we had received each. Olaf would often embellish his story with some new twist or boast that usually brought a grin to the faces of our elders. That, too, was a skill I had not yet developed, nor did I wish to. Whereas Olaf seemed to enjoy the theatrics, I felt less comfortable telling tales to an audience.

I could tell you that life's new rhythm fully replaced the nagging fear that tugged at me, but that would be a lie, and I am no liar. Anxiety was my constant companion. Battles and bloodshed and death filled my dreams, so much so that I feared to fall asleep. Wakefulness was no easier. I could not shake the thought that Holger and his men were coming for us. During our chores, my eyes drifted constantly to the woods, seeing shadows that appeared as men but were not. At night, strange noises filled the world beyond our walls — noises that my young mind morphed into murderous men coming to burn us in our sel.

I did not tell these things to my father or to anyone else for fear he or they would think me weak, but he was a perceptive man and soon noticed my distress. On the afternoon of our third day on the seter, he and I were sharpening axe blades on a whetstone when a twig snapped in the woods off to our left. My head jerked at the sound and I peered into the shadows for a sign of the warrior I was certain was there.

My father looked over at the woods. After a spell, he turned back to me. "There is a saying among men," he said. "Mayhap you have heard it. The witless man is awake all night, thinking of many things, but when the morning comes, his cares are just as they were." He sniffed and studied me, and I looked away, ashamed. "Set your worries aside, Torgil. Erik has men watching the approaches to our seter. When Holger and his men come, we will have warning."

"How much warning?" We had men posted on Jel too, and had barely escaped with our lives. I was not eager to repeat that.

My father shrugged, nonplussed by my question. "Enough."

At that moment, a pig waddled out of the underbrush where the twig had cracked.

"You see?" said my father. "It is only a swine."

I relaxed, though my mind had locked on my father's comment about Erik and his guards. "If we are certain Holger will come, then why do we stay here? Our tracks are easy to follow."

"Why should we run if Holger never appears? Traveling to the land of the Swedes is no trivial matter."

"And if we travel to the Swedes and Haakon is not willing to house us? What then?"

"If Erik says that Haakon will house us, I have no fear of that. Nor should you. Erik is a man of his word."

I felt somewhat better, though I was still not completely convinced of our security. I had seen nothing of these men who were purportedly protecting us and knew not how dedicated they were to our welfare. And Erik had not impressed me with his friendship toward us, especially his own grandson. Still, I knew better than to press my father. So I turned my attention back to my stone and axe and forced myself to silence.

On the sixth day after our arrival, Gunnar and Gunhild informed us that it was their rest day and that we would cease our work in the afternoon. "When you have finished your morning tasks, come to the sel," Gunnar said to us. "It is a good day to go fishing."

I could barely conceal my excitement at the prospect of catching some fish, though I was not as verbal about it as Olaf. As we hiked over the hill and up the stream, there was no end to Olaf's questions and chatter. My father had long since stopped responding to his babble and I was growing tense, as much at Olaf's nonsensical comments as my father's exasperated silence. It was Gunnar who finally turned to Olaf and put his finger to his lips. "By the gods, boy, you will scare the fish with your noise. Silence now, and watch."

We reached a spot where the rocky banks pinched the stream so that it formed a natural flood flow. At the base of the flow, a rope traversed the stream just above the waterline. Gunnar untied the rope on our side of the stream and ran the end of it through the cone-shaped fishing baskets he had brought along. He then handed the end of the rope to my father and submerged the baskets in the stream's current. "Retie the rope," he called to my father.

Gunnar emerged from the stream and passed each of us a stick. "You three will enter the water there." He pointed upstream beyond the weir. "Enter slowly, then in unison start slapping the water to scare the fish. As you do, move toward the funnel to scare the fish in my direction. Understand?"

We nodded.

"Come," said my father, and led us upstream to the spot Gunnar had indicated. "Ready?" he asked when we reached the spot. We nodded again, silent now in our mounting excitement. He grinned and slowly moved into the stream. We followed, careful to avoid the mossy rocks below the stream's surface. It was not difficult, for the water here was clear and we could see the rocks as well as we could see the darting fish.

Fish, I learned that day, do not swim backward. Only forward. So when our sticks hit the water, those fish facing downstream bolted in that direction, toward Gunnar and his baskets. We followed with our heavy footsteps and our slapping wands.

"That's it!" Gunnar called. "Keep coming!"

And so we came, driving the fish as a shepherd might drive his flock. Several silver streaks zipped past my feet, but I hoped more were swimming downstream, away from the churning water and the menace that was chasing them.

"Hey, hey!" he called and stayed us with a hand. "That's enough now! Lord Torolv, come help me with the baskets. Lads, move to the shore."

But Olaf was having too much fun and continued slapping the water and whooping his delight. I grabbed his shoulder and repeated Gunnar's command: "Olaf. To the shore."

Lost in the moment, Olaf shrugged my hand away. I know not why, but that move infuriated me. I know now that Olaf was just having fun and he did not want the fun to stop, but in that moment, I saw that shrug as a deliberate refusal to heed my word — or Gunnar's, for that matter — and that lack of respect set my blood to boiling. My body reacted out of sheer frustration, and I pushed him hard toward the shore. A little too hard. The lad lost his footing and fell sidelong into the stream.

He scrambled to his feet, drenched from head to toe, and rounded on me. "Why did you do that?" he sputtered, his face red with fury.

His tone put me on the defensive. "Did you not hear Gunnar's instruction?" I asked.

"No."

"Then you should clean out your ears. He told us to move to the shore, but instead, you continued to smack the water."

"Do not do that again," Olaf warned.

"Or you will do what?" I asked and stepped closer to him.

"Stop your bickering," my father growled, "and come help."

We scowled at each other for a moment longer, then scrambled to the baskets. The baskets were constructed of woven willow and in the gaps between those willow branches flopped several brown trout. I smiled and Olaf whooped, our spat momentarily forgotten.

Gunnar handed us one of the baskets. "Take it to the shore, lads. Carefully." We took the basket from his hands and moved to the shore. One of the trout worked its way free and splashed into the stream. "Don't let them escape!" Gunnar called after us, though I could tell he was smiling.

My father came after us with the second basket. Gunnar followed, carrying the third. "Set the baskets there," Gunnar said and nodded his chin toward a spot near his satchel.

"Look at them all!" Olaf exclaimed.

"A good catch," Gunnar acknowledged. "Though we cannot keep them all. Quick now, before they lose air, pull the little ones free and throw them back in the water. We keep only the big fish."

"Why?" asked Olaf.

"The little ones don't have enough meat on their bones yet. We must wait for them to grow before they are worthy of our table, eh."

I knelt by the first basket. A small trout's golden, black-spotted body was lodged between two willow branches and it was struggling mightily to get free. I pried the branches apart with my fingers and the fish flopped to the earth. Picking it up carefully, I tossed the slimy body back into the stream and watched it dart away.

Beside me, Olaf shrieked as he tried to dislodge another young trout from the willows and managed only to pull its head from its body. "Careful," I snarled.

"Boys!" my father warned.

I skewered Olaf with my eyes as Gunnar stepped in. "Do not pull the fish. Pry the branches apart and let the fish fall out. Like this." He demonstrated, using two to separate the willow. "Now you try."

Olaf concentrated on the next fish, his tongue visible between his lips as he delicately pulled the willow away from the fish's body. It flipped free and he smiled.

"Good," Gunnar said. "Now throw it back."

In all, we returned seven fish to the stream but kept twelve larger trout. These Gunnar knocked on the head with the blunt side of his knife blade to kill them, then placed them carefully in his satchel. "Come," he said when the last fish was in the bag. "We will give these to the women to clean and cook."

I assumed that we would take these back to the seter, but Gunnar led us past the trail that wound up to the cottage and followed the stream farther south. And then, quite suddenly, we emerged from the trees into an open area where a scattering of boulders split the stream into a patchwork of smaller streams and pools.

I froze at the sight ahead of us, not knowing quite what to do. Gunhild had just emerged from a pool where she had been bathing and was walking toward her clothing, which lay on a nearby rock. Near her, in a pool, Sigrunn combed Turid's red hair, their backs to us. In another pool, Astrid was scrubbing her face with her hands, her ample breasts visible for all to see.

My father who turned away first. Gunnar, then I, followed his lead. Olaf, of course, continued to stare. That is until I smacked his shoulder. At the same time, Astrid saw us and with a gasp, quickly moved her hand to cover herself. Gunhild scrambled to the rock on which her clothes lay and covered herself with them. I thank the gods that we had our backs turned when they finally saw us, for had they caught us gaping, there would have been no end to the awkwardness in the cottage that night. Still, the image of those women in their various stages of repose and nudity was seared into my brain and it would be weeks before I could clear my mind of it.

"March right back the way you came, husband," called Gunhild. "We will be done soon enough. And then you men can be about your business here."

"We caught some fish," Gunnar called back and held up the satchel. "We will leave them here for you. Once you are done, come find us at the fork. There we will be waiting."

He led us back down the trail to the place where the trail forked off to climb the hill back to the seter. We waited in silence, none of us quite sure what to say. When the women appeared at last, they carried the satchel and a separate sack filled with our newly washed clothes.

"You were faster than we expected with your fishing," was all Gunhild said to her husband as she set the sack on the turf. She ignored the rest of us. I tried to look at Turid, but she looked away.

"Fishing is easier with more hands," he responded. Which, in hindsight, I can now appreciate for its brilliance. It was a plausible excuse and a sad one, and it left Gunhild with no retort. Instead, she snorted angrily and marched off with the other women in tow. My father and Gunnar grinned at their backs, though I knew not why.

When the women had gone, we walked back to the watering holes to bathe. I wasted no time in stripping my soiled clothes from my body and jumping into one of the pools. Though I had no soap, it did not matter. Just the feeling of cool water on my skin was enough to make me feel clean. But the peace ended abruptly, for no sooner had I begun to relax when Olaf asked Gunnar how he had lost his arm. It was an innocent enough question, but my father, who sat in a nearby pool, did not like it and glowered. "Gunnar will tell us when and if he is ready, Olaf. It is not for you to ask a question like that."

Gunnar's marred face twisted with his grin, and he stayed my father with his meaty hand. "It is fine, lord. Olaf is young and curious. If he would like to know, I will tell him."

"It is up to you," my father said as he splashed some water on his face and rubbed at the grime on his hairy cheeks.

"Long ago, Olaf, I served Erik as one of his hirdmen. King Hakon had just taken the throne, but his reign was young and his hold on the land, tenuous. The Danes and Swedes had heard of his youth and came to test him. They came mainly to the Vik, for the lands on either side are fertile and the farms richer, and Hakon was then mostly in the west and too far away from the fighting to lend any help.

"One summer, we received a message from King Hakon that he was coming to end the Danish scourge and that we were to gather with King Trygvi in the Vestfold, at Kaupang, and wait for him and his men there. This we did and a mighty host we gathered, too. But we were also overconfident," Gunnar added with a sad shake of his head as his eyes traveled from Olaf to me. "It is one of the dangers of thinking yourself too strong, lads. Never forget that."

"What happened?" Olaf asked, his young face rapt.

"The Danes attacked before King Hakon arrived. We knew they were close, but never suspected they would attack such a host as ours. They came at us head on and hit us hard. In that first push, we were driven back, but with each step we gave, we tightened our ranks and held a bit firmer. By the gods, it was a fight." He clenched his fist. "The yelling. The cursing. The sword strikes and axe blows and spear play. The gods love their chaos and we men delivered it that day." He sighed. "I loved it. Every horrifying moment of it." He looked at us and must have seen the confusion on our faces. "It is hard to understand until you experience it, lads."

He went silent for a time, then started up again. "We were strong, but a shield wall, like a byrnie, is only as good as its weakest link. And when a second Danish force appeared on our left, that weak link was revealed. The bastards on that end were the local levy — farmers for the most part — and no match for the warriors charging at them. They broke and ran, scampering for the protection of the hill behind the town. And when they ran, they doomed us."

Gunnar turned his eyes to Olaf. "And that is when I was wounded, lad. When those bastards on our left ran, it distracted me and I turned my gaze from my attacker. Just for an eye blink, mind, but it was enough. Never, lads, never let yourself be distracted in a fight. Even for a moment. Because this is what happens." He held up his stump. "The first blade cut across my face and I reeled from the pain of it. And in that instant, I felt something hit my arm. I thought I had been smacked by a shield rim, but a quick glance revealed the truth of what had happened. My forearm had been cut clean through and lay on the ground with my shield. I did not feel pain, only confusion at seeing my arm where it should not be, and then fury at that Danish bastard who took it. I took his life for taking my arm, which gave me some solace. But more importantly, it gave me time to run."

"You ran?" Olaf was wide-eyed.

Gunnar laughed. "Before you think me the coward, lad, let me explain that most of my comrades had regrouped about twenty paces behind me to close their dwindling ranks. I was gravely wounded, but I was not about to let those Danish bastards take me out there in the open as my friends looked on. I wanted to keep fighting, see? To get to my comrades and take the fight back to the Danes." He smirked. "The battle frenzy can do that to a man. Make him think he's impervious to death."

My father grunted and nodded. I marveled at Gunnar, for I could not imagine having my arm severed from my body and still thinking that there was a chance to live. I could not imagine what he had gone through to survive, and it kindled within me a newfound appreciation for this farmer.

Olaf's mouth was agape. "So you ran back to them and kept fighting?"

"I made it back to my friends, but they would not let me fight. I was bleeding too badly. It was smearing their shining armor, see, and they could not have that." Gunnar grinned, and I knew he was fooling now. "So they ordered me back to the rear to find some help. I lost track of things then and blacked out. When I awoke, I was up in King Bjorn's hall in Kaupang with the other wounded lads. Someone had bound my stump and burned it to stop the bleeding. It throbbed horribly and took months to heal, but I survived."

"Who fixed you?" Olaf asked.

Gunnar shrugged. "I know not who. Come now. It is getting late, and I think I can smell the trout cooking. Let us finish our bathing and return to the seter."

We dressed quickly in our fresh clothes and hiked back to the seter. Olaf fought imaginary foes all the way up the hill, while I envisioned a steaming trout resting in my trencher. But reality soon interrupted our dreams. For there, at the door of the cottage, stood a strange man conversing with the women. With him were a hound, an ox, and a cart partially filled with goods. Astrid turned to us when we appeared, and in her eyes, I saw the hard truth.

It was time to leave.

Part II

To his thoughts the sacred name
Of his mother Astrid came,
And the tale she oft had told
Of her flight by secret passes
Through the mountains and morasses,
To the home of Haakon old.

The Saga of King Olaf

Chapter 8

The guide was a young man named Lodin who was as white as the snow that fell on our lands each winter. White skin. White hair. White brows. Only his eyes were blue — piercing, icy blue. An uncanny blue that set me on edge when he looked at me. A modest traveling cloak of coarse wool hung from his wide shoulders and a short, blotchy beard of white fell like ragged icicles from his jaw. He held in his hand a thick, well-polished spear that he used as a walking stick and wore two belts. The one at his waist held a small leather pouch and a seax. The other wrapped over his shoulder and supported a sword. Only a man of means or skill possessed a sword, and I hoped it was the latter.

The hunting hound seated by his leg was a beautiful dog, with a dark nose and a curled tail in the manner of our Northern hounds. It looked friendly enough, but when Olaf went to pet it, it bared its teeth and started to growl. "Careful," Lodin warned, placing a hand before the hound's face, which calmed it. "She is very protective of me. Would you like to know her name?"

Olaf nodded tentatively.

"It is Feilan," he said, which meant wolf cub. "I found her in the forest when she was a pup and think she might be half wolf."

"Lodin has come from my father's hall," Astrid interjected, "where the snake, Holger, sits this very moment. Lodin informs us that Harald has placed a bounty on my head, and that of my son. A sack of silver the weight of..." She could not finish the sentence, though her eyes shifted briefly to Olaf before returning to my father's face.

My father hissed a curse.

Astrid stood rigidly, her chin high, though I could see tears welling in her blue eyes, and I wondered if her insides felt like my own: knotted like a fist. "Lodin is to take me and Olaf to Haakon the Old. None of you need go. This journey is our fate, not yours."

My father spat in response, then pointed to me. "My son and I made an oath to your husband and we will keep it. We go with you."

This Astrid accepted with a nod of thanks. She turned to her maid-servants. "You and Turid should remain here," she said to Sigrunn more softly. "You are not thralls and can go if you wish. This journey will not be easy and though I would like your company, I do not wish to put you in any more danger than I already have."

"My lady," Sigrunn replied, "we have been with you a long time and are not about to let you run off without us. We belong with you, whatever the danger, and I will not hear another word on the matter." That was bravely spoken and made me reconsider my assessment of Sigrunn, whom I thought of as soft.

Lodin passed a small sack to Astrid. "Erik has given you this silver and some supplies for our journey, as well as this ox and cart."

Olaf's brows bent over his eyes. "My grandfather would have us walk to Sweden? He has horses to spare. Why has he not given us any?"

Lodin kept his face mild. "Because you have a bounty on your head and a horse will mark you as wealthy." He walked to the back of the cart and pulled a pair of simple trousers and a homespun tunic from the bed. These he tossed to Olaf so that they landed at his feet. "You will wear these."

Olaf lifted the clothes and gawked. "I am no thrall!"

My father rounded on Olaf and backhanded him across his cheek. The boy flew backward onto the dirt. The women gasped. "Erik is trying to keep you alive, boy. Be thankful for what he has given us."

Olaf rubbed his jaw as Lodin handed a simple shift to his mother. "You, too, will have to conceal yourself, my lady. As will the other two women."

Astrid snatched the clothes from Lodin's hand. "What of them?" she nodded to my father and me.

"They will remain as they are. From this moment forward, Lord Torolv, his son Torgil, and I are traders, heading to Sweden with our goods, which are in this cart. You will all play your parts. If we are stopped and questioned, and you forget your role, we are all dead. Is that clear?"

We nodded and eyed each other.

I was beginning to understand that life is never straightforward. Never predictable. It is just a series of random, yet unavoidable, events strung together by the Norns, those weavers of a man's fate who sit at the base of the world tree, Yggdrasil. I wondered as we quickly packed our measly belongings that afternoon whether the Norns cared about our predicament. Whether life was all a giant Hnefatafl board and they wanted to see whether we could overcome the moves of our adversaries. Or whether they wove our fate with the cold indifference of a stone, caring not at all if we lived or if we died. I wanted to believe it was the former, though the suddenness and relentlessness of life's recent trials made me think it was the latter. And that thought made me bitter. I wanted to rage at the Norns for the injustice of our situation, but I knew too that to do so would do no good. That, in my father's words, would be as useful as trying to change the direction of the wind by shouting at it.

It was not all bad news, at least. Turid would be coming with us and I was thankful merely to be near her. And despite the gold-seekers and fame-coveters who would soon be hunting us, our strange guide and his dog seemed capable enough and gave me some hope that we could survive this next trial.

"There are several more things I must ask of you, my lady," Lodin said to Astrid apologetically. He held in his left hand a leather collar and in his right, Gunnar's shears. Astrid, Olaf, and her maidservants wore their thrall clothes and stood in the half-light of the small seter, and even in that light, I could see the tears in Astrid's eyes. "We must hurry, my lady."

Astrid took the shears from Lodin's hands and without hesitation, grabbed a handful of her blond locks and snipped. She threw the hair into the hearth fire and snipped again. Olaf clenched his fists and turned his eyes to the ground. My father also turned away, though whether to give her privacy, to save her dignity, or out of shame for his foster daughter's fall from nobility, I cannot say, nor would I ever know.

When she was finished, she passed the shears to Olaf. "Cut your hair." He stared at the shears but did not take them. "Take them," she hissed, "or I will have Torgil cut your hair."

He grabbed them and started cutting, and as he did, Lodin tied the thrall collar around Astrid's neck. Meanwhile, Turid and Sigrunn helped each other complete their transformation from maidservants to thralls. My father and I removed any sign of wealth from our bodies and packed them away in the cart with my father's byrnie, our shields, and our extra weapons. Then we fastened cruder traveling cloaks to our shoulders. Mine hung nearly to the ground.

With our disguises complete, we took a teary leave of Gunhild and Gunnar, who had supplied us with ample amounts of hard cheese, dried venison, bread, water, and ale for our journey. I turned once as we descended the hill to see our hosts watching us. We had spent only a few days with them, but still, I would miss them and hoped one day I could repay them for their kindness.

Lodin set a comfortable pace from the seter, heading south. He held the ox's lead in one hand and his spear in the other, humming a soft tune. By his side ambled Feilan. My father and I strode behind him, our eyes scanning the forest for trouble. The women and Olaf plodded beside the cart that held our supplies, making a great show of their despair.

"We are walking south. Why?" I asked.

"How do you know we are headed south?" he asked.

"By the position of the sun," I responded, for I could see the angle of light streaming through the thick canopy of leaves above us.

"Good," he said. "It is useful to know such things."

I think I straightened my shoulders a bit more at my father's compliment, but Lodin was there to dampen my pride.

"Actually," he corrected, "we are traveling southeast, but more south than east. Away from the coast, anyway. Eventually, we will turn more eastward as we venture into Sweden."

My father glanced at me and rolled his eyes. I grinned, happier at that small gesture than his earlier compliment, or frankly, at any other gesture he had made toward me since leaving the borg.

Though the sun rarely sets during Northern summers, that truth does not hold exactly true in the forest. There, all is shadow, and as the night grows later, the gloom deepens. Only the faintest pinpoints of light mark the stars in the azure sky. It would have been pleasant, was it not for the threat of being hunted by men. And, of course, to my young mind, of being hunted also by the creatures of the night. Wolves. Malevolent spirits. The undead draugar. I saw them in every shadow and behind every tree. I lost count of the times I jumped at an unfamiliar sound and reached for my sword.

At one particularly noticeable flinch, Olaf sniggered. I scowled at him. "Shut up, thrall."

He stuck out his tongue at me, and it took all my self-control not to knock him upside his measly skull. I turned back to the road ahead, wondering if he was too young or dim-witted to fear the night as I did.

"Are you a trader?" My father's question interrupted my annoyance with Olaf.

There was a long silence as we waited for Lodin to respond. "Aye. Of sorts, I suppose."

"It is best not to ask?" my father surmised.

The man chuckled at that. "Ask what you wish to know. Whether I answer is another matter."

My father grunted softly but did not reply. The guide's responses verged on offense, but I sensed that he did not mean wrong — he was merely direct in his words and unwilling to lie. I think my father sensed the same, which is why he did not press the man.

When the sky began to brighten, we pulled the cart thirty paces off the track and cut branches to hide it. Lodin pointed Astrid, Olaf, and the maidservants to the space beneath the cart. "You should sleep. You will be safe under there." He looked at me and my father. "You too."

My father shook his head. "I will take first watch."

Lodin shrugged. "As you wish, lord. Feilan will sleep near me. Keep your eyes on her. She will sense something long before we do."

I did not sleep well that morning. It was warm and the ground hard, and my thoughts were filled with the imaginary men who pursued us — the men who became more vivid in my mind when my eyes closed. Beside me, Olaf slept soundly, but the others tossed and coughed. When Lodin woke to relieve my father, I rose with him.

"You should rest," he whispered to me as my father crawled under the cart and closed his eyes.

I shook my head. "I cannot sleep."

He beckoned me away from the cart. Feilan stretched and yawned and padded after us. I liked hounds, but I was wary of this one. I had seen how protective of her master she was and had no doubt she could turn on us too, if Lodin ordered it.

We sat at the base of a tall pine and Feilan joined us, sitting on her haunches next to Lodin like a sentry. He stroked her back. "You are fearful," he said, responding to my early comment about sleep. "If I was your age, I would be fearful too. But there are things you can do to help yourself."

"There are?" I asked, my curiosity piqued.

"To start, learn the sounds of the forest." He pointed to the branches above us. "Do you not hear the chitter and scurrying of squirrels at play?"

I heard them but could not discern that there was more than one squirrel or that they were at play.

"Listen to the leaves. Can you hear them rustle?"

I heard it.

"The trick is to learn the normal sounds from the foreign sounds."

"How did you learn?" I asked.

"I was raised in the forest." He paused, then explained further. "As a boy, people feared me." He held up his white arms as if to show me why, but I already knew. "I had no childhood friends. So I spent my time in the woods, among the animals. Animals never feared me." And then, quite suddenly, he added, "We must get rid of the cheese."

"What?" I responded, taken by surprise.

"The cheese. In the cart. It is an unnatural smell and does not belong in the forest. Any tracker looking for us will smell it and find us. Come." He motioned me up.

We walked to the cart and located two rounds of cheese among the cargo. He handed them to me. "Take your seax and bury the cheese over there," he whispered, pointing vaguely into the forest.

"Do we not need this for food?" I wondered softly.

"We have plenty of food," he responded. "Now, go."

I did as he requested and buried the cheese, but not before cutting a chunk from the round for myself. I could not remember my last full meal and though I was not fond of cheese, I savored the feeling in my gut as I buried the rounds in the soft earth. Around me, the forest continued its puzzling cacophony, and I endeavored to understand it. I failed, of course, but it gave me a better sense of control to do so, and so I promised myself to continue to learn. I was tired of fear and yearned to master it. Lodin's words gave me a path. It was now up to me to follow it.

When the group awoke, the women moved to the cart to find some food for our day meal. "Where is the cheese?" Sigrunn wondered.

"Gone," Lodin responded indifferently.

"Gone? Where?" she asked.

"We buried it."

Sigrunn's eyebrows shot up and her mouth sagged open. "You cannot just...that was...it was a gift." But she clamped her mouth shut when she saw Lodin staring at her.

"The cheese will get us killed," he explained. "Any tracker who knows his business will smell it a ways off. The same for hungry animals."

"He's right, Sigrunn," added my father with barely even a glance in her direction.

"But...should we not eat?" she asked, looking to Astrid for support.

"Oh, aye," Lodin responded. "Now is the time. There is bread and venison and fruit. We will leave as the air starts to cool."

With our fast broken, we headed back to the trail, only this time Lodin ordered the "thralls" into the cart with the rest of the goods. Olaf, of course, resisted, preferring to walk.

Lodin rounded on him. "I do not care if your prefer to walk, lad. Today you will do as I say and ride."

Olaf frowned, but Astrid managed to coax him into the bed of the wagon, where he sat with his arms crossed in a huff.

"No words today," Lodin ordered, then grabbed the lead rope and began walking.

I looked at my father, who had moved his cloak from his shoulder and walked with his hand on his belt, close to his sword. I did the same. Even Feilan seemed to sense the unease and padded alongside her master with her nose to the ground and her ears moving.

I know not what they sensed, but thinking back on it now, I am thankful for it, for I believe it is the reason we lived.

Chapter 9

The first warning came from Feilan, who uttered a barely perceptible growl as the hair straightened on her back. Lodin slowed his pace and showed his right palm to the wolf-dog's face, which silenced her. My father's hand moved to the grip of his sword, and he hung back until the cart came abreast of him. I glanced at him as he did so and knew from his eyes that there was trouble. I, too, made sure my hand was near my sword.

A burly man stepped from the forest some twenty paces ahead of us. Two smaller men flanked him. Movement to our rear brought my head around. Two more men stood there. All looked to be in their middle years, well-armed, and dressed in decent clothes. These were not mere forest outlaws come to rob us of our silver and provisions — these were warriors with a purpose. Even I could see that.

Lodin raised his hand to bring our party to a halt. "Greetings," he called to the man.

The corner of the man's mouth rose in a half-grin and he took a few steps toward us. There was a byrnie beneath the man's cloak and the long handle of a sword at his hip. "What brings you this way, traveler?" he asked.

Lodin shrugged. "Trade. I have thralls and some goods to bring to market. But I am happy to offload them here if you name a fair price."

The burly man's grin stretched. "I might consider your offer, but only if you have what I seek. We are on our lord's errand and are searching for someone."

Lodin acted surprised. "Whom do you seek?"

My eyes shifted to the men behind us, for they had taken several steps closer and their hands rested on their sword grips. I noticed another man in the forest to my left and guessed there was another off to the right, on the other side of the cart. Seven well-armed warriors against my father and Lodin, two boys, three women, and a hound. The odds twisted my gut. I did not want to die on that forgotten trail in the middle of that unnamed forest, remembered only by the wolves and ravens who picked the flesh from my bones. This could not be the end of my tale...

"We seek a woman and a boy. Much like those two you have in your cart," said the big-chested man, motioning to Astrid and Olaf with his brown-bearded chin.

Lodin scratched at his jaw. "And why do you seek a woman and a boy, might I ask?"

The man answered by moving Lodin aside with his arm and stepping toward the cart. His men moved with him and my hand inched closer to my sword. I sensed the men behind us moving closer too. The big man came to my side of the cart and pushed me aside. My heart thundered in my chest. "What is your name, thrall?" he asked Astrid.

Her response was not what I expected. She had been sitting dejectedly in the cart, her head down as the man asked his question. But now her face came up and with it came the sword she had taken from my father's hall. It was not a swing, but a powerful thrust, and it tore through the man's neck before he could dodge. Blood splashed across my face as I heard her yell her name.

The world erupted.

There was a sharp whistle, then a furious growl, and a man's shriek. I tore my sword from its sheath in time to block the brutal swing from the man coming from my right. That swing knocked me to the ground and away from the cart.

As I lay there, stunned, my eyes took in the scene. My father fought a man, though I knew not which one. On the ground near the ox, a man struggled to keep Feilan from his throat and howled when the half-wolf tore into his arm. In a flash of metal, Lodin sliced across the back of the man fighting my father, then into the side of the man in Feilan's jaws.

I turned my eyes to the cart. The man who had knocked me down had also knocked Astrid's sword from her grip and was struggling to pull her to the ground. Olaf had found the second blade and swung it hard at the man. He saw the boy's swing and tried to duck the blade, but it cleaved into the side of his skull, dropping him like a wet sack to the earth.

Behind Olaf, I saw a second man raise his sword to strike the boy. Just before his blade came down, a knife lodged in his chest and he stumbled backward, then fell.

I scrambled to my feet.

Something flashed overhead, so close I could feel the breath of it on my hair. It smacked into the cart. Another missile followed and I heard a cry. Across from me, Lodin whistled and Feilan barked and crashed into the forest. My mind could think of only one thing: evade the arrows. I was in the open and an easy target for a good archer. He had already loosed two missiles and narrowly missed me. A third one would not miss.

There was a small furrow on the side of the trail, and I dove for it. If I could reach it, the archer would need to be on top of me to hit me. My body slid into the earth's crease just as another man's scream tore through the air. Feilan had found her prey. And with that, the enemy nearest me crashed into the forest and disappeared.

I rose and scanned the scene. Lodin and my father were searching the men they had killed. Two more men lay dead near me. For a moment, I believed that we had somehow escaped without harm, but then I saw Turid. She was cradling Sigrunn's head in her arms, an arrow protruding from her mother's stomach. My heart sank.

I turned my eyes to Olaf, who stood over the man he had killed, staring down at the corpse. For a moment I thought he might hack at the dead man again, but at the last instant, he began kicking the body. Over and over, he kicked. "You pig!" he yelled as his shoe thudded into the man's ribs. "You dog! You potlicker!" His face was red and his eyes tearing. "This is what you get for hunting women and children, you coward! This is what you get!" He spat on the man.

"Enough!" Astrid screamed.

Olaf snapped from his fury and stepped back, panting. He then wiped at the spittle on his lips. I stared at him, still recovering from the shock of the attack and the rage I had seen in Olaf. The boy had a dark pit of anger in him. I knew its source, for I felt it in my own soul. Only Olaf was too young to be encumbered by morals or norms. He was too young to understand that kicking a corpse was irregular. I suppose there was a part of me that wished I had done it too to expunge the impotent rage I felt at the chaos that was our lives. But I was older than Olaf and had learned to swallow my rage, for better or worse. And so I just stared.

"Torgil! Check that man." My father pointed to the burly man whom Astrid had killed. "Take his weapons, his armor, and any wealth you can find. Hurry."

I rushed to the body, which had fallen flat on its back beside the cart. As I did, my father's voice called again. "Astrid. See to Sigrunn!"

My hands tore at the man's small purse. My eyes shifted to the man's face and his shocked, yet vacant eyes. As I pried his byrnie from his body, I tried not to look at the wound in his throat or the dark blood that flowed from it to pool around his head. When I was done, I dragged the booty to my father.

"How is she?" called my father to Astrid.

Astrid looked at him. "The arrow went deep and the wound is grave. She needs help." Astrid clearly wanted to say more but could not. Beside her, Turid wept as she brushed her mother's hair with her hand.

Olaf moved to the back of the cart and stared at her. "Will she live?" he asked with the bluntness of a boy who had seen only eight winters. As if to punctuate his lack of decorum, he dropped a sword and seax and sack of coins into the bed of the cart with a loud rattle of metal.

"Olaf!" Astrid scolded him. "Mind yourself."

My father climbed into the cart and studied Sigrunn. "We have no tools to remove the arrow, Astrid. And we cannot stop. We know not who might be following us or how close they are. If we find a steading ahead, we will see if they can offer help." His gaze shifted to Lodin, who stood near the ox, and in that glance, I saw the truth in his eyes. There would be no stopping. My father turned back to Turid. "Keep your mother warm, and do your best to stem the bleeding. That is all we can do for her now."

We dragged the dead into the woods on either side of the track, then Lodin whistled for his hound. Feilan came bounding back, her face a mask of blood, her tongue hanging from exertion. Lodin patted the hound's head, then called for us to move. "Olaf," he called. "Sit in the back of the cart and keep an eye on the trail behind us. If you see anything strange, call out. Do you understand?"

"Aye," said Olaf, then he dangled his feet over the end of the bed and rested his newly blooded sword on his lap.

And so we walked away from the carnage, and as we did, I marveled that the ox had survived the skirmish unscathed and did not seem spooked by the wicked affair. But then, that was life. Full of surprises and inexplicable mysteries.

My father was wrong about the stopping. We halted during the night at the sound of Turid's doleful wail. Sigrunn had bled too much from her wound and her life had drained from her despite Astrid and Turid's best efforts to stop the bleeding.

Truth be told, I was almost relieved, for her moaning had gotten worse as the night progressed and I feared it would give us away to our pursuers. I was not the only one who feared it. On more than one occasion, my father and Lodin cautioned Astrid and Turid to keep her quiet, but their efforts could not stop Sigrunn's complaints. I must say, it is a strange feeling to resent someone and mourn their dying in equal measure.

Her death, when it came, affected me more than I expected. I had not been close to Sigrunn, but she had taken good care of Astrid and Turid in life and had been kind to me, and for that, at least, I was grateful to her. A tearful Astrid said much the same at her graveside, which we dug in a pretty meadow near a stream. I fought to keep my tears inside as I watched a weeping Turid place wildflowers about her body, then lay honey and skyr and coins at her feet to aid her on her journey to the underworld. I did not just cry for Sigrunn, mind you. I also cried for Turid, who had suffered a loss no less than mine or Olaf's or Astrid's or my father's.

We laid stones over Sigrunn's shallow grave to fend off the forest creatures, then returned wordlessly to the cart. There was nothing really to say, though I suppose some comforting words for Turid would have been nice. Olaf and I were too young to think of those things and my father and Lodin too hard to show such care. Even Astrid seemed devoid of speech, choosing instead to wrap her arm over Turid's shoulders.

Without a word, Lodin pulled the ox forward. I glanced one last time at the meadow where Sigrunn lay, then followed Lodin down the path. As I did, I wondered silently whether more of us would die before we reached our destination.

Chapter 10

Just after leaving Sigrunn's grave, we passed into the kingdom of the Swedes and from there, the trail turned mostly east, as Lodin had said. The land was flat, though filled with all manner of terrain — rushing rivers and trickling brooks, round hills and lonely meadows, marshy ponds and windswept lakes. And all of it unfolding through curtains of spruce and pine, beech and oak. It was beautiful but deserted country, known more for its animals and outlaws than its inhabitants. In fact, if there were people thereabouts, we saw no cabins or signs of settlement.

Several days after Sigrunn's death, we eased our pace to regain our strength. Lodin used the longer breaks to teach us children about the forest and how to identify the sounds within it, such as the grunt of a mouse or the difference between the call of duck, eider, and grouse. We learned to stop and hide when birds took flight and how to watch Feilan for signs of trouble. He taught us how to identify different paw prints, which to be wary of and which presented possible food. It became a game and I enjoyed it — it took my mind off of our troubles.

"See there, Turid," he pointed at a nearby lake as we passed. "The red waterlilies?"

"Aye," she said.

"Do you know the story of those flowers?"

She did not and told him so.

"Then I shall tell you. Long ago, there was a poor fisherman who had a beautiful daughter. The small lake gave little fish, and the fisherman had difficulties providing for his family. One day, as the fisherman was fishing in his boat, he met a male water spirit, who offered him great catches of fish on the condition that the fisherman gave him his beautiful daughter the day she reached her eighteenth summer. The desperate fisherman agreed and promised the spirit his daughter. On the allotted day, the girl went down to the shore to meet the spirit. He asked her to walk down to his watery home, but the girl took forth a knife and said that he would never have her alive. She then stuck the knife into her heart and fell down into the lake, dead. Her blood stained the waterlilies red, and from that day until this, the waterlilies of the lakes here are red."

"That is a sad story," Turid remarked.

Lodin merely shrugged. "I do not make the stories."

Before leaving our camp each night, we boys trained with the men while Astrid and Turid prepared food, or washed clothes, or saw to their own grooming. Occasionally they would join us, learning the basics of weapon craft, though I admit, Astrid was already well-trained, having been raised by my father. It had been a long time since Turid had wielded her father's weapons, but she took to the training with a zeal that matched our own.

I enjoyed these moments of sparring immensely. Unlike Olaf, who, much to my chagrin and envy, often joked with Turid as they rode in the cart, I was shy and awkward in speech. Try as I might to join in their conversation, my words either felt inadequate or lame or both. Like an ill-shot arrow, they never seemed to hit the mark or make an impression. The sparring sessions gave me a way to interact with Turid, and I reveled in the closeness and the conversations they yielded.

But there was something else those sparring sessions provided. Turid had been miserable after her mother's death and spoke little to anyone. Training returned a brightness to her face, if only briefly. More, they gave her a way to expunge the pain and anger within her, which was plain to see in the ferocity with which she fought. After one such session with my father, he pointed his practice blade at her. "You fight with heart, Turid. That is good, but fighting with heart alone can get you killed." He tapped his temple. "Learn to fight with your head also and you will be formidable."

"That is high praise," said Astrid to Turid.

Turid grinned. "Thank you, Lord Torolv."

"It is the truth."

It rained the following two days. When it began, I welcomed it. We all did. It made our tracks harder to follow, and we needed that. But as the rain fell harder, drenching our clothes and turning the track into a quagmire through which our cart could no longer pass, my mood shifted from gratefulness to agitation, and then to teeth-grinding frustration. Whereas I had thanked Thor not much earlier, I now cursed our luck and the mud and water and cold he poured down on us.

Seeing the futility of our efforts, Lodin called a halt to our journey. We could not sleep on the muddy ground, so my father and Lodin constructed a flimsy tent over the bed of the cart and shared out some of the food we still had, most of which was now wet. Lodin took the first watch with a soggy Feilan by his side. The rest of us sat shoulder to shoulder among the cargo, listening to the rain patter on the tent as we silently and miserably ate our food.

I was about to bite into my venison jerky when Feilan launched into a cacophony of growls and barks. In the midst of the clamor, I heard Lodin yell. My father hastened from the tent, stepping on Turid's ankle and knocking the food from my hand as he did so. He flew out into the grayness with Olaf and me not far behind. But as we emerged, Lodin whistled and Feilan's barking subsided.

"What is it?" I asked as I stopped beside my father, sword in my hand, and scanned the rain-veiled landscape.

"I know not," growled my father.

Lodin appeared then through the trees with Feilan by his side. His hood was over his head, revealing just the white of his nose tip. "All is fine," he called. "It was a moose, I think. Something big, anyway. Feilan chased it away. I doubt it will return. Even so," Lodin added, looking at my father, "be vigilant when you take watch. If it is a hungry bear, it may have the scent of our food in its snout and return."

"I would feel better if I had Feilan with me," my father responded. I thought he was jesting, but there was no humor in his tone.

In the dimness of Lodin's hood, a smile stretched. "I am sure Feilan would not mind." Lodin scratched the top of the dog's head. The hound responded by shaking her body from muzzle to tail. "You should get some sleep, lord. Your watch will begin soon enough."

My father nodded and wiped his blade on his wet trouser leg before returning it to its scabbard. "I am grateful we have you as a guide, Lodin. Truly."

Lodin glanced at my father in a manner that suggested he was not altogether comfortable with the praise.

We encountered no more problems that night or the next, and when the rain finally ceased, we woke to find ourselves not an arrow's flight from a vast sea filled with crying gulls and terns. It twinkled in the morning light and brought a smile to my face.

"Behold, the Vanern," Lodin announced with a theatrical flourish.

"The what?" Olaf wondered aloud.

He laughed. "The Vanern. It is a mighty lake."

"This? A lake?" Turid added. "It looks like an ocean."

"Aye," Lodin said. "It does. More importantly, it means we are close. A few more days now and we will be on the threshold of Haakon the Old's farm, gods willing. Let us wash ourselves here and be on our way."

We moved on with our clothes and bodies cleaner and our spirits lifted, but all of that quickly changed. The trail rising from Lake Vanern was still thick with mud and hard to navigate. Here and there, the wheels of the cart got stuck, requiring us to push uphill to free them. Whatever cleanliness and rest we had enjoyed was soon a memory — by the end of that day, we were mud-streaked and tangle-haired yet again.

We pressed on, traversing the undulating landscape for two more days. It grew hot and we sweated in our dirty clothes. We stopped more frequently for water and breaks, though never long enough for my limbs or my body to fully recover. I refused to complain, though. Tired as I was, I was determined to emulate my father, who marched on resolutely, even as Astrid and Turid and Olaf rode in the cart and dozed.

We descended again on the third day and came to a flat, wooded place that reeked of smoke and something more pungent.

"Be alert," Lodin called.

"What is this place?" my father asked.

Lodin shrugged. "I do not know what they call it, but they make tar here. That is what you smell."

"A lot of tar, from the smell of it," said Astrid.

"Aye," confirmed Lodin. "Which is why we must be careful."

"I do not understand," Astrid admitted.

"Tar is valuable," he said. "Without it, kings cannot sail their ships. This place is prized by the lords for the tar it produces, so they watch it closely. As you can imagine, they are suspicious of outsiders."

We rounded a bend in the trail and stopped. There, before us, four men loaded barrels onto a large cart pulled by four oxen. Tar blackened the limbs of the men, who were collared like thralls and who were being ordered about by an armed warrior. All five saw us coming and stopped.

The warrior, whose belly was as large as one of the tar barrels, hooked his thumbs in his belt and approached. "Lodin? Is that you?" he asked.

"Is there another on this road who looks like me?" asked Lodin.

The man, whose red hair was covered in gray ash, smiled, revealing two rows of crooked teeth. "There is not. You are well met."

"As are you, Stig."

The man appraised our party with bloodshot brown eyes. "What have you brought for me this time? The blondy there? The younger one? Both?" He rubbed his hands together eagerly.

Lodin laughed. "Neither. I am afraid these thralls are spoken for."

The man frowned. "Truly? You know I pay well, Lodin."

Lodin grinned, and for the briefest of moments, I thought he might acquiesce. "I am merely passing through, Stig. Though —-" he raised his finger excitedly "—- I do have a gift for you. Ale! Some of the finest I have tasted, too."

The tar man frowned. "We have ale."

Lodin shook his head and took the tar man by the arm. "Not this ale. It is special. Strong and sweet. Given to me by the master brewer of a great lord. You will like it, I am certain." He walked the man to the bed of the cart and grabbed a small barrel. This he gave to the man. "Take it."

The man's frowned deepened. "This ale will not even last a night here. A woman, on the other hand..." His dark eyes moved again to Astrid.

Lodin wagged his finger before the man. "Careful, Stig. Or I will have Feilan teach you not to press your good fortune."

Stig eyed the wolf-dog warily, then raised his hands in mock surrender. "I meant no harm."

Lodin slapped the man's shoulder. "No harm done, my friend. Until next time." He grabbed the ox's lead rope and walked on. Stig stepped aside and we followed Lodin down the road, passing the other wagon and the miserable thralls loading it.

When we were beyond earshot, my father grumbled, "You should kill that smelly turd, Lodin, and end your troubles. He robs you."

"And then I will just have to face the next smelly turd that takes Stig's place. No. He may be a thorn in my side, but Stig is known to me and I to him. Besides, he is fearful of hounds," he chuckled.

"Will you truly bring him women next time you pass here?" Astrid wondered aloud, not attempting to hide her displeasure.

Lodin shrugged. "If a thrall woman will make Stig happy and give me passage, why would I not?"

I glanced sheepishly at Astrid and Turid. Though anger hardened their faces, they held their tongues. Behind them, Olaf was looking at the trees and whistling at the birds. I wondered if he had even marked the exchange.

The trail exited the trees then and entered a large meadow. In the distance stood the wooden walls of a borg. Lodin pointed to it. "That is Ormsbro."

"Who rules there?" my father asked.

"A lord named Ulf Ormsson holds his seat there. It is he who controls the tar pits we passed and sells the tar to lords in the north and east."

"Orm's bridge?" I translated the borg's name.

"That's right," confirmed Lodin as he moved to the cart and began organizing the wares in the bed. "The borg sits aside the trail and guards the one bridge over the black river. Ulf's father built it. It is our way east."

"Is there not another way?" my father asked. I could tell he did not like the idea of passing a borg with the prying eyes and silver-hunger of its guards.

Lodin shook his head. "There are no trails wide enough for our cart. We would need to leave it behind. Besides, Ulf's men guard all of the trails, so we might as well just pass through. Come. Help me hide our goods."

"Hide?" Astrid asked as my father moved to Lodin's side.

"Aye, my lady. Hide. The guards there have sticky fingers and usually take their cut before counting their lord's share."

"I do not like the sound of that, Lodin," said Astrid. "What if their 'cut' involves me or Turid?"

Lodin glanced at Astrid. "You look more like a thrall now than you did several days ago. To them, we are just traders and cargo. Worry not." He pulled up a plank from the bed of the cart to reveal a hidden compartment. "Place coins, swords, and anything of wealth in here."

"And if it does not fit?" asked my father.

"Then wear it or discard it. But if you wear it, you do so at your peril."

Lodin then motioned for Astrid, Turid, and Olaf to sit on the right side of the cart bed. There, he tied them by their wrists to metal rings.

"You are hurting me," Astrid complained.

"You are a thrall," Lodin responded mildly. "You need to act like one until we are past Ormsbro."

My father cursed and scowled. It pained him, as it did me, to see his foster daughter tied like livestock to a cart. Not a fortnight ago, we had been lords of vast lands and a favored family of a powerful king. We feared no man. Now we were just traders and cargo, hiding ourselves, our hard-won wealth, and our status from the greed of some tar lord. Whether he knew it or not, Lodin had just taken an axe to our pride and the blade had bitten deeply. I vowed to myself right then that I would kill the people who had driven us so far from our home and brought us so low. Under my breath, I swore to Thor that I would be his man forever if he helped me see my vengeance through.

"Come," Lodin commanded when he had secured the thralls.

What I had believed — and indeed, hoped — to be a small fortress was actually large enough for a small army. As we approached Ormsbro, the walls rose to thrice my height and encircled at least several halls, judging from the rooftops I could see within. Outside the walls, on the roadside, traders and farmers shouted and haggled as they hawked their goods beside their makeshift stalls. A small river flowed north to south on the west side of the fort, then curved around the front of the borg to head east. There, a small dock jutted into the river. Tied to the dock were several small vessels and a barge loaded with barrels. I could smell the rank odor of tar from where I stood.

To reach the borg, we needed to cross the bridge, which was guarded by two thick-chested warriors with spears. Several more warriors stood atop the walls, looking down on the bridge and the traders below. Even more warriors milled about the traders, ostensibly to keep the peace, though I suspected they were probably helping themselves to a little extra cut of the trade.

"What goods have you brought with you this time, Lodin?" asked one of the guards as we neared. He motioned with his spear to Astrid. "I have not seen you with thralls before. Are they for sale?"

Lodin turned and looked at the girls, then back at the warriors. "They are not for sale."

The warrior who had spoken had a runny nose, and this he now blew onto the ground. Only the snot did not quite dislodge itself from his nostril and hung in a long string. He grabbed the string between his index finger and thumb and flung it away into the tall grass beside the trail. Then he sleeved his nose with his forearm and eyed us one by one. Seeing nothing unusual, he approached the cart with his comrade and moved to the cart bed.

Using his spear, he moved our blankets and cloaks aside to reveal several stacks of pelts and a pile of ivory tusks. He opened jars and sacks, inspecting items he deemed of value. One such bag contained opaque amber. He lifted one of the stones and held it to the sunlight, then seemed to come to some sort of decision. "Three pelts and three amber stones and we shall let you pass."

Lodin looked unsettled. "That is a rich price."

The man blew another load of snot onto the turf. "It is a small price to pay if you are not willing to part with your thralls. Those two," he motioned vaguely to the women, "will fetch you a high price at Westra Aros. That is where you are headed, eh? Westra Aros?"

Lodin made a show of chewing on his lip and tapping the side of the cart. He eyed Astrid and Turid, then my father and me. "Will you not take three pelts and one amber stone?"

"No. Three pelts and three amber stones, or we take the thralls."

Lodin sighed. "Very well. Take it."

Snot Nose grinned cruelly and reached for a pelt. As he did, Feilan began to growl and bare her teeth at the guard. The man looked at the hound and went still. His comrade lowered his spear and pointed it at the wolf dog, though his fear was plain to see. "Call off your hound, Lodin," said Snot Nose.

Lodin silenced Feilan with a casual motion of his hand. As he did, he moved closer to the guards and said, "They say that hounds do not have memory, but I do not believe it. I think they remember with their noses and sense trouble that way. The next time I come through here, my hound may just remember you for your scent and the threat of your spears. I cannot be sure, of course, so the decision is yours."

In the end, the guards took only two pelts and no amber, and I learned a valuable lesson: men fear the attack of an animal far more than the blade of a man. To be killed by man is noble. If done heroically, it is worthy of Valhall. To be food for a beast is wretched and no way to die in the eyes of the gods, and so men feared it.

We left Ormsbro behind having paid barely our due, and walked on to what I hoped was our final destination, at least for a time. Through the day and into the evening we trudged, stopping only once for food and water and a short rest. Our path followed the black river until it reached a vast lake, at which point we turned northeast and followed a cart track along the shoreline. At some point in the night, we turned more northward and began to ascend low-lying hills until at last, Lodin called for us to halt.

"We are close now," he said as he sleeved sweat from his brow. He pointed east. "Just past that line of trees, our path will descend to Haakon's farm."

"What will you do once we reach it?" asked Astrid.

"I will stay the night and then complete the task that Erik has set for me."

"Which is?" This query came from my father, who was still waiting for an answer to the question he had asked at the beginning of our journey.

Lodin looked at him and smiled. "Let us rest here for the remainder of the night. Tomorrow I will take you to meet Haakon."

Chapter 11

Haakon was indeed old. He was a tall, thickset man who walked with a well-polished stick to support a noticeable limp in his left leg. Strands of white hair hung like cobwebs from his chin, which he scratched upon hearing Lodin's words. He looked at us with his rheumy cerulean eyes. They were kind eyes, I decided, with crow's-feet at the corners. "You say Eric Bjodaskalli sent you?" He spoke with a slight lisp that seemed at odds with the power in his frame. I ascribed that lisp to the two crooked and yellowed teeth that interfered with his lips when he spoke.

"Aye," responded Lodin. "This is his daughter, Astrid, and his grand-son, Olaf." Lodin motioned to the two with his chin.

The old man laughed. It was a warm laugh that made me smile. "These? Erik's kin? He is a rich man. I mean no offense, but these look like thralls."

"It is a disguise, Haakon," explained Lodin patiently.

The old man scratched his chin again. He had met us several paces from the front door of his hall. An elderly woman stood at the thresh-old, peering out at us, her body half concealed by the doorframe. Several more people stood at a distance, watching the scene unfold. From their clothing, I guessed they were Haakon's thralls. Mayhap a family member or two.

"And them? Who are they?" He motioned to my father and me with his crooked index finger.

"My name is Torolv Torgilsson. My friends call me Loose-beard."

He glanced at my father. "Loose lipped, more like," the old man said, though there was no malice in his tone. "My question was for Lodin, not you."

I did not dare look at my father for fear of seeing his embarrassment or his ire. Near me, Olaf sniggered. Had he been closer, I would have smacked him.

Lodin chimed in then. "He is who he says, though you should also know he was one of the most trusted lords of King Trygvi of Vingulmark. He is also Astrid's foster father and one of Erik Bjodaskalli's closest friends. The boy next to him is his son, Torgil." He then motioned to Turid. "And that young woman is Astrid's maidservant, Turid."

Haakon regarded my father briefly before letting his eyes travel to the rest of the group. "You are well met," he said to us. He turned back to Lodin. "So, why are they here, exactly?"

Lodin explained the circumstances of our arrival. As he did, I noticed the others on Haakon's farm moving closer to hear his tale.

"So Erik is in need of my help," Haakon concluded.

"Aye. They need a place to stay until things have settled in their homeland."

"To stay or to hide?" asked Haakon. It was clear that Haakon did not mince words. He attacked matters directly, if not abruptly. At his age, I suppose he had that right.

"Both," said Lodin flatly.

Haakon scratched his jaw again and turned his eyes to the ground. At last he lifted his gaze and turned to my father. "I do not have much. As you can see, it is a humble hall and a humble farm. It will be a hard winter with so many mouths to feed."

I did not know why he said that. It seemed a rich farm to me. The hall was large and well kept. There was a separate storehouse made of stone, a barn, a privy, a work hut, and a pen for pigs and sheep, though that livestock grazed now in the fields to the north of the farm. Beyond the hall were three small fields for crops, and beyond that, a wide river. To my eyes, it was a beautiful piece of land, lush and for the most part, well kept.

"You will be paid well to have them here," offered Lodin.

"And we can help on the farm," added Astrid.

My father was not used to begging, especially with a man whose measure he did not yet have, and so he held his tongue.

Haakon raked his eyes over us. "Very well. But for this winter only. Then you must move on. If you are hiding, then someone is searching for you. I am too old for trouble, especially if it is the trouble that comes from kings and queens and heirs. Grab your things and bring them into the barn." He pointed to a structure off to our right. "We will make space for you there until we can add some beds to the hall."

We slept on the hay in the barn that night, and for the first time in many days, I slept the entire night.

Lodin left as the sky blushed with the dawn. I, for one, was sad to see him go. He had been a good guide to us and had seen us safely to our destination. He had also taught me much in our time together. But above all, he was an attachment to the world I had known and left behind. As he disappeared down the track with Feilan by his side and the ox cart behind him, I felt as if my old life was walking away from me, leaving me with a strange, lonely feeling in the pit of my stomach.

There was little time for melancholy, though. No sooner had Lodin left than a thin, aging man who introduced himself as Bursti beckoned us into Haakon's hall. The portly woman who I'd seen at the doorway the day before ushered Turid and Astrid into the kitchen. I would soon learn that her name was Tala.

"Haakon would like your beds to be situated here," Bursti announced. "The platforms already exist, as you can see, but we will need feather and wool and skins for your beds. I will show you where the feathers and furs can be found. It will be up to you to collect them. How good are you with a bow?"

My father grinned.

That very afternoon we hunted. Bursti led us downriver from the hall to a place where the reeds grew thick. We sat among them, still as stones, until the waterfowl settled in. Bursti referred to the river as Goose River, and I could see why. The water echoed with the honks and calls of that bird. My father shot four that day, which we carried to the hall and handed to the women. After a fortnight of bread and dried meat, I cannot remember a meal I enjoyed more. It was a feast of fowl, though amazingly, they supplied only enough down for Astrid's pillow.

I would like to say that we boys hunted like that every day, but that was rarely the case. That task fell to my father alone. The women, under the guidance of Tala, milked the cows and sheep, prepared the meals, and tended to the myriad other tasks that filled a day. We boys and Bursti saw to the fields with the other male thrall, whose name was Gamal. The grass on the edges of the farm had already been cut and collected for hay, so our loathsome task was to painstakingly weed

Haakon's crop fields before sowing the rye seeds. Olaf did not seem to mind the work, but I hated that task. Bending and standing until my back screamed. Grubbing in the dirt like a foraging pig. It was menial work. Thrall work.

When I complained to my father, he showed no mercy. "You are a guest on Haakon's farm and you will do as he asks."

"But —-" I tried to plead.

"Save your breath, Torgil," he called as he marched away. And so I bit my tongue and groveled in the soil.

When we were not rummaging for weeds, we helped Bursti build the bed frames in Haakon's hall. This I liked better, for it involved working with wood and tools in Haakon's workshop to produce something that would last. I liked the delicate task of planing and the smell of wood that filled that place. I liked hammering the pegs and the feeling of completion when we finished a frame. Strangely, Olaf's mind strayed with this kind of work, and he complained to me later about how boring it was. It was to him as weeding was to me.

At night, we five — Astrid, my father, Olaf, Turid, and I — sat with Haakon at his table and talked. We learned early on about Haakon, and how he had come to have the farm and how he knew Astrid's father.

As a lad, Haakon had ridden the wave-steeds south and west with his friends and earned his share of booty from those fights. Erik had been with him on some of those raids and had saved his life on one occasion, which is why Haakon had not — could not — refuse our request for lodging. It was a debt and Erik had finally called for his payment.

Haakon used his earnings from his raids to buy a plot of land from his lord and to take the hand of a woman he had known all his life. His dream had been to raise a family and work the land, but life did not unfold in the manner he expected. Instead of peace and prosperity, famine and disease came to his door. It was an enemy he knew not how to fight.

"That is why you are alone here?" Astrid asked delicately.

Haakon sighed deeply and slurped from his ale cup. "Aye. Disease took my wife that very winter. I raised my boys by myself, hoping they would enjoy farming as I did, but they had other dreams. My oldest son went a-viking and died in the east. I raised a runestone in his memory, which stands up on the hill to our north. After that, I forbade my other boy to go, but he left anyway. I am told he now lives in Irland, but I have long since given up hope that I will see him again. He and I parted on bad terms, as you can imagine."

I looked at my plate because I was not quite sure how to react to such a sad tale. I was not alone in that. No one else spoke either. "I am sorry," Astrid finally offered.

My father, who was never comfortable with sorrowful tales, turned the conversation to a more practical subject. "Who will run the farm when you are gone? Do you have other family near?"

Haakon shook his head. "I do not. Mayhap I will give it to you." He chuckled, then backhanded the air before him as if to brush away a fly. "We shall see. In any case, it is good that you are here. I have missed gatherings at my table." He raised his ale cup. "Sköl."

"Sköl," we responded.

We completed the beds just as the rye fields began to ripen. Haakon waited for a string of warm days before declaring that it was time to harvest. On Jel, our thralls had seen to the reaping and binding, but on Haakon's farm, every person was employed in the task, save for Tala, who made sure we were fed. It was my first time taking part in a harvest, and it was every bit as hard as felling trees for our borg on

Jel. We rose before dawn, toiled all day, and stopped at night. By the end of it, when the sheaves were safely stored in the barn, my hands were calloused, my body tanned, and my muscles sore from toil. My only solace was that our beds were now inside and just a few steps from the table and the crackling hearth fire. Most nights, I fell asleep on top of the skins, fully clothed.

At the harvest's end, Haakon sent word to his neighbors to come for a feast. The women prepared for days, pounding some of the new grain into flour for bread, making cheese and butter, or gathering nuts and honey from the nearby woods. We men pulled trestle tables and benches from the back of the barn, repairing those that needed it, and placed them in the field beside Haakon's hall. The day before the feast, we fished in the river and cleared a pit of debris. Above it, we erected a spit. On feast day, with the sun high over our heads, Haakon gathered his guests about the pit — roughly thirty of us in all. There, he called to the gods, thanking them for a good harvest and beseeching them for a mild winter to come. With practiced skill, he then slit the throat of one of his finest pigs and collected its sacrificial blood — its hlaut — in a wooden bowl. This he passed around to his guests to drink.

When the bowl reached me, I repeated my prayer to Thor, asking for his help to see my journey through. I would not quit, I promised, until Holger and his king, Harald, lay dead. This I swore above the bowl, then I drank of the acrid liquid and passed the bowl to Olaf. He, too, said some words above the blood, though I could not hear them.

The sacrifice over, Haakon ushered us to the tables, which had been festooned with wildflowers of blue and yellow. I did not know the names of those flowers, but they were beautiful. Among them stood pitchers of ale, water, and milk, as well as baskets of warm flatbread and plates of butter and cheese. My stomach growled as Haakon took his seat at the head table and bade us sit.

"We heard that Haakon had visitors. From whence have you come? We have not seen you before."

The question came from the man sitting on the bench across from my father. I wondered, as I watched him take a long sip of his ale, what he might answer.

"And you may not see us again. We are just passing through," my father replied.

"How do you know Haakon?" asked the man. I tensed. It was just small talk, I knew, but his questions were coming perilously close to subjects we would be fools to discuss.

"He is a friend of a friend," my father answered casually, which was true.

Astrid sat to my father's right and placed a hand on his wrist. "We are headed to the East. To Holmgard. My brother is there. He is a trader and we wish to join him."

The curious neighbor's eyes widened. "To Holmgard? That is a long voyage for the likes of you." My father must have frowned, for the man held up his hands. "I mean, for three children. The East Way can be perilous."

"We will manage." My father drained his cup, then rose.

"You must forgive my husband," said the redheaded woman seated next to my father's interrogator. "He likes to talk and often oversteps. It is a blessing and a curse." She shrugged. "He means no offense."

"I meant no offense," the man repeated as his eyes followed by father's retreating back.

"None taken," Astrid responded pleasantly, though I could see the color rising in her cheeks.

To my right, Olaf was feeding some bread to one of the neighbor's hounds. I smacked his shoulder. It was common enough to give hounds scraps after a feast but wasteful to feed them before the feast had yet begun. "People eat before the hounds," I chastised him.

He looked at the half-eaten bread in his hand, then smiled his mischievous smile. "Here," he said, and tossed the dog-slimed bread into my trencher. "Then you eat it."

I recoiled, bumping into Turid, who had just taken a sip of her water and had not yet returned the cup to the table. The water splashed onto the table and washed onto her lap. She jumped to her feet. "Torgil! Look what you have done!"

I gasped. "I am sorry, Turid. I did not mean—"

She didn't wait for my apology, but stormed off into the hall. I made to rise and follow her, but Astrid stilled me with a hand. "Let her be. It was an accident, Torgil. Besides, it was only water."

I sat back down and glared at Olaf. He smiled haughtily at me, as if he had won a victory of some sort. But I had had enough. I backhanded him so hard that he fell off the bench and hit his head. Before he could rise, I was on him, my fist connecting with his face. Once. Then twice. Then three times. There was no thought of my duty to him. There was only a vicious need to make him feel pain for his indifference to wasting food, to embarrassing Turid, and to teasing me.

As I was bringing my fist down for the fourth blow, strong arms yanked me up and whirled me away from my prey. Delirious with rage, I kept throwing punches and kicking, but the arms that held me were like vises. They carried me into the barn and threw me to the ground. I wheeled around to face my assailant but never did see his face. I later knew that it was my father's fist, but it may as well have been a hammer that connected with my jaw. With a sudden flash of pain, my head jerked backward, then everything went black.

We never spoke of the incident. Nor did I ever apologize for the bruises on Olaf's face. I did tell Turid I was sorry for spilling water on her dress, though. She accepted the apology with a nod but kept her distance from me after that. I suppose my attack on Olaf, however warranted, was the cause of her distance, but I was too young to broach that subject with her. I sensed that Astrid, too, was a bit more wary of me, but what could I do? Olaf deserved the beating, and I did not regret giving it to him.

The snows came early that winter and fell in thick mounds upon the ground until the world was covered in a beautiful, silent mantle of white. Taken by surprise by the sudden snow, we chopped and collected wood, and slaughtered those animals deemed weakest. And then we settled in to wait out the long, cold days and nights.

I hated that winter. It was not like the winters on Jel, which were milder. This one was severe and lung-searingly cold. It was our captor and the hall, our fetters. We were stuck indoors, with our eyes stinging from the smoke of the hearth fire and our noses filled with the odor of wood and bodies and animals and shit. Our stomachs grumbled constantly from lack of food, not because we had none, but because we knew not how long winter would last and so we had to conserve what we had.

There was still plenty to do, of course, but none of it was fun or interesting. I did not have the patience for the long board games my father and Haakon played, and there were only so many baskets I could weave or clothes I could mend or blades I could sharpen or sticks I could whittle. Understandably, I suppose, Olaf would not play with me, nor would Turid, though they did play together, much to my chagrin. Astrid spent much of her time at the loom, or helping Tala in the kitchen, or in talks with my father and Haakon, so I rarely interacted with her. And so I spent that winter surrounded by people, yet deeply alone.

My solace came in sleep and training. But even sleep was interrupted by Olaf's incessant shifting and rolling at night. We slept in the same bed, you see, and his body moved constantly, even in slumber. Many was the night I would wake with nary a cover to warm me and have to pry the furs from his grasp.

Training was different. Olaf and I took turns at the far end of the hall, where there was space to move, just one of us boys against my father. Because of danger to others in the cramped hall, we moved through our attacks and parries slowly, methodically. My father would stop mid-slice or -thrust to adjust our arms to the right position, or shift our feet, or move our shield. He would say nary a word. If we made a mistake twice, he would smack our arm with the flat of his wooden blade. On occasion, my father would invite Astrid or Turid to train. Turid liked it. Astrid tolerated it. But neither ever refused. There was an unspoken understanding among us all that we might need the skills my father taught, and so we did as he instructed without complaint.

For nearly ninety days we remained indoors, sitting, pacing, training, sleeping, biding our time. I know this because I counted those days with notches on my bed frame. And then, one day, winter's freeze released its grip on the world and the sun returned. The days warmed and the snow turned to rain, and the white mantle of my prison melted away.

That first spring-like day, I ran from the hall into the mud and the lingering chill. It was drizzling, but I did not care. Like a caged hound suddenly released, I sprinted for the river, frightening geese into flight, then circled into the foothills and finally back to the farm. I did not invite Olaf, but he ran with me, echoing my whoops and hollers as we sank into ankle-deep snow and splashed across puddles. I knew then that our camaraderie had reached an understanding. But more importantly, I knew that Olaf would be more wary of our relationship. He would not always listen, but he understood that I would not hold back, and that gave me confidence.

Which was good, for I would need it in the days to come.

Chapter 12

Trouble came that spring.

We had just begun plowing, for the ground was now soft enough to turn. My father, Bursti, Gamal, Olaf, and I were in the fields, either turning the wet earth with shovels, clearing rocks from the turned soil, or running a plow behind. We had hit a tough patch and were struggling to get the plow moving when men appeared from the woods on the south side of Haakon's farm. Bursti straightened and, after observing them for a time, went to meet them. Haakon, who sat wrapped in furs near the hall doors, rose to join Bursti. The rest of us stopped our work and watched.

I recognized one of the men as my father's interrogator from the harvest feast. My stomach tightened, and I glanced worriedly at my father. If he felt the same apprehension, he did not show it, though he sensed it in Olaf and me. "Easy, lads," he cautioned. "We have nothing to fear."

It was a good reminder, for we did look different now. More spartan in our clothing; less groomed. We boys had grown and thinned from toil. My father had clipped the beard he loved so much and now wore it close to his jaw. I never thought I would see him do that, for he had been proud of that beard. It had been part of his identity — his name, even — but he answered our questioning gazes as we watched Astrid trim it with a shrug and one of his sayings that even now I can hear in my head: "Hair grows back. Life does not."

I was under no illusion that the interrogator did not recognize us. His business at the farm may have been purely innocuous — a simple visit to check in on Haakon. We were too distant to hear their words, but we could see Haakon and the men gesturing as they spoke. Eventually, Haakon turned to his hall and beckoned the men to follow. The interrogator glanced in our direction briefly, then turned to follow Haakon. Bursti rejoined us in the field.

"Neighbors?" my father asked.

"Aye. One is Haakon's neighbor. You must recognize him from the feast? The other two are his friends from the nearby village," he responded as he picked up his shovel.

"What do they want?" I asked.

He shrugged. "They would not discuss it in front of me. They wished to speak with Haakon alone."

My father glanced at me. "We will know soon enough what their business is. Come, let us finish this work."

The men left after a short time and vanished into the woods. As soon as they were gone, Astrid came to us with a pitcher of water and some wooden cups. She did not usually run water to us, and so we gathered around her, sensing some import to her mission.

"So?" my father said as he took a cup from Astrid's hand and gestured with it toward the trees. "Should we be concerned?"

She nodded as she filled his cup. "They have come to tell us about men in Westra Aros who are asking questions. The king's men."

Westra Aros was the closest village to Haakon's farm. It lay at the point where a river east of the farm flowed into what the locals simply called the Lake. Due to its access to the East Sea and its proximity to the interior of the Swedish realm, the village had long been a trading site for Swedes and eastern traders.

My father scratched his beard. "There are many men who think themselves king nowadays. Which king is this?"

Astrid stopped pouring the water and looked up into my father's face. I could see the concern playing in her eyes. "The king of the Swedes. Erik. He who rules in Uppsala with his brother, Olof."

I had not heard of these men, but if they ruled in Uppsala, the ancient seat of the Swedish kings, I knew they must be important. "Are these men asking questions about us?"

"Aye," Astrid confirmed.

"Why would they do that?" I wondered aloud.

"Because other powerful men are asking," my father grumbled as he half turned to me. He finished his water and handed his cup back to Astrid. "Did they say how many men are in the village asking questions, Astrid?"

"No exact number. He just said 'many,'" she answered quietly, and that one word set my heart to racing.

My father sighed, then cast his eyes on each of us in turn. "We will soon need to leave. Let us speak with Haakon tonight and start to plan."

"I asked those men who came here today to return here on the morrow when the sun is high," Haakon told us that night after our meal. "They will bring a boat to take you downriver to the Lake. They will also send a messenger to a trader named Sigvard in Westra Aros and alert him of your coming. If he is there, he will help you."

"Do you trust this Sigvard?" asked my father.

Haakon grinned. "More than I trust most traders. He was a friend of my son's and is like kin to me. It is he who brought me word of my son's death in the east. He still trades in the East Sea and knows it well. For a price, he can bring you to the trading outpost Aldeigjuborg in the land of the Rus. From there, you may need to find another vessel to take you to your brother, wherever he may be."

"And what if Sigvard's ship is not there?"

Haakon pursed his thin lips. "Then we shall have a choice to make, eh?"

"What about you and the spring planting?" asked Astrid.

He smiled fondly at her, giving us a glimpse of the two yellowed teeth remaining in his head. "You are good to ask, but we have fared well before, and so we shall again. Do not worry." He sat hunched at the head of the eating board and passed his gaze over us and our gloomy faces. "Oh, come. Why the melancholy? Should we not be thanking the gods for our time together?" He hefted his cup and waited for us to do the same. When we did, he cleared his throat and said, "I will not soon forget the pleasure of having you in my hall. The sound of family was music to my old ears. I have missed it, these last winters."

Haakon's mind had grown noticeably softer since our arrival, and I had lost count of the times he had told us that. Across from me, Olaf rolled his eyes, and I kicked him. Our host did not notice, but my father did and stayed us with a fiery glance.

"So I thank you," Haakon was saying, "and I thank the gods for the gift of you. To the gods!"

"To the gods!" we responded dutifully. Each of us tipped our cups and let a small measure fall to the rushes in sacrifice before taking a sip.

"Could the king's men come tonight?" Turid asked when the toast was done. It was an innocent enough question, but it set me on edge. Astrid's smile vanished, as did my father's.

"If they learn of your presence here, then I suppose it is possible," Haakon replied. He looked at Bursti, who sat on the nearby platform, eating from his trencher. As close as he was to Haakon, he was still a thrall and did not eat at the main table —- at least when we were present.

Bursti shrugged. "They could sleep in the barn," he suggested, meaning us. "Might be safer there."

Haakon pursed his lips. "It is a good idea, though if we are planning for trouble, we should then plan thoroughly. Gather your things and bring them with you to the barn. My thralls can assist you. If trouble comes, it is best you have your things."

"And what of you?" Astrid asked. "If trouble comes, you will be in here. Alone."

Haakon patted her hand, which lay on the table near his. "I fear more for your safety than my own, Astrid."

"I am sorry we have brought trouble to your threshold," she responded.

Haakon smirked, though his eyes remained steady and earnest. He patted her hand again but held his tongue.

"We travel as we did before," my father announced. "We will draw fewer eyes to us if we appear as traders with thralls to sell."

Olaf's face pinched. "Can we not have Torgil play the thrall this time?" He nodded in my direction.

I wanted to kick him again, but I knew he had a valid point. He was a king's son, and if it came to a fight, he would be just as handy as me, if not more so. My father looked at me and raised his brow in question. I nodded at him. "I will play the thrall, Father, if that is what you require of me."

My father nodded and turned back to our host. "One day, Haakon, I hope we can return the kindness you have shown us."

He grunted and waved my father's comment away, then rose with a grunt. "Come. The night is growing late. You should prepare. Bursti and Gamal, make the barn ready. Tala, help them gather their things."

I do not remember much of that night except that, after spending time in a warm bed near a hearth fire, I was uncomfortable and cold, the more so because my hair had been cropped in the manner of a thrall and I was not used to the chill on my neck. To heighten my discomfort, the hay poked me and my rough blanket made me itch.

I struggled that entire night, until finally, in the gray light before dawn, I rose bleary-eyed and walked to the barn door to relieve myself. But as I opened the door, my eyes caught sight of shadows moving toward the hall. Many shadows. Then a man appeared in the midst of those shadows with a lit torch. The flame cast its wavering glow on him and those around him, and on the metal that protected their heads and bodies.

I froze. And so, too, did my heart.

Chapter 13

I closed the door as quickly and quietly as I could and retreated into the shadows of the barn to seek the sleeping form of my father.

He sat up abruptly when I shook him. "What?" he growled.

I held a finger to my lips. "Warriors. Outside." I pointed to the barn door.

My words stirred him into motion. "Wake the others. Quietly," he hissed as he rose and moved to his possessions stacked against the nearby wall.

One by one, I nudged the others awake.

"How many?" Astrid asked me quietly as she stood.

"Mayhap twenty or more."

She passed my father a concerned glance. He looked at her, then pulled from his belongings the four seaxes, the two old swords, and his own sword. "Each of you take a seax," he whispered. "Boys. Grab the swords."

Outside, we heard the warriors pounding on Haakon's door.

"Cover our things with hay," he commanded quietly. "Then hide."

We did our best to quietly place hay on our bags. As we did so, my father moved to the barn door and peered out into the darkness, his sword firmly in his grip. I moved to a spot to the right of the door —

behind a pile of hay that lay in the shadows — where I knew a peephole to be. I crouched and peeked through the aperture.

Outside, the men had gathered in a group before the hall's door. Before them stood Haakon with his sword in one hand and his walking stick in the other. Behind Haakon, near the hall door, stood his thralls. Haakon stepped down onto the turf and limped up to the apparent leader, who removed his helmet to reveal his black hair and gaunt profile. The breath caught in my throat as I recognized Holger. I glanced over at my father but he had not moved from the doorway.

Holger gestured toward the hall and Haakon shook his head. Though I could not hear his words, Holger's anger was clear. The man next to him, who stood nearly a head taller than Holger, held up his hands as if to calm Holger, but Holger kept up his tirade, motioning to another man. That man moved up to Bursti and yanked him forward. I heard my father hiss a curse as the warrior forced Bursti to his knees. Holger pulled his seax from its sheath and pointed it at Haakon, then at his thrall.

Please, no, I thought. *Not Bursti.* I closed my eyes to shield myself from what I knew would come next.

"Stop!" my father roared and exited the barn.

I opened my eyes as the men spun to face this unexpected threat. My father stopped but kept his sword in his hand where the others could see it. I knew not what to do, so I remained hidden, watching through the peephole with my heart thumping in my chest.

Holger strode to my father and stopped just beyond his sword's reach. The others followed him, including Haakon and the tall man who had stood at Holger's side. "You have not been easy to find, Loosebeard," said Holger.

"Who is he?" asked the tall man. He had the lilt of a Swede and the bearing of a lord, though I did not recognize him.

"This is Torolv Torgilsson, the foster father of Astrid Eriksson. He used to be a lord in our lands, but is now a nithing. A runaway from the true king, Harald."

"You did not mention that Astrid would have others with her."

"I did not know if he would still be by her side," Holger answered with a glance at the taller man. He studied my father with his dark eyes and a wicked grin suddenly stretched across his thin face. "But you are a man of honor and her foster father. You would not abandon her, would you?"

"If you want Astrid and the boy, Holger, you will have to fight me for them," said my father.

Holger's grin widened. "For the troubles you have caused me in finding you, it would be a pleasure to lay you low, Torolv. But in all candor, you are not worth any more of my sweat. I have others who would relish killing you, and I will still take Astrid and the boy."

"What is this talk of fights and killing?" asked the taller man, visibly confused and angry now. "You told us that Queen Gunnhild wished to foster the child. That this was a mission of goodwill."

His words made my thoughts spin. Gunnhild was the former wife of Erik Bloodaxe and the mother of the man who called himself King Harald, the very same man who had killed Olaf's father, Trygvi. By all accounts, she was a calculating and wicked woman who some said was a witch. Her desire to foster Olaf made no sense unless it was to see him killed.

I was not alone in my shock. "Goodwill?" asked my father incredulously, then laughed.

Holger seemed to remember himself then and grinned. "That is indeed the case, Dag. Thank you for the reminder." He looked my father full in the face. "Gunnhild wishes to extend peace to your charges, Torolv. And as a token of that peace, offer Olaf a place in her home as a fosterling. He will, of course, be treated as befits his station and his lineage as a king's son. We shall return Astrid to her father. She will not be harmed. You have my word."

"As King Trygvi had your word when you invited him to raid with you?" my father retorted. "Your word means nothing, Holger."

Astrid and Olaf appeared then at the barn door and peered out at the men. Holger noticed their presence and smiled his serpentine smile. "My lady," he said with a brief nod in her direction. "Queen Gunnhild, the mother of King Harald, has offered a place in her home for your son as a fosterling. He will not be harmed, nor will you."

"So I heard," responded Astrid sourly.

"Gunnhild has kings enough in her family," continued my father, meaning Harald and his remaining brothers. "You and I both know that Olaf is a threat to those sons. I can see no reason to put him in Gunnhild's care."

"I am not privy to the reasons of a queen," Holger said evasively. "I have only her promise of friendship and this sack of gold to repay you for the losses you have suffered." He motioned to one of his men, who lifted a sack as large as a man's fist. "There is enough here, Torolv, for Astrid, you, and your son to live comfortably until your final days."

"And what of my lands? My title?" asked my father.

He lifted his hands as if the matter was beyond his control. "I am afraid those are now gone. But with that much gold, you can easily start over."

"Is that as large as the ransom you placed on our heads?" called Astrid from the barn.

"Ransom?" asked the man, Dag. This exchange was clearly not what he had been expecting.

"Aye, ransom," Astrid repeated to Dag. "This man and his lord killed my husband and have been pursuing us ever since." She then shifted her fiery gaze to Holger. "Tell your lord Harald and his mother that they may not have my son for any price."

My father looked at her, then at Holger. "Astrid has spoken and as her oath-sworn protector, I am honor-bound to ensure that her words come to pass," he said. "Queen Gunnhild will need to look elsewhere for a fosterling. Olaf will stay with his mother."

Holger's face pinched into a scowl. "Very well, then, I shall take the boy by force." He pulled his sword from its scabbard.

"You will do no such thing, Northman!" hollered Haakon. "These people are guests in my house and guests they shall remain. Dag, since when have we allowed Northmen to come to our lands and threaten violence or break our laws?"

The old man's words struck a chord with the Swedes, and especially Dag, who stepped forward. "Put your sword away, Holger. You too, Northman," he said to my father. "There will be no violence this night. The boy and his mother are guests in this hall and free to decide their fate. If they do not wish to go with you, Holger, then that is their right. Besides, I now see that there is something more at play here and that you and your men have been dealing with us in half-truths." Then, to add salt to Holger's wound, Dag said, "Holger, you shall give Haakon one of your gold coins for his trouble. Come. We are done here." He whirled and motioned for his men to follow.

My father faced Holger for a long, tense moment. He was ready to fight if Holger made a move. Holger must have sensed it, for he held himself in check. "There will be a time for you and me, Torolv Loosebeard." He spat in my father's direction.

"I will welcome it, Holger."

Holger sheathed his weapon, then turned to go. My father stepped back and returned his own blade to its scabbard. There was a part of me that ached to rush forth and ram my seax into Holger's back and fulfill the oath I had made to the god Thor, for I blamed him more than the faceless King Harald or his mother, Gunnhild, for our plight. But I knew, too, that even if I managed to reach Holger, I would fall to his comrades' blades before I could pull my own blade free. And so, instead, I stabbed the wood planking of the barn wall and cursed under my breath at the retreating snake.

And Holger slipped away into the gray morning.

Later, we sat in Haakon's hall, debating our journey as we broke our fast on porridge. With Holger's sudden appearance, we knew not which was the better choice: staying on Haakon's farm or chancing a trip to Westra Aros where Holger might be waiting.

"I would not put it past that snake to be camped downriver," Astrid said sourly, "just waiting for us to make our escape."

"One thing is clear to me," said my father as he sleeved some porridge from his mustache. "We cannot stay here and endanger Haakon any more than we have. Holger could easily have killed Bursti this morning, and that does not sit well with me. I also believe that Dag would not allow Holger to lie in wait for us. Dag now knows Holger's true mission and was ill-pleased at having been deceived by him. He will be keeping a closer eye on Holger and his men, I think."

"And if Holger and his men are waiting for us in Westra Aros?" asked Astrid. "Or worse, they are there and Sigvard's ship is not?"

My father turned to Haakon. "Do your neighbors know Sigvard's ship?"

"*Sigvard's Swan?*" asked Haakon. "Every local knows it."

"So it will be easy to spot if it is there? Or if it is not there?"

"Aye. It is unmistakable."

My father nodded, having made up his mind. He looked at us. "We go. Let us grab our things from the barn."

As planned, Haakon's neighbors came later that day to collect us. They arrived in a shallow riverboat and helped us load our meager possessions into the vessel. Haakon and his household gathered on the riverbank near his humble dock and watched in silence as we prepared for our journey.

We went to them when we were finished loading to say our farewells. I, being more reserved than the others, took my place at the end of the line. The others hugged and said their well wishes or shared a laugh. I did not. Rather, I mumbled my awkward words to Tala and Gamal and Bursti. It is not that I did not care for them or feel the loss of leaving them — I simply did not know how to show it. They responded with a pat and a kind word, but said no more, perchance knowing that any greater outpouring of emotion might embarrass me. If that is true, then they were right — it would have.

When I came to Haakon, he studied me with his rheumy eyes, then motioned me to him. I stepped forward and he placed a gentle hand on my shoulder. "Walk with me." We took several steps away from the others. "I have some words for your ears alone, Torgil. These words are not to share. Not even with your father."

My curiosity piqued, I nodded.

"You have in you two gifts: your silence and your mettle," he began in his direct manner. I felt my cheeks flush at his words, for I knew not where they were headed and already they made me uncomfortable. "I have seen both. But I also sense an uncertainty in you, perchance born from your circumstances. It is understandable. I want you to understand that you cannot change your circumstances. They are woven into your life threads. The gods wish to see how you react and if you are indeed worthy of their favor. I have seen that you have the gifts to react appropriately to those challenges and they will not only serve you well, they will keep that brave but foolish charge of yours alive. Do you understand my words?"

"I think so," I responded.

He straightened and looked in my eyes. I had a hard time meeting his gaze and so looked down. He brought my chin up with his crooked finger. "Be watchful. Be considerate. And be fierce when you decide to act. The world is vicious and you must be ready for it."

I nodded, understanding a little better now, but still not fully.

"Fare you well, lad."

"Thank you," I managed to mutter and turned to go.

I climbed into the riverboat and waved briskly to Haakon and his household, hoping the knowledge he had imparted to me would become clear soon.

Chapter 14

Westra Aros was a fetid place.

By the gods, how it reeked. Rotting fish. Manure. Smoke. Urine. Before I even set eyes on the village, those foul aromas invaded my nose. I covered my face with my forearm, but it did little to mask the odor. Olaf, who sat before me in our small vessel, covered his face in his tunic.

Wilderness met civilization in that strange town. Yet it seemed to my young eyes that the two had not yet reconciled how to coexist. Long a trading center of the Swedes, its shelters huddled on the tree-thick banks of the Lake like lots cast haphazardly by the hands of giants. Tall pines loomed over the structures, their branches casting the place in a sinister shadow from which echoed the faceless cackle of revelers, the bark of hounds, and the hum of conversation. There were three docks against which larger trading vessels rocked in the current. Smaller ships lay strewn on the shore in no particular order. I could see pockets of people moving about and hear the call of tradesmen hawking their wares. To the west of the town, on the beach, two men fought with swords surrounded by a group of cheering men. To the east, women washed laundry, oblivious to the fighting or the men who pissed in the water not twenty paces from where they toiled. I sensed that this was a place where men came to lose themselves and where hopes and dreams grew and died in equal measure. I dreaded it instantly.

"Do you see Sigvard's ship?" called my father from the shadows of the ship's small prow where he sat.

"Aye," responded Aki, the man who had interrogated us at the harvest festival and who owned the small vessel in which we sat.

"Pull us up beside the ship," my father ordered as he ventured a peek above the gunwale to see the ships. Olaf and I sat behind him and followed my father's lead, peering into the darkness at the ships' hulls that glowed in the firelight of the village.

"Oars up," whispered Aki from the stern. "Bjarni, fend off the ships."

The man named Bjarni raised his oar as we angled toward the easternmost dock, glided slowly past one ship, and sidled up to another. This one, he tapped with his oar to keep us from hitting it too hard. The ship was large, its hull nearly twice the length of our small vessel, its gunwale high above our heads. Unlike a warship, this was a trading ship, or knarr, designed less for speed and maneuverability and more for holding cargo.

"Who is there?" came a gravelly voice from the ship's aft deck. A face appeared, a wrinkled graybeard wearing a woolen cap.

"It is Aki. I have the cargo we discussed."

"Get 'em aboard. Quickly, now."

We did not need more coaxing. I grabbed my sack of possessions and my weapons and lifted them into the knarr, then followed Astrid and Turid in their climb over the gunwale. The old man grabbed each of us in turn and hoisted us aboard.

"Into the hold," he hissed, indicating the sunken space between the fore- and aft decks. The space was already crowded with sacks and barrels and ropes and spare oars. We climbed down and sat wherever we could find space.

"Get you gone," the graybeard said to Aki and Bjarni, and I realized with some guilt that we had not thanked them for their help. The old man then turned to us and pointed to two metal pots in the middle of the hold. "There is food in one o' those pots. The other is your privy. Do not mistake one for the other. We will see you in the morn." And with that, he shoved a plank in place to cover the hold, then another, until we sat in complete darkness.

I sensed some movement to my right, then heard Astrid say, "Come. Bring your spoons. I have found the food."

Though we could see nothing in that dark place, we could still smell and feel and hear, and so we worked our way to Astrid and the pot that she had found. I fumbled for the spoon I carried in my belt pouch and felt my way to the pot's opening, then lowered it until I felt my fingers touch warm liquid. Lifting my spoon back to my nose, I sniffed and was greeted with the smell of fish and potatoes. I ate. After several spoonfuls, I retreated to an empty spot and tried to position my goods to form a pillow under my head.

For what seemed like an eternity we waited in that dark space with the rank smell of Westra Aros in our nostrils. To take my mind from my discomfort, I tried to discern the various sounds, parsing order from misconduct, sobriety from intemperance. I could not — it all blended into one grating cacophony that seemed somehow fitting for that strange place.

"I want to see what is happening," Olaf announced impatiently and made to rise.

"No," my father growled in the darkness.

Olaf ignored him and began working on one of the planks that formed our ceiling. I was lying near him and as soon as I found the wool of his trousers, I pulled him back. There was a thud as he careened off a barrel and another as he hit the ship's ribbing. He cried out and his voice sounded like thunder in that small space. I did not know if he was truly hurt, but at the moment, I did not care. "My father said 'no,' " I hissed.

"Quiet, you fools," the graybeard jeered above our heads. "Men are coming."

I noticed the footfalls on the dock, distant at first but getting closer. Their approach did not unsettle me. Holger could not possibly know of us. It was probably just more crew. That is, of course, until the graybeard asked, "Who are you? What do you want?" With his words, my calm evaporated.

"We want what you have in your hold."

I recognized Holger's voice instantly and now my heart thundered. I knew not how that snake had found us. I knew only that there was no way out of our watery prison.

"And what is that? Furs? Amber?" asked the graybeard. "It is not yours to take."

"Torolv?" Holger called, apparently tired of the graybeard's game. "Is that you in there, skulking like a rat? Have you fallen so far from that mighty hall of yours?" His words prompted some laughter from the others with him, though how many others, I could not tell.

The slow rasp of my father's sword sliding from its scabbard answered Holger's accusation. I could not see my father, but I could sense his fury, and wondered if he might leap from the hold to slice the tongue from Holger's mouth. Holger, too, must have sensed it, for I heard blades sliding from scabbards out on the dock. The sound raised the hair on my arms and reminded me of my own blade, which I now readied by my side.

"What are you doing? You have no right to board this ship," the old man protested.

"Silence, or I will feed you to the fish along with the friends you hide. Remove these," Holger commanded.

Heavy feet climbed onto the deck above our heads. To my left, a plank slipped from its spot. Though it was dark outside, it was lighter than in the hold. I could suddenly see the shadowed forms of my father, who sat across from me, and Olaf, to my right. Astrid and Turid were to my father's left, though deeper in the hold. As the men moved a second plank, I slithered farther into the shadows and tightened the grip on my blade. My father showed me the blade at his side and pointed directly above me, where a man stood. I knew then what he intended and he confirmed it by pointing at me, then at the deck above his head. I nodded my understanding.

Sweat beaded at my temples, though it was not a warm night. My stomach tightened, and I felt a sudden urge to piss. I said a quick prayer to Thor for courage and safety, then looked to my right. Olaf was on his knees, blade in hand, smiling that mischievous smile of his. *Wait*, I mouthed to him and held up my hand, but he ignored me.

As the fourth plank slid away, Olaf darted forward. I heard Astrid scream just as he launched himself up the hull's interior and over the gunwale. My father and I stood as one, but rather than rush for the man above me, my father catapulted himself over the wale.

Across from me, one of Holger's men fell backward in surprise. That left the man above me. I spun and swung my blade as hard as I could at the first thing I saw: a leg. That man, too, had shuffled backward at the sudden appearance of Olaf and my father so that my blade ripped across his shin rather than taking his leg off at the knee. He wailed and stumbled farther back.

I was vaguely aware of blades ringing to my right, followed by a scream, and a splash. I had no time to look, for I knew the man behind me would soon be approaching. I turned in time to see his blade angling for my chest, coming fast. And then, suddenly, Astrid flashed up from the shadows and drove our one spear into the man's side. The surprise on his face was matched only by my own.

I spun then, knowing well the other man was still behind me. He had recovered and was limping toward me, though more cautiously after seeing his comrade fall to Astrid's spear. I brought my blade up and readied myself.

"Halt!" came a cry in the night.

I ventured a glance in the direction of the voice and saw a group of men running toward us. Turning back to my assailant, I yelled at him to come at me. That, I realize now, was foolish, for he was far larger than me and could easily have killed me, but after all of the injustices we had suffered and the great distance we had traveled, I wanted nothing more than to lay that man low. In the end, he did not attack me. With this new threat approaching, he backed away.

To my right, my father and Olaf stood on the dock, facing Holger, who bled from a gash on his cheek. Behind him stood another of his henchmen. I did not see the old man.

"What is this?" called the leader of this new gang, a tall, slender man whose loose blond hair fell to his shoulders and partially covered his face. "Who are you?" The man pointed his sword at Holger.

"My name is Holger and I am the emissary of Queen Gunnhild and her son, King Harald," said Holger calmly. "We have come to return this boy to the queen."

"And you have been told that the boy does not wish to return to your queen," came another voice from behind the first man who spoke. The man stepped forward and I smiled. Dag. "Not only have you told me your half-truths to deceive me and our king, you now come like thieves to steal the boy from his mother." Dag pointed at Astrid, who stood in the knarr.

"And you board my ship unlawfully to do it," said the slender blond man, who I now knew to be Sigvard.

"Arrest these men," ordered Dag.

"I am the queen's emissary," responded Holger indignantly. "You cannot arrest me."

Four men stepped forward with their swords drawn. They wore byrnies and helmets and carried shields. Holger and his remaining warriors, who had come to take us stealthily, were ill-equipped to fight them. They wore no helmets or chain mail shirts and carried no shields. Still, they did not budge. Rather, they stood with their swords pointed defiantly at the new threat.

"Lay your weapons down, and it will go easier for you," called Dag.

"You know not what you do, Dag," Holger growled.

"I will say it once again, then no more. Drop your sword, Holger."

With a curse, Holger placed his sword on the deck. His henchmen followed his lead.

As Dag's men escorted Holger and his henchmen away, Sigvard came forward to survey the scene. The man Astrid had killed slumped over the gunwale. Another body floated in the water. I knew him only by his clothing. Aki, Haakon's neighbor.

"Now we know how Holger found us so quickly," growled my father to Olaf and me. He spat at the corpse.

To my right, the graybeard lay on his back on the dock, his arms loose by his sides. His eyes gazed blankly at the dark sky. There was a puncture wound in the poor man's chest and a pool of blood below it.

"I am sorry," said my father.

"Who killed him?" asked Sigvard.

"Holger," said Olaf, pointing in the direction of the retreating mass of men.

Sigvard rose and stormed down the dock, back the way he had come, leaving in his wake a gang of nine men who stared stonily at us. Finally, one of them turned to the others. "Get that dead bastard off our ship. And fish that one out, too," said the man, pointing to Aki's corpse in the water. "I will not have their corpses bringing their bad luck to our ship." Several of the men fingered the talismans at their neck as they moved to do his bidding. "Careful with Arne, you louts!" he called to two of his comrades who fumbled with the graybeard's body. The man then turned his hard eyes on us. "He was a good man. You lot had better be worth his life."

The following morning, Sigvard gathered his crew and told us to stay close to the dock. He and his men were going to bury Arne's remains in the graveyard on the east side of town, but did not want us to come. As we waited for their return, a crowd gathered on the beach. Shouts carried to us over the water as the group grew in size and moved close to the water. At the same time, one of Dag's men approached Sigvard's ship and beckoned for us to come. Wordlessly, we gathered our weapons and followed him to the beach and the gathering crowd.

Even before we reached the strand, I could see what awaited. The group had formed a crescent around several men, one of whom was Holger. They faced a fire that crackled in a pit on the beach, their bodies bound by ropes. Across the fire stood Dag, as silent and rigid as an oak tree in the midst of the townspeople. To his left, at the head of the crowd, Sigvard stood with his crew, their arms crossed and their faces masked with anger. Our guide led us to Dag and ordered us to face Holger and his bound men.

"Holger Einarsson. You and your men have attempted to take this child, Olaf," he gestured at Olaf, "against his mother's will and, in so doing, have killed an innocent man and broken the peace of this place. In addition, you have lied to me and to my lord, King Erik. As a consequence of these actions, you and your men will be punished."

Holger scowled. "I act at the behest of my lord and my queen and with the support of your king. If you punish me, you bring punishment on yourself."

"I will take my chances," replied Dag. "For the life of Sigvard's crewman, you will pay him two hundred silver coins."

Holger tried to speak, but a warrior rammed the butt of his spear into Holger's back, knocking him to his knees. The crowd cheered as Holger collapsed.

Dag continued, unfazed. "For disturbing the peace, you shall pay another one hundred coins. And for lying to my lord, the king, and attempted kidnapping, you will each be given a choice. You shall lose a hand or an eye. Since Olaf Tryggvason was the subject of your crimes, it is he who shall exact the punishment."

The four men with Holger accepted Dag's words with stoic courage. Holger did not. His face pinched and his cheeks flushed. He spat at Dag and yanked at his bindings until his guard rammed his spear butt into Holger's back again. The crowd cheered that wretch's misery and I felt a smile form on my face.

Dag did not delay the punishments. A guard brought the first man forth while Dag extracted a sword and a spear from the fire, the metal on each glowing orange and blue. The guard shoved Holger's man to his knees before a wood block and asked which he preferred to lose, his arm or his eye.

The man looked from Dag to Olaf. "Take my left hand, for I can still fight with my right. And I wish to see you with my eyes when I come to kill you."

"Bravely spoken," Dag responded as he handed Olaf the sword.

My heart thundered as I watched my young charge walk forward. He took the sword and stepped toward the man whose left hand was now being tied in place on the wooden block. The criminal watched Olaf warily and set his jaw. "Strike truly, boy," he said.

Olaf gripped the sword in both hands. The glowing sword arced into the air. Astrid and Turid looked away. I stood mesmerized by the horror and the anger pulsing in me. The blade dropped hard onto the man's wrist and bit into the block.

Surprisingly, there was little blood as the man's left hand dropped to the pebbled beach. There was only the man falling backward, holding his bloody stump before him as he struggled courageously to keep his scream inside. His guards grabbed him and pulled him free of the block, then used a leather strap and stick to form a rough tourniquet around his lower arm.

Olaf handed the blade casually back to Dag, who thrust it back into the flames as a guard ushered the victim away. There was a grin on Olaf's blood-speckled face, and I knew he was enjoying this. My stomach roiled. The men deserved their punishment and the punishment was just, but the sight of Olaf's boyish, smiling face speckled in blood lifted the bile in my throat.

Holger was made to watch as all of his men received their sentences. Each chose to lose his left non-fighting hand, and each accepted his punishment with varying levels of stoicism. About us, the crowd cheered each stroke of Olaf's blade. Those cheers swelled now as the guards brought Holger forth.

"This is not the end of my pursuit, Olaf," Holger hissed. "I will find you, and I will kill you."

Olaf smiled as the guard tied Holger's arm to the block.

"Go ahead, boy," Dag coached.

He had not done so with the others, but this time Olaf yelled his fury as he brought the blade down. It struck with such force that Holger's left hand flew from the block and into the fire. Holger stumbled to his feet, then stared in horror at his dismembered limb. The guards came forth, bound his arm as they had the others, and marched him away.

"We shall collect your silver," said Dag with finality. "Justice has been done."

Sigvard approached my father then, his face grave. "That was a bad business, lord, and an inauspicious way to begin our voyage. We have lost a good man and friend. If I were not such a friend to Haakon, I would leave you all here."

To my surprise, my father took no offense. "I understand your words, and I owe you a debt that I cannot readily pay," he said. His eyes then turned to Dag. "I owe you both a debt."

If Sigvard heard my father's words, he did not react to them. Instead he said, "Before we cast off, we shall give a sacrifice to the gods, for we will need it now more than ever." He walked away with his crew in tow.

Dag, on the other hand, nodded to my father. "You owe me nothing. Vanish from this place and do not let me see you or that boy again. For I sense if we do, there will be a higher price to pay."

And with those ominous words hanging over us, we left that wretched place.

Chapter 15

We sat on the foredeck, boys on one side, women on the other, doing our best to stay out from under the feet of the crewmen. I was weary and tried to doze in the cramped space beneath the fore gunwale. Across from me, Turid wept quietly, though I knew not why. Astrid soothed her with whispered words, and I suppose that was the best remedy, for the weeping eventually ceased.

I do not remember falling asleep, but I awoke to the call of ducks overhead and the sensation of water on my cheek. I sat up quickly, stiff from slumbering on the deck planks. A thin layer of water had splashed onto the deck and I had been lying in it. I peered over the gunwale and was greeted by a crisp, gray day.

We sailed with the shoreline to our left, heading east into a climbing sun that a shroud of gray clouds muted. A flock of ducks passed above our billowing sail, heading west. Sigvard stood in the aft deck holding the steer board, his loose blond hair blowing about his head in the breeze as his eyes scanned the water before us. Beside him stood my father. About the deck sat the crew — nine men in all — in various stages of repose. Some gambled. Others chewed on bread and hard cheese. One juggled with knives. They were a rough-looking lot who stole glances at us when they could. Several looked resentful or angry, others just curious, as if they were trying to piece together the puzzle of our presence on their ship. I tried to ignore them.

My father returned from the aft deck and slid down next to me with a partial loaf of bread in his hand. He tore at it with his teeth and chewed for a moment. Across from me, Astrid sat upright with her eyes closed. She was wrapped in a thick hooded cloak that hid all but a few strands of her cropped, golden hair. Her face, I realized, looked altogether different from that of the woman I remembered in my father's hall the previous summer. She was thin now — almost gaunt — and tanned from her work on Haakon's farm. Dirt streaked her cheeks and forehead.

Suddenly, her eyes opened, and she looked straight at me. "Why do you look at me so, Torgil?" she asked.

Startled, I looked away, too embarrassed to respond.

"You'd best eat, Torgil," interrupted my father as he offered me the bread in his hand. "We will not have good bread and cheese for the length of our journey. Soon enough, the bread will mold and we will be eating dried cod, nuts, and anything else that can last. Believe me, you will be sick of cod by the time we reach Aldeigjuborg."

"How far is it?" Olaf asked, twirling his knife on the deck in his boredom.

My father shrugged. "It depends on the weather, the winds, and the seas, lad. If all goes well, we could reach Aldeigjuborg in half a moon. At least that is what Sigvard just told me. I have never been there."

I smiled at my father's words and the promise of reaching someplace new, far away from Holger and the reach of Queen Gunnhild and her son, Harald. It would be good, too, to start afresh and to prepare for our return home, whenever that happened to be.

The Lake was actually a long bay. It opened into a broad waterway near Westra Aros, but east of the village, in the direction we were traveling, it narrowed into a patchwork of tree-strewn islands and labyrinthine waterways. For two days, we wove our way through the channels, coming ever closer to the East Sea. As we neared it, the slack tide sucked at our ship's hull, as if some invisible hand pulled us inexorably toward our fate and Sigvard was only there to steer us to it, a ferryman to the unknown. The closer we came to the sea, the more treacherous the channels grew, the threat of hidden sandbars, floating logs, and hull-crushing stones ever-present. It did not help that we sailed in a wide, heavy knarr — more a plodding ox than a maneuverable serpent, especially with our extra weight and its burden of trade goods.

It helped that Sigvard and his crew knew every stretch of these shores. He knew where hazards lurked and those places to avoid —- where a bad tide could leave us stranded or dangerous logs could be floating, and where the inhabitants were protective of their lands and less than friendly. He knew, too, the coves where bathing was best and the women could have some privacy, or where the hunting was choice, or where the pike grew as large as baby seals and could be hunted with spears, or where a farmstead was willing to trade and add to his chance of profit in Aldeigjuborg.

Our captain was not a man who took chances. When he knew he could not reach a particular waterway by nightfall, he would steer into the safety of a quiet cove and wait for morning or a shift in the tide. Even with the sun high and visibility fair, Sigvard waited for the tide to lift his hull rather than attempt to snake his way through hazards. His caution suited me well, but not my father, who was mayhap more anxious to be clear of the Lake and away from the reach of Holger. One night, when Sigvard had gone ashore to barter with one of the locals for some fresh food, my father commented on Sigvard's caution to his second in command, a surly fellow named Tostig.

The man regarded my father for a moment before speaking. "I do not know who you are or what has brought our paths together. I know only that traveling the East Way requires equal measures of skill and fortune, and we did not begin this journey with the best of fortune," Tostig said as he fingered the hammer amulet at his neck.

My father frowned but did not push the matter further.

Still, no matter how interesting the scenery or wildlife that surrounded us, it was difficult to remain stationary from morning until dusk with the sun baking our skin and nothing but wind, the lap of water against the hull, and the creak of ship's rigging to fill our ears. To pass the time, we boys practiced juggling with our seaxes, or took our turn bailing water from the ship's hold, or learned the ways of the rigging and sail. At anchor, we tiptoed along the gunwales, trying to make it from stern to prow and back again, but more oft than not, and much to the enjoyment of the crew, ending up in the water. The crew would cheer or guffaw or curse our feats, so much so that my father recommended that we stop distracting the men and make ourselves useful. Sigvard heard my father's words and stopped him. "Let the boys have their fun, Torolv. The men enjoy it!"

On the evening of the fourth day, just as the sun began to sink below the treetops behind us, we angled for the shoreline. The wind had died on us earlier in the evening, so we approached under oar. Olaf and I raced to the bow and gazed at the muddy beach materializing before us.

"What is this place?" Turid asked to no one in particular.

"You will see," answered a crewman.

We did not moor offshore as we had in other places. Instead, we pulled the ship ahead until the hull bit into the soft mud. The crewman who had answered Turid hopped over the gunwale and tied the ship to one of the trees.

"Get the logs!" ordered Sigvard.

More crewmen leaped overboard and disappeared into the woods, emerging a short time later carrying some small logs between them. These they placed next to each other so that they stretched, side by side, from beneath the ship's prow to a point midway up the narrow beach. Meanwhile, two more men tied ropes to iron hooks on the ship's hull and ran them up to a tree into which two deep grooves had been carved.

"Off, you louts," called Sigvard as he jumped into the shallow sea, "and to the ropes!"

The crew rushed to do his bidding, half of them grabbing one rope, the other half grabbing the other.

"Everyone pulls!" Sigvard called to us. "You too, women! We need all hands for this!"

The five of us joined the tug of war, and together we pulled and grunted until our hands stung from the hemp ropes and sweat glistened on our brows, and still we tugged. Ell by ell the wide-hulled ship moved across the logs until we could see the barnacles and seaweed clinging to it keel.

Sigvard pointed to Tostig and ordered him to start a fire. Wiping his hair from his sweating forehead with a sweep of his hand, he turned to us. "We stay here to make final repairs to the ship," he said to my father. "It will be our last chance to rest and prepare ourselves before the long journey across the sea. It would be wise to fill your bellies and to pray for a safe passage." His eyes briefly shifted to the sky, and I felt my good mood slip from me like the water dripping from the knarr's hull.

We rested that night around two separate fires, the crew at one, our group at the other, sharing bread and cheese and some of the salted venison for which Sigvard had traded. The crew drank ale, and with each round finished, the jokes and songs grew lewder, the farts and burps louder. Now and again, the men would cast an eye in the direction of our women and mumble something to each other, then break into peels of laughter. It was unsettling.

Our group could not have been more opposite in demeanor. The crew knew what dangers awaited them. We did not. And that unknowing turned our words and thoughts inward. Across the fire from me, Turid cast tense glances at the men as she worried a piece of cloth with her fingers. Astrid stared into the fire and chewed silently, her thoughts elsewhere. Olaf whittled a stick with his knife. My father and I sharpened our sword blades with whetstones. None of us spoke.

Eventually, I settled on the ground with a cloak as my pillow, doing my best to ignore the crew's boisterousness. Beside me, the fire cracked and popped, throwing its smoke and ash up toward the trees that towered over us like silent sentinels. Only, from them, I sensed not protection but foreboding, as if they somehow knew what awaited us yet could not say.

I was not aware of falling asleep, only of starting awake for some inexplicable reason. To this day, I am not sure if it was a sound I heard or something more divine that pulled me from sleep. It was the dead of night, that moment when the summer sky is darkest. I started to put my head back down when I heard rustling in the woods nearby and lifted my head to look. Across the fire, among the trees some twenty paces away, something moved. Limbs. Forms. A glint of steel flashed.

I did not think, but reacted. Rising with a shout, I drew my seax and readied myself for the attack I thought was coming.

Only we were not being attacked.

The forms were dragging something between them, and this they dropped when they heard my shout. Around me, people scrambled from their bedding and came to my side. As I stepped around the fire toward the dropped bundle, the assailants retreated into the shadow of the woods. The bundle moved then and my father rushed forward. I followed and then stopped, for the form sat up and I could move no farther.

Turid.

We never did discover who dragged Turid into the night. The crew searched the woods but found nothing. The two guards on the ship swore they had seen nothing. My father and I investigated the following morning and found footprints in the mud, but whether these belonged to the assailants or the crew who had carelessly trampled the area in their amateur investigation the previous night was impossible to say. Turid was no help either. She was struggling with the trauma of the event, and all she would tell Astrid was that it had been men who had tried to take her. Men with a sword at her throat and ale on their breath.

"Today we will see to the ship," Sigvard said to all of us after we had broken our fast. His eyes scanned his crew and finally fell on us. "What happened last night is a bad omen and I do not wish for the likes of it to happen again. Tonight we will double the guard and put away the ale. Tomorrow, we leave."

As the crew mumbled their understanding and saw to their individual tasks, Sigvard stepped over to us. "I am sorry for the...for what happened."

Astrid had been sitting with Turid, and she now rose to face the captain. "You know it was members of your crew, do you not?"

Sigvard cocked his head as if considering her words. "Careful with your accusations, Astrid. It is a long walk to any towns from here."

As he turned on his heel, Astrid stepped closer, her fists clenched at her sides and her cheeks red. She wanted to say something more, I could tell, but my father raised his arm and blocked her path. "Leave it, Astrid. It will do us no good."

I glanced at Turid. Tears filled her beautiful eyes and streaked her thin cheeks. Several leaves clung to her red tresses. I wanted badly to make her feel better, but the stony countenance on her face told us all that she was in no mood for words or comfort, and I guessed that that was especially true for men. So instead, I sighed in my helplessness and went to join the crew.

We left that strange place the following morning, as soon as the wind was up and the tide slackened toward the sea. Our crew had added fresh caulking to the ship and so it was with the scent of wool and pine resin in our noses and a cloud of suspicion in our minds that we left our campsite behind and pointed *Sigvard's Swan* toward the east.

And the unknown.

Chapter 16

We headed northeast from the land of the Swedes. It was a beautiful day, bright and clear, with the wind blowing mostly north. Above us, seagulls circled and dove and called out belligerently. Small fishing boats hugged the coves and islands of a coastline that grew ever more formless behind us. Soon it would be but a dark line on the western horizon.

I stood in the prow beside Olaf, our eyes filled with nothing but the green and blue and gray sea, the white tips of waves, and the light blue sky above. Overwhelmed by its beauty, Olaf raised his arms and yelled at what he saw. I blushed at his foolishness and the crew chuckled. Behind us, Turid sat against the steer board wale, her arms wrapped about her knees, her eyes focused on the ship's deck. I looked away.

By early nightfall, we reached an archipelago that rose like the humps of some sea monster as we neared. We anchored on the lee side of one of those humps — a rocky island upon which stood a few windblown clumps of greenery. The sea was quiet here in the bay, the wind calm. The only locals we saw were the squawking ducks and the snorting gray seals that huddled on rocks washed white by bird shit.

"We sleep on deck," Sigvard announced to us as soon as the anchor dropped. "It will be warmer here and easier to escape, should trouble find us." He turned to his crew. "No tent. We sleep under the stars."

"We should kill some of those pups before we leave," called Tostig, his eyes on the seals.

"No time," responded Sigvard flatly. "If we find some closer to Aldeigjuborg, we can grab them there."

Tostig spat over the gunwale and shrugged. "A shame."

"Are we expecting trouble?" Astrid asked as she swept a fly from her face with a dirty hand. Turid studied Sigvard with her wide blue eyes.

Sigvard's face was as bare as the rocks near which we floated. "I always expect trouble," he said, "especially out here." He rolled the pendants at his neck between his fingers. "Besides, we have experienced enough mishap already for one voyage."

I looked at Astrid, then at my father. "Sleep with your blades to hand," my father advised as one of the crewmen offered us a strip of dried cod. My father took it with a nod of thanks and handed it to Astrid. "I will take first watch. Torgil, you will take second."

"What am I looking for?"

"Anything that seems out of place."

The gods left us alone that night, though there were times when the winds blustered out of the south, bending the trees on the shore so that it sounded like a company of archers pulling their bows. I knew, of course, that could not be, but I still kept my head low. Around me, most of the men snored peacefully. Nearby, the seals grunted. Turid slept in Astrid's arms. Beside them, Olaf rolled and turned in his sleep as he was wont to do. He had never been a good sleeper and on a hard, windswept deck, he was even worse.

We moved on the following morning. The sky was but a smear of gray. Within the islands, the wind was blustery and unpredictable, so Sigvard had the men pull the ship from its mooring under oar. The seals watched us go with their dark, melancholy eyes. In that moment, I envied their safety in that rocky cove and their seemingly simple life, and I prayed that we would know that feeling once again.

My father's voice tore me from my thoughts, and I rose to join him at the bow. Olaf stood by his side, wrapped in his cloak, gazing outward.

"Which direction are we headed?" my father called above the wind when I reached him. Though his hair was pulled into a ponytail, several strands had broken loose, and these now flapped about his face in the wind.

"East," Olaf and I called in unison.

"How do you know?"

Though it was still early and the sky was but a sheet of gray, the light shone brighter to our right, where it had been since entering the land of the Swedes. "The sun is southeast of us," I said.

"And why do we not set a sail?" he asked.

"Because the wind comes from all sides," said Olaf.

"Good," he said. "One day, you both will command a ship. It is important to know these things. Here," he pointed to the low-lying islands through which we navigated, "we have clues for traveling. Like a trail. Sigvard and his men know these islands and use them as guides. Out there," he pointed, meaning beyond the rocky forms, "we may not always be so lucky, and in those instances, the captain and his crew must know how to read the wind and the sea, the tides and the clouds, the birds, and the sun and the stars. Do you understand?"

We nodded.

From one island to the next, we made our way east until, at last, we reached the open sea. But even here, the wind gusted and swirled, and I did not like it. Behind me, the men sat on their sea chests, pulling slowly, rhythmically, on their oars. Between grunts, they tossed lewd jokes at each other like kids in a snowball fight. I concentrated on their ribaldry, for it brought a smile to my lips.

Later, my father took a turn at Tostig's oar to give him a break and had us boys sit beside him. He pulled as we lightly held the oar so that we could get the feel and the rhythm of the stroke. I liked rowing. It quieted my thoughts and focused them on the movement and pulse of the sea. There was something soothing about twisting the oar as the blade came up and twisting it again as the blade bit down into the sea. Something controllable about it. Olaf, of course, was a natural at it, but could not keep his mind on it for long. His concentration flagged, and time and again he glanced over his shoulder to glimpse the sea before us.

"Lose your attention on your stroke, Olaf, and the oar will rip you from your seat," my father remonstrated.

He smirked. "I intend to command a ship, not row it."

Behind us, a man snorted.

My father spat over the gunwale. "Men will not follow a captain who cannot row his own ship."

"Why not?" Olaf asked.

I could feel my father tensing. "Would you follow a lord who cannot wield a sword? I think not."

My father's words turned my thoughts to Olaf's father, King Trygvi, who had always been so brash. He had been a man of action, not plans, and because of that, we now sat here in the middle of a gray, desolate sea, running for our lives while in the hold near our feet, Astrid, who had once been a queen, bailed.

I spat the rising bile of anger from my mouth.

The wind shifted later in the day, concentrating in a southeasterly direction and bringing with it a dark mass of clouds. I heard Tostig grumble that he could smell rain. At the steer board, I watched Sigvard study the clouds for a long time before commanding the crew to hoist and trim the sail. The crew leaped to their tasks, though I could see some cast nervous glances out beyond the port wale at the dark mass gathering in the sky. I peered beyond the bow into the distance but saw no sign of land —- no sign of anything, save for the gray sea and the now churning whitecaps.

Above me, the sail ballooned. The ship tilted beneath my feet as it bit into the sea and picked up speed. We dove into a trough and smashed into the oncoming swell. Sea spray shot over us and the crew cheered. Olaf joined them with a hoot of his own. I managed a smile even as my stomach lurched. Across from me, Turid's face turned as gray as the ocean.

I gazed out at the clouds to the north of us —- or I should say, what used to be the clouds. No longer were they a distinct mass from the sea. Now, a dark veil stretched from sky to ocean, like a gray tapestry hanging in a hall.

"A squall," my father called above the wind and pointed, though I knew not what a squall was.

"A what?" I asked.

"A storm. They happen from time to time. Come at you suddenly, like this one. That sheet of gray you see is rain and judging from the wind, it is headed this way. Sigvard is running before it, trying to get us as far as he can before it hits."

"What happens when it hits?" I asked.

"Depends on its strength. Could be just some rain and wind. We will see when it reaches us."

And so we did, though I wish we had not.

The rain began to fall shortly after he spoke those words. Big, fat raindrops that fell slowly, almost lazily at first, splatting on the deck and upon our heads. I prayed to Thor to be easy on us, but He did not oblige. By late afternoon, the sky had darkened further, the winds had picked up more force, and the rain had begun to fall in thick sheets that rolled across our deck, drenching us. The crew scrambled to cover and tie up loose barrels, secure their sea chests, and rack the oars.

"Secure the sail!" called Tostig. "You too, lads," he commanded us. "No one sits on their arse!"

"Come!" my father yelled to Olaf and me, and guided us to a group of men who were working the rigging to lower the yard. The deck rolled under our feet, and a man careened out over the sea, only to be saved by the mindful grasp of the crewman next to him. When the heavy beam reached us, we worked with the crew to secure the sail, though I felt more a burden than a help, for the yard and rain-pregnant sail were far heavier and clumsier than I ever would have imagined and I could barely see for the water streaming in my eyes. More than once, I caught my fingers in the ropes and had to stop my labor to pull them free.

Nearby, an oar dislodged from its rack and slid across the deck, smashing into the shin of one of the crewmen to my left. He cursed and stumbled, and the sail pitched precariously.

"Astrid! Turid! Collect the oars and tie them up!" Tostig called.

On hands and knees, the ladies scrambled into our midst and worked below our feet to gather the loose oars and secure them to their racks.

"Now the oar holes! Plug them! When that's done, get in the hold and bail!"

The ship pitched mightily just then and Olaf fell to the deck and rolled into the gunwale beside me. I did not have hands to help him. Another man tripped on a rope that had shifted out of position. He righted himself and continued his toil.

Still the storm grew. The sea rose and crashed over the gunwales to splash across the deck. The rain thundered down and the wind howled so that we could barely see or hear each other. With the men unable to row and the sail unusable, it was left to Sigvard at the steer board to keep our prow true to the wind and the swells. The rest of us could do nothing save cling to the ropes and wales and pray.

At one point, I ventured a glance over the gunwale. There were only the angry sea and the bottomless swells and the gray chaos of sky and cloud. If we lived, it would be because the Norns had decided to save us and that was all. Despite all we had been through, I had never felt more helpless or more terrified.

A mighty wave crashed over the prow. I heard a scream and peered into the stinging spray to see Turid sliding toward midship. I dove for her outstretched arm. There was no thought behind it except to save my friend. I could see her mouth open in a scream, her eyes locking on mine. I slid, reaching, my ears full of a hollow roar that was the storm and everything in it. Before me, Turid hit the mast fish with her feet and spun. As she did, I clutched her ankle, which in turn spun me sideways so that my ribs slammed into the mast. The blow knocked the wind from my lungs, but still I clung to her. I would not let go.

Then, mercifully, I felt hands pull us to the safety of the gunwale and wrap ropes around us to keep us safe. I lay there, my face upon the sea-slimed deck, Turid bundled against me, until the rain stopped and the winds calmed and life returned to order.

Slowly, gingerly, I rose and looked about me. My father, Astrid, and Olaf slept in heaps near me alongside most of the crew. Tostig manned the steer board on the aft deck, with Sigvard asleep at this feet. Several of the crewmen pulled slowly at their oars, while another two bailed water from the hold. Turid sat with her back to the port gunwale. She eyed me curiously when I rose.

"Where are we?" I whispered to her.

She shrugged.

I peeked above the gunwales and saw nothing but calm sea, blue skies, and the sun's orb low on the southern horizon. No birds. No other ships. No islands or distant shores. Just us, alone in a strangely quiet sea. I rested my back against the gunwale beside Turid and scratched at my head.

"Thank you for saving me, Torgil," she whispered. "Again."

Even in my exhausted state, I could feel my cheeks heat. "You are welcome."

A long moment stretched between us in which I heard only the lap of the sea against our hull, the creak of the deck, and the men bailing water from the hold.

"Do you ever get the sense that we are cursed?"

I frowned. "You should not speak of those things. It will bring ill luck."

She snorted. "Ill luck? Have we not already had enough ill luck to last a lifetime?"

"Luck can change," I said.

"I hope so," she responded.

Another long stretch of silence. Near us, the crew began to stir. So did my father and Olaf. Astrid slept on.

"I was sorry about your mother. I never told you that."

"Thank you," she whispered.

My father sat up abruptly and wiped his face. He took in the scene quickly, then gazed at Turid and me. "Thank the gods." He rose unsteadily and looked around. "I will speak with Tostig," he announced and walked stiffly back to the aft deck.

"Your father is a good man," Turid said.

"He is a good man," I concurred, "though hard at times."

"He needs to be, I think," said Turid.

I knew she was right but could not bring myself to say it, for she had not experienced his hand or his belt as I had. Still, I was glad for his strength and his mettle now.

At the steer board, he spoke briefly to Tostig before weaving his way through the sleeping forms and loose ropes and sea chests back to us. "The storm has pushed us to the south," he said when he reached us. "We need to head northeast — away from that coastline." He pointed to the distant dark line to the south of us, which I had not noticed on my first inspection. "When the crew wakes, we will set the sail and see to the ship and food."

"Why do we need to get clear of the coastline?" Olaf asked. The question had been on my mind, too.

"That is Estland, a place whose people are no friends to the Swedes. It is best we stay clear."

The steer board wale dipped, and I gazed at the distant shore, wondering what had started the feud between the two peoples. As I pondered that, the crew began to pull themselves from their slumber and see to their tasks. Food, trade goods, and the ballast were inspected.

Furs and skins were pulled to the deck to dry. Bread, fish, and water were distributed. The bread and fish were soggy and foul-tasting, but my father urged us to eat, for we knew not when we would have another chance.

As we forced the food down, the crew set the sail and Tostig pointed the prow northeast. The wind was light and the going was slow. To pass the time, we helped organize the ship's deck and took turns bailing water from the hold. It was not easy work but it was necessary, and it made me feel more useful.

"Sails! Off the steer board wale." Sigvard's call rang above our heads, bringing our eyes to the right. It was late afternoon now, and the sun was high in the cloudless sky.

I shielded my eyes from the glare and peered out across the sun-touched sea. It took a moment, but eventually, I saw them: two sails, coming in our direction.

Sigvard was midship, staring at the approaching vessels. Several of the crew had joined him. He glanced over his shoulder at my father and I marked the tightness in his gaze. "Warships."

A lump hardened in my throat.

Chapter 17

"Get the goods below deck!" Sigvard yelled. "And get our guests down there too!"

"What is the plan?" my father asked.

"We cannot outrun them — all we can do is try to deceive them, make ourselves look less desirable. If they are Estlanders and think we have goods to take, they will take them, and kill us. Now go!"

My father did not question Sigvard. He seemed to understand that whoever approached was most likely hostile. "Come," he called to us. "Get in the hold and hide."

I did not argue, for I knew it was pointless, but Olaf did. "I want to stay on deck. I can help if it comes to a fight."

Thunder rolled across my father's face. He pulled Olaf by his arm to Astrid, who stood near the hold. "Take your son, Astrid, and hide him." He tossed Olaf toward Astrid. "If it comes to a fight, do not let him help. The same for you. Stay hidden. Do you understand?"

She grabbed her son and nodded.

He turned to me as they disappeared below deck and placed a heavy hand on my shoulder. His dark eyes bored into mine. "Protect them, Torgil."

I nodded dumbly. I knew what he was saying and knew, too, that there was nothing I could say or do to change his mind or the situation.

"Come out only when I call you or when the ships are gone. Do you understand what I am saying?"

I nodded again.

He patted my shoulder and smiled. "Go now."

I scrambled below deck. Astrid and Olaf and Turid had squeezed into a spot behind several barrels, below the foredeck. I joined them, finding a narrow space in the pool of seawater between the ribs and beams. The crew hastily packed in trade goods and ropes and other loose items around us.

"Keep your weapons near," I hissed as the deck planks slid home and darkness enveloped us. I eased my sword from its scabbard and laid it across my lap.

For what seemed like ages, we waited in that leaking hold as the ship rolled beneath us and lines of light from the cracks in the deck planking shifted about us. My fist clutched the sword's grip, and my heart thumped so loudly in my chest that I was certain it would be heard above deck.

"Ho!" I heard Sigvard call.

There was a distant voice, but I could not hear what it said. Sigvard responded in a language I did not understand. The language of the Estlanders, I assumed.

There was a long pause, then a rough crash of wood as hulls knocked against each other. The force of it shifted our knarr sideways and threw us against each other. Sigvard's voice came again, this time a bit more quickly. A rougher, deeper voice responded to him. Footfalls landed on the deck above us — men boarding Sigvard's vessel — and I ducked instinctively. Beside me, Turid whimpered, and I shushed her quietly.

For a long, tense moment, Sigvard and the man with the gruff voice conferred, their voices calm but hard. Gradually, the calmness slipped and tensions rose. I could hear Sigvard's voice rising and quickening, and I tightened my grip on my sword, silently cursing my blindness and the questions it conjured in my head. What were they saying? Did they plan to search the holds? Should I use my blade if they did? How many men were there?

Suddenly, a shout, followed by the sound of wood sliding and the flash of light as the men opened the hold. We shrank as low as we could behind the barrels that hid us. Men splashed into the wet body of the ship. A peek from my hiding spot revealed four men at least. Two started handing furs and ivory and other goods up to their comrades on deck, while two more lifted lids from barrels, peering into their depths, laughing and blabbering to each other in their strange language as they worked ever closer to our spot.

What would my father do, were he in my position? The answer came instantly. He would fight. And so I gripped my blade tighter and gathered my feet beneath me to find more purchase. I could hear the gruff-voiced man up on deck, barking orders as goods came to view, and I knew, without seeing, that he was taking them to his ship. The injustice of that — of robbing the men who were helping us — infuriated me and steeled my nerves for what was to come.

The Estlanders moved closer to us, working their way into the darkness under the foredeck. I knelt behind the barrel before me and readied my sword to thrust. Beside me, I sensed movement from Astrid and Olaf. To my right, the light played off Turid's seax as she edged slowly to a more advantageous position.

Then, suddenly, the men were upon us, prying off the tops of the barrels behind which we hid. I did not hesitate. As the Estlander before me lifted the container's top, I drove my blade up and into his gut. He wore no armor, and the blade slipped beneath his ribs with surprising ease. He sucked in a breath, dropped the lid, then collapsed backward as I yanked my weapon free.

His comrades turned to see what was the matter, and as they did, my friends struck. I could not see their attacks clearly, just dark forms moving in my periphery and metal gleaming. There were shouts, the curses of men, stumbling, and crashing. A man cried out. Then another. I was certain it alerted everyone on deck, but there was nothing for it now.

On deck, I heard shouts and the ring of steel and thought instantly of my father. I worked my way forward, toward the exit and the light. There was no resistance, only dead Estlanders and my friends, their blades and faces speckled with gore. They followed me through the congested space.

I peeked up on deck, trying to make quick sense of the chaos that greeted me. Men fought in two groups: on the foredeck, where my father stood, and the aft deck, where Tostig and Sigvard fought. Half the crew were dead, as were several of our assailants. Amidships, near the hold's entrance, Gruff Voice shouted commands and urged his men into the fray. To my right, more men leaped from a ship with their weapons drawn.

Had I been older and wiser, I would have seen that the fight was already over. By sheer numbers alone, we could not prevail. Yet my father fought and I could not let him die alone, not without trying to help him. As I contemplated my next step, Olaf sprang forth and rolled up onto the deck, flitting past the Estland leader and hacking into the legs of a man attacking my father. The man fell with a shocked cry, and I, who had quickly followed my friend into the fray, hacked my blade into the man's skull to finish him. Beside me, Astrid swung her blade into a man's unprotected shoulder, opening a wicked gash with such force that he stumbled sideways and collapsed. Another Estlander turned to the new threat but never came full about. As he turned, he met Turid's wicked slash that caught him hard across the face. He screamed and stumbled away.

The one remaining Estlander rejoined his leader near the mast, where a knot of pirates now stood. Across the knarr, Sigvard and Tostig stood shoulder to shoulder, alone now and wounded, crewmen and Estlanders dead around them. Facing several men with shields and blades, they stood little chance. I itched to get to them — to help them — but the knot of men at the mast stood in our way and more men were streaming aboard. Just then, a grappling hook tossed from a second ship smacked the deck and dug into the steer board wale.

"Grab shields," my father commanded us. "Quick."

We each rifled through the corpses and yanked several shields free, then stood back and formed a crude shield wall on the foredeck. There were two crewmen with us, so together we numbered seven. A paltry force we were, but at that moment, I believed we could win. That, of course, was the battle frenzy telling me so.

"Torgil and Olaf, stand behind us," my father uttered from the side of his mouth. "Astrid, you and Turid behind them, closest to the prow." We arranged ourselves accordingly.

"Fight and you will all die," called Gruff Voice in a heavily accented version of our tongue. "Lay your weapons down and you will be spared." He was a tall, gaunt man with grimy, weathered skin and a wild beard the color of polar bear fur that wrapped around his chin and neck like a scarf. Were it not for his byrnie, dented helm, and sword, he looked more a farmer than a leader of men. Except for his eyes. So starkly did those blue orbs contrast with his weathered skin; so coldly intense did they stare at us, as if perceiving everything but revealing nothing. Wicked eyes. Calculating eyes. They came to rest on Astrid and Turid, two women dressed as thralls yet with blades in their hands. The eyes narrowed, and I knew that he understood that all was not as it seemed.

"I will say it again," he said, more calmly now. "Lay your weapons down and you will be spared."

"How many men is this ship worth?" responded my father.

A grin stretched slowly across the Estlander's face. "My men understand the price they must pay. Do yours?"

As they spoke, I could feel the fight slipping from my body and the fear seeping in. I watched as more warriors joined the throng of Estlanders at the mast and felt my confidence wane. Moments ago, I would have rushed into that fray. Now I felt indecision and weariness gnawing at my limbs and at my thoughts.

Before my father could answer, the Estland leader raised and dropped his hand. Four arrows zipped into Sigvard and Tostig, penetrating their chests with a sickening thud. Turid screamed as the two men grabbed at the shafts protruding from their bodies, then crumpled to the aft deck. I stared in disbelief. They had done nothing but try to deliver us to our destination and now they lay dead beside their crew.

The Estlander lifted his arm again, and my father raised his hand in surrender. He knew we were doomed, as did we all, and so he gave in. The physical part of me raged at his surrender, yet the practical side of me understood. He was saving us and saving our fate for another day. "Stop!" he called. "We will lay our weapons on the deck. But we expect you to keep your word and spare us."

The Estlander nodded slightly.

My father nodded too, as if silently sealing the deal. He dropped his sword to the deck and ordered us to do the same, which we did. Then he turned to me. "I leave you to keep my oath. Remember, a noble name will never perish."

The words took me by surprise, but I could not ask what he meant, for my father had already turned back to the Estlander and stepped forward. My eyes turned instinctively to Olaf. He was smiling that mischievous smile. In his hand was his knife, which he held by the blade point, as if he meant to throw it.

I opened my mouth to stop what I knew was about to happen, but the next moments happened faster than my words would come. As my father took another step, he pulled his seax from where it rested, behind his back on his belt, and drove it into the neck of the Estlander nearest him. At the same moment, Olaf tossed his blade. My shout reached Olaf as his blade spun over my father's left shoulder, across the deck, and into the shoulder of the Estland leader, where it lodged. The man staggered but did not fall. The rest of his men tried to come to grips with what was happening, but by then my father was among them. He dropped three more Estlanders to the deck before the men had time to recover their wits. Beside him, the crewmen were plunging into the fray with my father, doing their best to stay alive.

My eyes spun to the bowmen who had just killed Sigvard and Tostig and were turning their weapons on us. "Shields!" I yelled just as the arrows began their brutal assault. "Stay low!"

I looked left again, toward my father. A giant man stood before him, swinging an axe at my father's head. My father ducked and jabbed his blade into the man's groin. The man dropped his weapon and crumpled, and as he did, my father tore the axe from the man's hand, spun, and slammed the blade into another man's shield. The man fell backward and my father ripped the axe free, rose, and slammed his shoulder into the next man before him. That man, too, fell away, and suddenly my father was facing the Estland leader. The man had found his footing and stood with Olaf's blade in his shoulder and a hand axe in his grip.

My father did not hesitate. He swung the axe over his head, meaning to cleave the Estlander's skull in two, but the Norns and their tapestry of fate intervened. Two arrows slammed into my father's back, staggering him. Yelling his fury, he righted the blade and brought it down, but the Estlander sidestepped the awkward blow, bringing his own hand axe up and into my father's temple.

"No!" I screamed as he collapsed, lifeless, to the bloodstained deck. I ran to his side, heedless of my own safety. The other crewmen were dead now too, and I could have joined them, had the Estlanders not let me live. I looked at my father briefly, at the deep gash in his head, at his lifeless eyes, then turned away. I could not stomach seeing him so. My eyes shifted to the Estlanders, then back to Olaf and Astrid and Turid, who crouched behind their shields near the prow, their faces a mixture of shock and pain.

The Estland leader yelled at his bowmen to lower their weapons, then yanked the knife from his shoulder and tossed it aside. I rose with my seax to meet him, but he merely swatted me aside with his shield, then kicked the seax from my grip as I fell to the deck. Grabbing a fistful of my hair, he forced me to stand before him and to stare into his hard face. He did not speak — he just stared, moving my face first left, then right. Finally, coming to some sort of conclusion, he barked another order at his men. They came forward now to bind my wrists and hustle me to the Estland ship. I was joined shortly by Olaf, Astrid, and Turid.

I watched, then, with tears in my eyes and rage in my heart as the Estlanders unceremoniously tossed my father and the crew of *Sigvard's Swan* over the gunwale and into their cold sea graves. "I will kill him," I hissed, meaning the Estland leader, though my grief had constricted my throat and I had a hard time getting the words out. "As Thor as my witness, I will kill him."

"I shall join you in that," Olaf responded.

"Your father died well," Astrid said as the pirates tied our knarr to their ship and made ready to sail. "Mark my words, Torgil. His bravery will not go unnoticed. He died with his sword in his hand and will be feasting with his ancestors soon enough."

The Estlanders left the trade goods on *Sigvard's Swan* and turned their prows south, toward their home. And as they did, our dream of reaching Holmgard and Astrid's brother slipped forever from our grasp.

Part III

Then strange memories crowded back
Of Queen Gunnhild's wrath and wrack,
And a hurried flight by sea;
Of grim Vikings, and the rapture
Of the sea-fight, and the capture,
And the life of slavery.

The Saga of King Olaf

Chapter 18

Life is not so unlike the multiple worlds of the Norse cosmos. Worlds for gods. Worlds for giants. Worlds for men. Underworlds. Each with their own joys and sorrows and horrors. While there was only one world for men — Midgard — there were varying degrees of how one existed in that world. A royal. A karl. A thrall. In short order, fate had moved me from the top to the bottom rung on that ladder. One rung lower and I would be dead, though arguably, that might have been better than the market at Eysysla, which in the local tongue was called Saaremaa.

The market was not a town, but rather a smattering of stalls grouped near the shoreline on a deep bay. I sensed it was a makeshift market — a place that existed to process the thriving movement of pirated goods in that area during the warmer months. Still, a group of warriors met us at the beach to collect their harbor fees, suggesting there must have been some organization to the market.

Our captors untied us from the mast and marched us from the beach up a trail that wound through stalls, huddles of traders, and lounging warriors drinking near their tents. It was a bewildering place and for a moment I was lost in my fascination, for there were things there I had never seen before. Men with dark hair and dark skin dressed in foreign garb haggling with Northmen in a language I did not understand. Pots filled with colorful powders that I would later learn were spices from the south. Furs of more shapes, sizes, and colors than I thought imaginable. Weapons and shields and armor and axe-heads and tools and jewelry and pottery and even raw iron on sale. This last item, the iron, caught my eye not for the bars that lay on a mat outside a stall, but for the man who sold them — a man with rough-hewn features who stopped his haggling long enough to make me uneasy with his staring. And that is when I understood. In the midst of all of these strange sights and smells and sounds, we were just another item to be sold.

That horrid fact became even more clear as we left the stalls and trudged over a small rise behind the market. On the opposite side of that rise lay a field of tall grass and fetid pools in the midst of which sat two large wooden cages with mud for floors. Females stood in one cage. Males stood in the other. Crows called from a nearby tree. Rats scurried between the cages and around the feet of those within, seeking food where there was none to have. As we arrived, the captured thralls crowded the cage walls, begging for food scraps with outstretched arms from our escorts but receiving only curses or a wad of spit in the face for their troubles.

Our captors cast us into our pens, and I stared at those within mine: a young man and three small boys. All were wide-eyed creatures with mud-caked hair and a layer of dirt for skin. All wore ripped and soiled clothes. Two of the boys were shoeless. Another boy was there, but he ignored us, choosing instead to focus on the oozing mud that he dug with his hands. He found a writhing worm, which he held up victoriously for us to see before plopping it into his mouth. He smiled even as he spit tiny globs of mud on the ground from the carcass that writhed between his teeth. I grimaced, thinking then that I had reached the living version of the underworld called Hel.

Olaf appeared unbothered by the disheveled group. "I am Olaf," said my friend. "Who are you?"

The young man cocked his head.

Olaf tapped his chest. "Olaf." He then pointed to the man.

Understanding, the young man tapped his chest in reply. "Herkus."

"Herkus," Olaf repeated and nodded. He then pointed to me. "Torgil."

The man repeated my name, then pointed to the children. He shrugged his shoulder as if to say he did not know their names. Olaf introduced himself to all of them, but I did not. We would soon be sold or dead, so to me, knowing their names was a useless distraction. Instead, I turned away and gazed at the women. Their conditions were no better than ours and, in one way, far worse. For no sooner had we settled in our cages than the leader of the Estlanders, whose name we learned was Klerkon, appeared and entered the female cage. The women cowered before him. All, that is, save Astrid, who stood before him as if to say that he might have captured her but he had not broken her.

I admired her courage, but in the end, it was folly. He grabbed her by her wrist and tried to pull her from the pen. She punched him in his wounded shoulder, and he roared his fury, backhanding her so hard that she slammed against the wall of the cage and collapsed, unconscious. The big man then lifted her onto his shoulder, closed the pen, and walked away.

"Bastard!" Olaf yelled after him. "I will kill you!"

There was a hiss behind us and we turned. Herkus had his index finger to his lips, urging Olaf to silence. Do not yell at them, he seemed to be saying.

Olaf scowled and turned back to the sight of his mother being carried away. I spat at Herkus and his weakness. The man took no offense. Instead, he smiled, his eyes telling me that I too would learn. Beside him, the other boys merely stared at us or let their gaze travel to the departing figure of Klerkon and the woman bobbing on his shoulder. Their indifference sickened me.

Later that night, Klerkon's men returned, pulling an unconscious Astrid between them. In the torchlight that illuminated our cages, I barely recognized the former queen. Her eyes were mere slits in the purple mass of bruises and welts that was her face. Blood trickled from a wound in her head and her lip. Her legs were too weak to support her, and so she collapsed into the mud when they threw her into her cage. Turid rushed to her side as Olaf kicked the wood slats of our pen, yelling at the men with curses and obscenities I had never heard before heard him utter. The Estlanders called to Olaf, mocking him as they staggered away into the night. I could do nothing but smolder in silence at my helplessness.

For two days we rotted in those cages. The Estlanders fed us some sour gruel in the morning — which Olaf and I refused to eat and our cellmates devoured — and nothing else. If it pleased them, they came for the women in the afternoon, pulling a different one each time. They left Astrid alone. I suppose she was too weak and battered for them now. Turid, too, remained unscathed, though I am not sure why. Mayhap it was her young age. Or mayhap, her slenderness did not appeal to them.

I slept little, for anger consumed my thoughts and I could think of nothing but escape and revenge. Of how I might find Klerkon and avenge my father. Of how I might find Holger and destroy him. Olaf paced, his eyes flitting from the female cage where his mother recovered to his feet and back again. Herkus tried to make conversation, but neither of us would speak with him. The worm eater tried to share some of his catches with us. I stared at him as if he were sick in the head and hoped that I would never lower myself to his mud-hunting level. Looking back, I know now that it was pride holding me back and that, between us, the worm eater was probably far smarter than me. Of all of us, he was the only one staying somewhat nourished. The rest of us were slowly starving.

On the third day, the Estlanders came to our cages, bound us, and led us like sheep to the marketplace, where a small group of men had gathered. Klerkon stood before them, speaking in his tongue, pointing to us. The men raked their eyes over us as we appeared, then turned back to Klerkon.

"Stand straight," Astrid slurred to Olaf. She stood two places behind Olaf, with me between, all of us tied together by the rope at our waists. Ropes bound our wrists, too. "You are a king's son and an heir to the High Seat of the North. Remember that."

"I *was* a king's son," Olaf hissed back at her.

"You are a king's son still and always. Trygvi's blood runs in your veins. Do not forget that. Do not lose hope. We are to be sold now and it is unlikely that you and I will be sold together. It is more likely that I will never see you again. No matter what, Olaf, you must never forget who you are or from whence you came. You must survive and avenge us."

"I will try, Mother," he said, and I could tell he was trying to hold back his tears.

"You must, Olaf. Whatever the cost. And you will help him, Torgil."

Here we were, bound for the blocks. We may as well have been standing on the edge of a cliff, waiting to be kicked over its edge, yet Astrid was beseeching us not only to survive but to avenge the wrong done to us. It was ludicrous, yet I could not help but feel inspired by her hope and her mettle. "I will," I said solemnly, though I am not sure I wholly believed it.

"Thank you, Torgil," she responded, quieter now. I could not see her face and so I will never know, but it seemed like relief I heard in her voice. That all she wanted from her son — from someone. A glimmer of light in a world whose light was fading. I hoped then, as I hope now, that I gave it to her.

No sooner had she thanked me than the girl at the front of our line was untied and led to Klerkon's side. She could not have been much older than me — a girl on the verge of womanhood with an entire life before her — and I wondered from whence she had come. It mattered not to the men. To them, she was merchandise, a thing over which to barter. With a practiced hand, Klerkon untied her wrists, lifted her arms, and pulled her muddy shift over her head so that she stood naked before the men. She tried to cover herself from the leering eyes that appraised her, but Klerkon pulled her arms back and held them firm so that her skinny, naked body stood there for the entire group to see. As the bidding started and her head fell in shame, I looked away.

One by one, Klerkon paraded us before the buyers. Like the females, we males were stripped. Klerkon held up our arms and made us tighten our muscles for everyone to see. My cheeks burned with the humiliation of it, but I could do nothing to stop it. I wanted to scream at the haggling men, but I knew to do so would only result in more misery, and so I bit my lip and focused my attention on the mud at my feet.

Every thrall sold that day. Astrid went to an older man who had come by boat to the market and did not seem to mind her battered face and bruised body. As she was led away, she glanced over at Olaf and mouthed the words *be strong* to him. He nodded back and wiped the tears from his cheeks with his bound hands. At that moment, I felt the weight of my father's words on me like a stone and knew not how to carry that shame. I had failed to keep my promise to him and Astrid's departure from us was living proof of that failure.

Herkus and several of the younger thralls, including Olaf, Turid, and me, sold to the man who had stared at us when we arrived: the iron merchant. As he appraised us, I was struck by his rich cape and fine boots and how neither could distract me from his short stature, his thick black hair, his wobbling girth, or the mallet-sized hands that protruded from his sleeves. Simply put, he was a walking contradiction, like the iron he sold. Crude in appearance yet notable. Thick, yet gelatinous. Powerful, yet soft.

"Swedish?" he asked me when he completed his appraisal.

"Norse," I responded softly.

"You are kin to the man who killed my sons." His statement took me by surprise.

"I do not know your sons."

"They fought for Klerkon. They were his guards. On the ship, there was a man who killed many men before Klerkon killed him. This man was your kin?"

I knew not where this man was venturing with his questions, but it felt perilous nonetheless. Still, I would not disavow my father, whatever the consequences. "He was my father."

The iron merchant stepped closer so that I could smell his wretched breath. "He was a lord?" he asked.

I do not know why, but I held my tongue. I suppose I thought that if I told him the truth, he would use it as leverage, though just how he might use that leverage was beyond me.

"You will answer," said the man, his fleshy cheeks flushing with his command.

We held each other's eyes for a long time before he finally grinned and patted my cheek. "Smart boy," he said. "Still, I plan to repay you for your father's sword work, for he took my sons from me. Do not worry — I will not kill you. I need you. That is why I purchased you." He turned his back to me and walked several paces away, then turned back again. "Come. Stand here."

I stepped to the spot he indicated and stood there, waiting. Inside, my stomach twisted as my mind conjured one possibility after another. Sensing something was amiss, other merchants and warriors began to gather about us. I glanced at them and as I did, the iron merchant struck.

His first blow hammered my cheek. Bright lights shot across my vision as my head jerked to the right. I do not remember falling to the ground, but that is where I found myself when my head finally stopped spinning. I pushed myself to my knees and tried to rise. The second blow came, this one on my other cheek. I spun and landed hard on my shoulder. A third strike came from a shoe as it connected with my nose, breaking it with a loud crack. I felt the warmth of blood gushing over my lips, and still I tried to rise. A fourth blow slammed into my ribs — another foot — and I felt rather than heard a snap where the foot connected. I gasped and rolled onto my back, and for a long, panicked moment, I sucked desperately at the air, trying to breathe.

The air returned just as rough hands pulled me to my feet and held me there. I tried to lift my head to see what was to come. Somewhere a shriek, then a fist connecting with my stomach. I tried to double over but the hands held me firm. A shoe connected with my groin, and I felt I would vomit from the pain of it. The hands released me then and I doubled over. As I did, something collided with my chin. For a moment, I was light. Weightless. And then I landed hard on my back and what little air I had in my chest shot from me again.

I had lost count of the blows now. My reality was a fog of pain that seemed to envelop my entire body. I must have tried to rise again because another fist crashed into my face. There was no pain this time — only a flash of light, then nothing.

Chapter 19

I remember little of the ensuing days save for sweat and shivers. Some-one kept a blanket over me that I cast aside as soon as the fever in my body rose. My dreams were frantic and filled equally with visions of pleasure and pain. Of welcome times spent in my father's hall. Of laughter with friends. But also of fire and bloodshed and chaotic fear from which there was no escape. Often, I would lurch from sleep to wakefulness to find someone by my side, shushing me back to my dreams with a gentle stroke on my brow or a drip of water on my tongue or a calming hand on my shoulder. Days and nights blended together like stew in a pot, swirling ceaselessly. I lost track of time and knew only the pain and heat that held me in its grip.

Until one morning when I suddenly woke.

I wish I had not, so great was my agony. My entire body throbbed. Through the slits of my swollen eyes, my vision swam, as if I were on the deck of a ship in a rough sea. I could make little sense of my surroundings — it seemed just varying shades of darkness. There was someone by my side, though I knew not who. There were other voices too — whispers, really — but I knew not whether my mind had man-ufactured those or whether they truly existed.

"Do not move," came a voice I recognized as Turid's. "You are still badly hurt. We set your nose, but your other ailments are internal. You must remain still."

Of course, I turned my head to the voice and nearly shouted with the explosion of pain in my head and ribs. A wave of nausea rolled over me, and I moved my head back to a spot where the throbbing settled somewhat.

"I told you not to move," she scolded me. She lifted my head gently and brought a cup to my lips. I sipped at the water within, then coughed painfully as the cold liquid slid down my dry throat a bit too quickly.

Her hand came to my forehead, and I knew then that it was Turid who had been by my side all along. "I am sorry," she whispered. "I did not mean to hurt you."

"I know." The silence stretched until I could bear it no longer. "It was you, was it not?"

"I do not understand," she said.

"It was you by my side. Here," I said, though I knew not where "here" was.

"Aye," she whispered.

"Where am I?"

"The thrall quarters in the home of our new master," she whispered. "A pit-house." She made no attempt to conceal her displeasure. A pit-house was a shelter partially dug into the ground. It was normally used to store things. In this case, it was us being stored.

I cast aside that sorry thought and latched onto the next. "New master?"

"Aye. The man who beat you. His name is Heres."

"Heres," I repeated, though my muddled memory could not conjure a picture of him. "Has he other thralls besides you and me?"

She looked at me strangely. "You do not remember?"

"No," I admitted. "Is Olaf with us?"

"Aye. We came with several others besides."

I lay silently, trying not to agitate my ailments as my eyes adjusted to my murky surroundings. Around me were stone walls through which sunlight snuck, catching dust mites in its rays. Above me were decrepit wooden beams supporting a roof of old thatch, all held aloft by posts. My head lay on a pillow of straw that poked my scalp. I sensed movement and guessed that there were others in the hall as well.

"Tell me more of Heres," I asked.

"He is a property owner who smelts iron that he sells in the market," she said. "We dig the iron from the nearby bog and he and his men smelt it down. He is married to a woman named Rekon and has one son named Reas who helps him make his iron. His other two sons died fighting us."

"Iron," I repeated.

"Aye. All day long we search the bogs for it. It is hard work."

So that was to be our fate, helping our master find bog iron. I knew little of the work or the process of creating it but imagined it would not be easy work. Not like weeding a field or building a bed. "Tell me more of Heres. What sort of man is he?"

She bent closer to my head. "He is a cruel man, Torgil. A man not to be crossed. He and his men beat us for the meagerest infraction."

I shifted the subject before my bitterness took hold of me. "Where is Olaf?"

"He is here. Asleep. All the new thralls are sleeping. They are not yet used to the work. I sense that Heres is eager for you to heal so that you can also help. They have tasked me with seeing to it. I suppose I will be working in the bogs with you when you are better. Here. I have made some pea soup," she said, grabbing something by her side and holding a spoon to my lips.

I slurped from the spoon and swallowed. Its warmth coated my throat and soothed my hollow gut. "I have never had soup so good," I said, and it was not a lie.

Turid's cheeks lifted with her small grin. I smiled despite the pain in my head, for I had not seen a smile on her face since we had lived in Haakon the Old's home. It felt like ages ago. She shifted her eyes to the bowl in her hands and slipped the spoon into my mouth again. I swallowed dutifully, luxuriating in the earthy taste and the warmth in my stomach.

After several more spoonsful, she set the bowl aside and gently brushed my forehead once again. "You must not eat too much. It will upset your stomach. Rest now, Torgil. I will be back soon."

I wanted to ask her to keep stroking my head, but I had not the nerve. And so she left me to my pain and the sleep that soon swallowed me.

Olaf came to me later and woke me with a nudge. The interior of the shed was yet dark, so mayhap it was still night. Or mayhap it was morning and dawn had not yet broken. It was hard to say in our gloomy quarters.

Olaf moved his face close to mine. His hair was matted and his face streaked with something black. Ash? Mud? I could not tell. "You are better?" he asked eagerly.

"No," I answered and winced at some shock of pain in my side. I was hungry again and my stomach growled.

Olaf's face collapsed. "I understand," he whispered.

I wanted to lift his spirits but knew not how. I could not think of many worse situations in which to find ourselves, so I had nothing to offer Olaf in the way of humor or distraction. "How are you faring?" I finally asked.

Tears welled in his eyes. "It is hard here, Torgil," he started. "Heres and his men treat us no better than oxen. We work from daybreak until after nightfall, digging for ore and hefting it to the furnaces. One misstep earns us a whipping. I have been whipped countless times already. I know not how long I can take it."

I am not sure what Olaf thought thralldom would be like, but everything he described fit my imagination of our new life. Still, I felt for Olaf. He was a tough boy, but like a rusted ring in a byrnie, that toughness was showing signs of weakness, and there was nothing I could do. Nothing, at least, until I was healed. When that day came, I hoped I could deflect some of the attention Heres currently reserved for Olaf onto myself. "If I could help you now, I would. When I am better, I will help you. You must persevere until then, Olaf."

He nodded, though there was still sadness in his eyes. "I know," he muttered.

I grabbed his arm then and looked at him full in his grimy face. "Hear me, Olaf. Do not forget your mother's words. You are a king's son. You cannot be broken by these swine. It may take some time, but we will find a way clear of this piss hole. Do you understand?"

He nodded hesitantly.

"Do you understand?" I hissed.

"Aye," he said fervently.

I forced a grin to my face, despite the pain it caused. "Good."

He moved away and I closed my eyes, exhausted by the exchange.

One morning, after the others had left for the bogs, Turid came to me to examine my wounds. She prodded the ribs on my right and I winced, though the pain had abated somewhat since I'd regained consciousness. Suddenly, I felt the familiar fullness in my bladder that usually accompanied my morning exams. "I have to piss," I said indelicately.

"Shall I bring the bucket?"

"No," I responded. "I would like to walk to the privy."

She nodded. "That is a good sign."

Gently, I rolled to my side and pushed myself up to my feet, gritting my teeth at the pain in my ribs. Turid tried to grab my arm but I politely shirked her proffered assistance. Step by awkward step I walked across the pit-house to the door, then outside. The pit-house was a gable-roofed, A-framed structure that sat on the top of a small rise. Its design and location kept rain from its interior. As I descended the wooden steps outside our door, I shielded my eyes from the daylight that greeted my face.

Turid urged me forward until I had taken some thirty awkward steps. There, I rested my hand on a birch tree as I took in my surroundings. To the west of me was a flat meadow of green dotted by clumps of wildflowers and random groupings of birch trees. To my right, north, was a hall that filled my vision with its size, as well as a storehouse and a barn. The hall was an awe-inspiring structure, with beautifully lain stones for walls mixed with high gables carved like serpents and a thatched roof that had been freshly placed. Our master, it seemed, was not poor. Near the main door, two stones stood, each with some sort of inscription on it. I guessed they were markers to commemorate the sons whom we killed. I took some pleasure in that.

Turid followed my gaze. "That is Heres's hall. It houses his family and his men. Those who oversee the iron production," she muttered.

"Where are all of the people?" I wondered aloud.

"Reas is in the hall, and you can bet that one of Heres's henchmen is watching us."

I gazed about me but saw no one. Instead, my eyes took in the sunshine glinting off the fluttering birch leaves, the serenity of the meadow, and the blue of the sky. "This would be pretty, were we not thralls."

"Aye," Turid conceded. "It is pretty here. But walk five hundred paces up that path," she said, pointing to a trail heading west into the forest, "and you will find a different place entirely."

"Where are we?" I asked. "Where is *this* place?" I pointed to the ground on which we stood.

Turid shrugged. "I am just beginning to understand the language of these people. I believe we are on the eastern side of the island the locals call Saaremaa in their tongue. Behind us, to the east, is a small bay where Heres keeps his ship. I have heard some of the thralls say that another island lies to the east of us and, beyond that, the mainland of the Estlanders."

Her words formed a picture in my head. I sighed, feeling suddenly very far from Holmgard and from the future that was supposed to have been waiting for us there.

"Please turn your back," I said as I fumbled with the ties on my trousers.

She blushed but did so, and I emptied my bladder on the birch.

Over the following days, I made it a point to become more aware of my surroundings. As I have said, we lived in a pit-house, a structure that was buried two ells in the ground. In theory, it was designed to protect us from the elements, which, for the most part, it did. However, a wall of poorly lain stone climbed from the turf to the old thatched roof, and both seeped air through their cracks and holes. At night the air washed over us, chilling any exposed skin. Our shelter's interior was cramped, with just enough space for twelve straw mattresses laid an ell apart from each other along the walls. A rectangular hearth lay in the middle to keep our feet or head warm, depending on which way we slept. Wooden pegs lodged in the stone walls held our clothes at night. Our privy was an exposed trench on the back side of our pit-house. Though it lay outside the walls of our dwelling, a slight wind blowing in the wrong direction was all it took to fill our noses with the stench of it.

The thralls with whom we lived are etched in my memory like the lines on a runestone. Most of them were Prussians, for the unprotected coastline of Prussia was close to the island and easy hunting for the Estlanders. Of them, Herkus and Raban were the eldest. Herkus was with us at the slave market. An earnest and friendly man he was, and a rule follower besides. I rarely saw him earn the ire of our masters, though many were the days he would offer me a helping hand. Raban was there when we arrived, and he was our jester. I remember him for his missing teeth, his babbling, and his flatulence. It mattered not what we ate for our meals, you could count on him to foul the air with his skinny arse and, in the confines of our pit-house, flash us a toothless grin for the gift of it. Besides that, he had a habit of talking to himself, so much so that even the guards ignored it.

The worm eater from the market was Pipin. He was small and mangy, but I have yet to meet a more resourceful lad. Most nights, he would produce something from the folds of his tunic — something he had found in the bog that day, such as a frog, cranberries, or blue-berries — that we could eat at night. It was not much, but it kept us nourished.

Agi was the other boy. He was a clumsy, oafish lad who seemed to mope his way through the days, though that may have had something to do with the brutality of our work. There was a Prussian girl as well: Sigdag. She was a blond mute, but fierce in her demeanor and as tough as the iron we dug from the earth. Cross her and she spoke her mind with gestures and prods that were as clear as any words she might have uttered.

Our other two housemates were Swedish siblings: a boy named Egil and a girl named Eydis, both roughly Olaf's age and almost as pale in hair and skin as Lodin had been. Twins they were and, perchance because of that, inseparable.

Not long after my excursion with Turid, I sat on my mattress, awaiting the arrival of the others. To surprise them, I had collected wood on my own and started a small fire in the hearth. I was blowing on it to build the flame when the door to our pit-house opened and in marched the others, water-soaked and smelling of earth and sweat. Rather than appreciate my gift of warmth, they regarded me — and it — solemnly, then moved to their mattresses.

"What is the matter?" I asked Olaf, who was removing his muddy shoes.

He glared at me. "Agi is gone."

"Gone? Gone where?"

"In the bog. Gone."

I looked at Herkus, then at Pipin, for further explanation, but neither would meet my eye. Instead, Pipin moved to the fire to warm his hands. Finally Egil spoke. "It was near the end of the day. One moment Agi was there, and the next, he was gone. When we noticed, we ran to the spot he had been and saw only a muddy pond. He must have fallen into it with his heavy sack. His pole lay there, but he was gone."

Olaf gestured toward the door with his chin. "Bastards tried to save him by pushing his pole into the water in the hopes he might grab it. They probably just pushed him deeper into the hole." He spat his disgust.

I was about to reply when the door to the pit-house flew open and Heres's rotund body filled the doorframe like an oversized toad. It was a warm night and even from a distance, I could see the dark stains of moisture in the armpits of his soiled tunic. He squinted into the gloomy interior. Eventually his hard eyes found me, at which point he waddled over and appraised me for a long, silent moment.

"On the morrow," Heres said in the Norse tongue, "you and your caretaker," —- he motioned to Turid —- "will join us in the bogs. We lost a thrall today and need more hands. A broken boy and a weak girl should make up for a healthy thrall."

I nodded my understanding. He snorted, then marched from the pit-house. I looked back at Olaf.

He looked from me to Turid. "I am sorry." He need not say more, for in those words was all of the information I needed. Gingerly, I moved to my mattress and lay my head on my pillow. Turid, who lay behind me, grabbed my arm and squeezed. I placed my hand on hers and squeezed it back.

There was nothing more to say.

The following morning, we awoke and shuffled out into the chill of pre-dawn. A teenager who I later learned was Heres's son, Reas, handed each thrall an empty cup and a slice of stale bread. The cups we filled in a bowl of water in which blades of grass and dead bugs already floated. The others did not seem to mind, but I fished out a dead bug in my cup and flicked it away.

"There is no time for that," Olaf coached me. "In a moment, Reas will take us to the bogs and if you are not finished, you will not eat."

I forced the bread into my mouth and swallowed a mouthful of water, doing my best to avoid the other creatures circulating near my lips. I failed and ended up spitting them from my mouth in disgust. Pipin looked at me as if I were a dolt.

"It may be the only meat you will see this day," Olaf explained. "You will learn."

We left in short order, following a bull of a man named Tarmo. His height and brawn made me wonder why he was here, guarding some lowly thralls and not on a ship in the employ of a lord like Klerkon, making a name for himself. He wore a sword on his hip and carried a switch in his hand made from a birch branch. Reas followed us with two other men, also with swords on their hips and switches in their hands.

Tarmo led us down a path and into the birch forest, the breaking dawn casting a pale pink hue on the white bark of those wooden sentinels. The leaves flickered green and silver on the gentle breeze, displaying a beauty that seemed to mock our forlorn figures as we passed beneath them.

A hundred paces into the trees, we came to a clearing in which dozens of low, circular structures stood. I could smell the remnants of wood smoke and something besides — an earthy, almost muddy, aroma that I could not identify. "Furnaces," Olaf said as we stopped to collect poles and bags, one each for every thrall. "We hunt the iron with our poles," Olaf instructed as we moved again, "and collect it in the bags. At the end of the day, we bring it here. When there is enough to smelt, Heres and his men burn it down in the furnaces to create the bloom."

"The bloom?" I asked.

"The bloom is the material that our masters manipulate and tease into iron billets. Billets are what are used to create tools and weapons. They sell the billets at the market each summer."

I was trying to picture it, but the process was somewhat lost on me, the more so because the forest was beginning to thin and the bog was presenting itself, distracting me. It was, in a word, ghostly. A mist hung motionless above the landscape, painting the entire flat place in a soft gray that sucked the color from the shrubs and made the lonely trees that dotted the bog appear like lost souls in an empty world. Birdsong carried to my ears, but it sounded more like creatures trying to find each other in the gloom than the happy sound of animals greeting a new day. All of it stopped me in my tracks, forcing Olaf to hiss at me to keep me going, lest I feel the sting of Reas's switch on my back.

We followed a path of reddish-orange mud about two arrow flights into the bog, then turned right and wound our way through dark ponds and rivulets of water and clumps of bog sedge until the bearman Tarmo stopped and pointed us off to the right again. He gave us a few instructions that I did not understand.

"We are to work in pairs. Starting here," Olaf translated. "Come. I will show you how."

To this day, I cannot think of another task as grimy, backbreaking, and mind-numbing as hunting for iron in a bog. There was generally no skill needed. Just step, prod, prod, step, until your pole hit something hard, at which point you dug with your hands in the turf to see what lay beneath. If you were lucky, you found a pebble or small stone of gray-brown iron, which you then placed in your bag. Sometimes oil appeared on the surface of the bog water, indicating that iron was near, though you still had to prod the muddy pond bottoms until you found it, and that, again, required only luck.

That first day, I found five measly pebbles of bog iron, which I placed in my sack and carried back to the furnaces, though I could have carried them in my fist. I was, like the other thralls, soaked and muddy and too tired to speak. My hunger tore at my stomach and robbed me of strength. My back screamed from bending and pulling. I had twisted my right ankle on a clump of grass so that each step sent a twinge of pain up my leg that carried to my right rib. It had been Turid's first day as well, and she appeared to me as tired and mud-caked and pain-wracked as I felt. By the time we reached the furnaces, she was dragging her feet so severely that Olaf and I were forced to hold her upright to keep our masters from prodding her with their switches.

Back at the pit-house, our masters gave us a bowl of watery vegetable stew with a chunk of gristly meat, a slice of stale bread, and a cup of water. We sat outside the thrall quarters, unwashed, and devoured the meal wordlessly. Turid fell asleep halfway through her meal. Others grabbed her bowl and shared its contents between them. I could not blame them — I would have done the same, were I seated closer to her when it happened. Not long after, I collapsed on my sleeping mattress and instantly fell asleep.

So began my bondage in Heres's household.

Chapter 20

For four winters, we struggled to survive as thralls in the household of Heres and Rekon.

The days took on a strange uniformity so that we marked time only by the seasons and the variations of our work. Mostly, we dug in the bogs. Only in the dead of winter, when blizzards blanketed the landscape and made it impossible to locate the iron, did we break from that toil. In the late spring and through the summer, if we had collected enough iron ore already, we dug at the soil for peat, then carried it to the furnaces, where Heres's men would carve the chunks into brinks and set them out to dry. When we had enough iron and enough dried peat, we worked at the furnaces, pumping the bellows until our arms could pump no longer.

Like the iron we harvested, Heres had smelted our lives down to its most basic pursuit: survival. We worked. We slept. We ate whatever we could get our hands on, which was not much. If we were lucky, we were thrown an extra scrap of meat over which to fight, much to the sadistic enjoyment of Heres and Reas, Tarmo, and the other men who served them. We were the playthings of our masters, our treatment worse than the mangy hounds lying at the Estlanders' feet. Our skin seared in the summer sun and the biting cold of winter. Our nails cracked and bled. Our muscles ached. Our teeth fell out. We thinned and sickened. Yet still, we worked. And if we failed to work, or slowed in our toil, we felt the switch on our skin for our dereliction.

Only at the height of summer, when the market appeared again on Saaremaa, did some of us get a break from the backbreaking routine. Those among us who had been good were chosen to help Heres carry the iron billets to market, which was in no way a break from work. I, of course, was not always the most submissive thrall and so I never had the "honor" of accompanying our master to market.

It was clear that Heres cared little for our welfare, save for our ability to keep him and his family prospering from the iron we dug from the bog on his lands. The same held true for Reas. He saw his father's treatment of us and mimicked it, reveling in his ability — his power — to bring us low. I suppose this had something to do with his own low status in his household, for he had not yet earned the right to smelt the iron, a task that required great skill and for which Heres had others. To counteract his inferiority, he would target us with his sadistic whims. They were simple things, like a pebble in our shoe he would not allow us to remove. Or a thrall caught in a water hole he would not let us help. Or a switch to the back for working too slowly. It was incessant and infuriating, and random, and we could do nothing to protect ourselves from it.

Life was harder than it had ever been, yet in the midst of our brutal plight, we managed to find moments of distraction. During the dark nights, we mended each other's wounds — those seen and those internal — or bathed each other discreetly with wet rags, or combed the tangles and lice from our hair. Olaf proved a gifted storyteller, recounting to us tales of heroes and kings and monsters that he had heard in his father's hall as we munched on berries or a morsel of frog found by Pipin that day.

In the winter we snuggled tightly to keep warm, caring not about the smell of our bodies. Occasionally, when the wind kicked up and hid our sounds, we whispered jokes to each other and laughed until our emaciated sides hurt, or shared dirty secrets about the Estlanders, or plotted the escape that one day soon we would accomplish together. If we had the energy, which was rare, Olaf and I would grab sticks and brandish them like swords, practicing the moves my father had taught us, much to the wide-eyed wonder of the other thralls. Simple acts they were, yet critical, at least for me. They were the balm for my bitterness, keeping my temper in check when my body screamed to retaliate.

Through it all, we grew from children to young adults. Though Olaf's seed had not yet spilled, dark hair grew on my chin and jaw, chest, and groin. My skin blemished and my voice cracked. Turid, too, changed, as did the bodies of the other girls. Soft mounds grew on their chests. Whatever softness clung to their youthful bodies fell away. Their faces became masks of guarded severity, like ice that forms over a waterfall. It pained me to see it so, though I understood it. Our bodies had become the product of our toil. As we stretched, our faces and physiques tightened, every muscle defined and chiseled by our pain, our labor, our malnutrition.

Sadly, I was not the only man to note the changes in Turid or the other girls. Heres and his men saw them too and cast upon them their lecherous gazes — gazes that eventually transformed to comments and prods and gropes. It was one more indignity in a life of fleeting dignities and it all came to a head on a rest day in early autumn, one of the few rest days we had had that season.

Most of the other thralls were down by the ocean, washing their clothes and bodies and resting in the sunshine. Olaf and I were lounging in the shade, casting stones at a target we had erected at the base of a nearby tree, when a yell suddenly rent the morning air, scattering birds into the sky. The two of us stopped our game and looked back toward our pit-house. The cry came again, only more muted this time. But in it I heard something familiar and so I scrambled to my feet and sprinted toward the thrall quarters. Olaf came behind me, and though he was smaller, he was faster and rushed ahead.

He disappeared into the structure ten paces ahead of me. I arrived shortly thereafter and stopped at the door. In the murk stood Reas above a prone, half-dazed Turid. Her shift had been torn at the neckline. A trickle of blood dripped from her bottom lip. Reas held a knife in his hand, facing Olaf. My mind raced. Together, I knew Olaf and I could kill the bastard, but I knew, too, that we would die for it. I glanced at Olaf and watched as that mischievous smile crept onto his face.

"Olaf, no," I said in our Northern tongue.

Reas scowled at me, and just then, Olaf moved. Though younger, he was just as tall as Reas and much faster. By the time Reas reacted to the threat, Olaf was a step away from him. Reas slashed wildly at Olaf with his knife, but Olaf blocked Reas's arm with his left hand, then punched the boy squarely in his left jaw, dropping him hard to the hay. His knife skittered away as he hit the ground. Olaf kicked the blade from Reas's reach and bent to grab Reas's collar.

"What is happening here?" a voice boomed from behind us.

We thralls moved away from Reas and stared wordlessly at our master.

"What has happened here?" he repeated, this time with more ire and with his switch brandished in his fist.

Reas sat up, rubbing his jaw, and pointed at Olaf. "He hit me."

"He was attacking Turid," Olaf shot back.

Heres's eyes moved for the first time to Turid, then back to Olaf. "I can kill you for striking my son, thrall."

Olaf shrugged. "You can try."

Heres did not take the bait but rather snorted and turned to his son. "Are you such a fool that you come to take with force that which is already yours? If you want her, you need only ask." He looked as if he might say more, then he pointed to the knife. "Pick it up and take her to the house." He turned to us. "Do not resist or you will suffer."

Reas grabbed his weapon, then reached for Turid's arm. She moved it away. We moved toward her to help but she held up a hand to us. "Do not. It will only make matters worse for us all." And with those words, she followed Heres and Reas from the pit-house.

We could only watch them go.

Turid returned to us that night, walking slowly. She was dazed and bruised, both on her face and body. The other thralls stared at her as she walked silently to her mattress, looking only at the ground. Perchance the two other girls — Sigdag and Eydis — were wondering when a similar fate would befall them. Olaf and I moved to her, but she flinched and retreated and would not let us come close. Later, as the darkness deepened around us, I heard her soft sobs, and still, I could do nothing to help her.

The following morning, Heres roused the thralls early and marched Olaf and me to a nearby stand of trees, where Reas waited with a thick stick. He was bending it between his hands, testing its strength and durability. Tarmo lifted my arms and tied my wrists to two separate trees so that I stood like Thor's hammer before the others. I did not try to resist — to do so, I knew, would only bring more pain.

"Yesterday," Heres explained to the thralls as I awaited my punishment, "two thralls attempted to interfere in the actions of my son. Interference of that nature will not be tolerated. You are all my property and will accept the words and actions of my men as if they have come from me. Is that clear?"

The thralls mumbled their understanding. I looked at Turid, who gazed at me with tears in her eyes. I could say nothing to her to ease her distress and so I looked away and steeled myself for the pain I was about to endure.

"This," Heres continued as he motioned to me, "is their punishment." He nodded to his son. "Proceed."

Reas's first stroke tore through my rough tunic and into my skin, opening a groove that would take months to fully heal. I winced and whimpered, but did not cry out. He struck again and I bit my lip until it bled, keeping my teary gaze on the ground, away from Olaf and Turid and the others, lest they see my weakness. Three more strikes and my back was a patchwork of bloody crisscrosses, my mind delirious from the searing agony. Tarmo untied my arms, and I collapsed to the ground. He kicked me clear of the space so he could bind Olaf's arms to the birch.

Olaf fared worse than me. He was defiant and cursed Reas with each lashing, which only made him strike harder. By the seventh strike, Olaf had stopped his cursing and was spitting blood and saliva onto the dirt. Yet remarkably, he still had enough strength to remain on his feet.

Reas snarled and drew the stick back to strike again, but Heres caught his arm. "That is enough. We need our thralls in the bog." He untied Olaf's hands and let him drop to the ground like a corpse.

Chapter 21

Two more winters passed. Two more winters of toil and hardship, of longing and loneliness. Two more winters in which the gods shat upon us thralls while Heres, his family, and his men enjoyed the warmth of their high-timbered hall and the profits of our labor.

Unless you were Turid, Eydis, or Sigdag.

They endured a different fate that in many ways was worse than ours. Their burgeoning womanhood saved them from the bog and our cramped pit-house, but it did not save them from the beds of men. Of course, I was too engulfed in my own misery to truly grasp their particular brand of horror. All I saw was their transformation. They looked better rested, bathed, and groomed. Gone were their smelly, mud-caked shifts. Gone were the emaciated limbs. Unlike us, they no longer had the look of death upon them. Guardedness, aye. Bitterness, certainly. But death, no. And that transformation enraged me.

Occasionally, I would see Turid and our eyes would meet, but one of us would invariably turn away. I do not know why she hid from me, but I know why I could not gaze upon her. The gods help me, but the sight of her incensed me as much as it confused me. I was thankful for her well-being, but I was jealous of it too. My young mind could not grasp how violated she must feel. All I could think of was better rations, better sleep, and an occasional bath. If being the toy of women could guarantee me those things, I would do it gladly. Which begged the question: did she perform her new tasks readily, or did it sicken her to do so? To think on it tormented me, so much so that I began to go out of my way to avoid her.

I saw a change in Egil, too. When his sister was finally pulled to the main hall, I think he took on his twin's pain with his own. He became bitter and pinched in expression. When spoken to, he answered in short, clipped responses. When our guards appeared, his malignant gaze followed them closely, as if he were trying to kill them with that look. A few of the guards finally took exception to him and beat him nearly to death, then tied him to a tree for a night. It did not cure him of his anger.

When I confided in Olaf about my feelings, he just shrugged it off. It was early summer and we were working together as we had done for the past six summers, only now, Olaf's voice cracked with his new-found maturity. "You speak as if Turid has a choice in the matter. You know as well as I that to fight her duties is to be punished or killed."

"I know," I responded sourly. "Still, it eats at me. As it eats at Egil. I can see him rotting from the inside out."

"It eats at me too, Torgil," Olaf confided. "And one day, we will set it aright. These bastards will pay dearly for their cruelty."

After six long summers, I was no longer so hopeful, but I held my counsel on the matter.

We returned that day from the bogs to find Heres waiting for us at the pit-house. "Five days hence," he announced in the Estland tongue when we were assembled, "begins the market on Saaremaa. We had a good haul from the bog these past months, so I will need two of you to assist us."

As I mentioned, this task normally fell to the thrall who had caused the least havoc over the previous three seasons. It offered a break from the monotony of our digging, so we all wanted to go, though Heres normally chose only one of us. Our rule-follower, Herkus, was oft chosen, though Raban and Egil had also gone. Being bigger troublemakers, Olaf, Pipin, and I were overlooked. Still, the prospect excited us and so we all listened closely to Heres's words in the hope that one of us would get lucky.

"This summer, I will take Raban and Olaf."

I whooped involuntarily and clasped my friend's shoulder, receiving a captious gaze and frown from Heres. Olaf grinned at my joy and mayhap at his own luck, then quickly sobered, lest his chance to go was revoked by our master.

"Over the coming days, you will all help load the ship."

When our master was gone, I pulled Olaf aside and spoke a thought that had jumped into my head. It was a delicate topic but one I felt compelled to say. "If you get the chance to escape, take it," I whispered to him. "Get to your uncle, if he still lives."

Olaf studied me with his blue eyes. "I cannot leave you or Turid. You know that."

I knew he would say that and was ready with a reply. "Then come back for us when you have the means and rescue us."

He was about to respond when Reas tossed me a bowl for the night meal. Olaf turned to catch his.

"You must," I said quickly, then moved away to get my food.

Four days later, we walked together with Heres's household to the shore. Heres was there already, making a final examination of the boat and its oars. Those men headed to the market with him were saying their farewells to their comrades and family members. I clasped Olaf on the shoulder and whispered to him, "Remember my words, Olaf."

He nodded. "Keep well," he said with a glance in my direction and a slight smile. Then he moved to the ship and climbed aboard.

As there were many people milling about on the shore, I took the opportunity to seek out Turid. I knew not what I would say to her, only that I must say something. It had been two summers since we had spoken and despite my anger at her, I felt the need to at least acknowledge her. Mayhap it would help quell my ill feelings.

I found her on the fringes of the gathering, standing with Eydis as she watched Olaf settle himself in a spot on the ship's deck beside Raban. I snuck up behind her, for I feared she might try to avoid me if she saw me coming.

"You look well," I said into her left ear.

Startled, she partially spun and, seeing my face, blushed and turned away. In that quick glance, I saw the bruise on her left cheek and the cut on her brow, and my stomach twisted.

"Do not move away," I whispered quickly, trying to get the words out before I lost her again. "I wished only to greet you. It has been some time since last we spoke."

"I know," she said. She kept her face averted.

"My hope is that they are treating you well, Turid, but I can see that is not the case. I am sorry."

She snorted bitterly "They plump me up, just like their pigs, so that they can justify beating me when they spread their seed."

"At least they feed you," I replied sourly before I could stop the words.

She glared at me, red now from anger rather than embarrassment. "A curse on you, Torgil," she seethed. "I would rather starve to death than have one of those bastards force himself on me again."

Her words were like a slap to my face, and I struggled to apologize. Unlike Olaf, who could spin words like the Norns could spin thread, I was clumsy with language. She did not wait for my lame apology but shouldered past me. I stared at her retreating back for a long moment, feeling utterly foolish, then turned my eyes back to the departing ship.

At least it would have no harsh words for me.

The ship returned nearly a fortnight later, during the day. We thralls who had been in the bogs noticed the men and activity as soon as we shuffled into the settlement for our night meal. Raban was there, eating from a bowl in the fading light. Near him were four children — three boys and one girl — looking frightened and dirty, the more so when they saw us thralls appear with our bog-caked skin and dirty clothes. They looked so young, and yet, they were probably as old as I when I first arrived.

One of our master's men handed us a bowl and a cup of water as we returned, but I did not take mine. Instead, I moved to the pit-house door and opened it, finding myself almost giddy with the prospect of Olaf's return.

Except he was not there.

Nonplussed, I moved to the privy, thinking to find him occupied, but he was not there either. Concern began to creep up my spine as I returned to the front of the pit-house where the others now ate. I ignored their prying eyes and approached Raban.

Before I could even ask, Raban babbled something in his thick Prussian accent that sounded like, "If it is Olaf you seek, the lucky bastard is gone."

"What?" I asked, thinking I had misheard.

"Gone," he repeated the one word. "Olaf is gone."

A wave of panic washed over me, for that one word could have many meanings, most of them bad. "Gone?"

"Aye," Raban said as he flashed me a toothless smile. "Gone. A man came to him in the market and asked him his name. A lord, he was, this man. He asked Olaf his name," Raban repeated, "then the names of his kin. Must have seen something in the boy that was familiar to him." He shrugged. "Anyway, he purchased Olaf's freedom on the spot. Right there. Handed Heres a sack of silver coins. Paid more for him than he was worth, in my opinion. But still, paid for him he did. A sack of silver. One moment Olaf was a thrall, and the next, he was not." Raban barked a laugh and shook his head. "Lucky bastard."

I could barely believe the words I was hearing and for a long moment thought Raban's flatulence might have traveled to his mouth. It had to be some sort of jest. I looked at the others now, who were chattering excitedly at the news, then at our guards, thinking that I would find the lie of it in one of their faces. I must have been shaking my head as I searched, for Raban pointed at me. "No amount of head shaking is going to change my tale, Torgil. He is free. Gone from here."

"What man freed him? Do you remember his name?" I asked.

Raban shrugged. "I know not. Though judging from the price he paid for Olaf and the size of his ship resting in the harbor, I could tell he was important. A lord from somewhere."

"Try to remember," I urged him quietly, lest the guards overhear my talk. "Was his name Sigurd?"

Again, Raban shrugged.

"And he freed Olaf? You are sure of that? He did not just buy him to do his thrall work?"

"Of that I am certain," Raban said. "Heres cut Olaf's collar from him right there on the spot. Like I said, one moment he was a thrall and the next, a free lad."

I was stunned, and yet I had no time to process the information, for one of the guards blurted, "Back to your shit-house!" They had called our pit-house that for as long as I could remember, and the name still made them chuckle. We, of course, were immune to the name by that point and shuffled wordlessly to our mattresses. Herkus ushered the children to their new beds, where they sat in wide-eyed silence.

I lay down and stared at the moldy thatch above me, ignoring the chatter and questions that flew about the pit-house about Olaf and his release. It must be Sigurd. Who else could it be? Erik, Astrid's father? It was possible, but less likely. He would not waste his time on his daughter when he had sons.

In the end, it did not matter. What mattered was that Olaf was gone. I suppose I should have been overjoyed at my friend's release, but I found myself vexed by his departure and grieving the loss of a vital part of me and my life. Even though I had told him what I expected, I had not truly believed he would leave us behind. And yet he had, and now we were alone.

It was time to plot my revenge and my escape, for I did not know how much longer I could last in that Hel.

Chapter 22

The absence of Olaf was a dull ache. I missed his presence, his voice, his inattentiveness, his energy. It was like a shadow, following me through my days and lurking in the dark at night. But the ache was not for his absence alone. It was also the ache of fading hope. I had thought in the early days of his departure that mayhap he would come in Sigurd's ship to rescue us, but as summer slid into fall and then into winter, that hope slipped further from me.

His departure, of course, was not enough for the Norns. They had to stoke the torments of Olaf's loss by weaving even more misery into our lives.

It started in early fall, when an unseasonal cold snap fell across the land. For days the skies remained clear, the air bitter in its chill. Then suddenly, a mass of angry clouds rolled over us as we worked in the bog. Icy rain dropped from the sky, pummeling our heads and limbs and chilling us to the bone. Tarmo was with us that day and pulled us from the fields, but as we jogged to the safety of the birch forest, one of the new boys — a straw-haired, freckle-faced lad named Ilo — fell headlong into a half-hidden pond. I ran two paces behind him and leaped to the edge of the water, then fell to my knees and snatched at his flailing arms. Catching a section of his tunic, I pulled him to the water's edge and dragged him up. He thanked me with a nod and we moved on.

Two days later, Ilo fell ill. It began as a raw cough but quickly turned to a rattle in his thin chest. After several days of it, he could barely rise. Herkus helped him get to the bog, but by that time, his skin was sweat-streaked and his forehead as hot as an iron furnace. We beseeched Reas to let the child rest, but he refused. The poor lad collapsed before the sun had fully brightened the sky. Herkus and Raban carried him to his mattress, but he never awoke. Sometime later that night, he died.

"Allow us at least to bury the lad down near the beach," Herkus begged Reas when we told him of Ilo's passing at the morning meal.

Reas regarded us, then the sky that was brightening into another crisp, clear day. A smirk broke on his face and my heart sank at the sight of it. "No. A morning spent burying his body is a morning of lost iron. You can toss him in a bog pond on your way to your tasks."

"That pig," Pipin mumbled as Reas departed. "One day, I will feed his body, piece by piece, to the salamanders."

I used his anger to hatch my plan. In the fields over the following days, I spoke to him in hushed tones about my ideas. It was a risk to involve him, I knew, but I knew I could not exact my revenge or escape alone. I would need recruits and so I offered up my thoughts. I did not know what to expect, but he did not oppose me. He accepted my invitation enthusiastically, adding elements and wrinkles to my plans that I had not yet considered. He was a clever lad; some of his ideas brought a malicious grin to my face.

The cycle of hardship did not stop with the loss if Ilo, whom we weighted down with peat to help him sink in that desolate bog. Soon after, Eydis began to show signs of pregnancy as we neared winter. She tried to conceal it, especially from her brother, but eventually there was no way to hide the growing mound of her belly. While we did not know who the father was, we all understood what it meant. Giving birth was difficult even when you had the best of help, but who knew what help Eydis would receive? She was a thrall, after all, and just as likely to be turned out as helped. To make matters worse, none of Heres's men claimed the baby. The unspoken truth of it was that no man wanted that responsibility if the babe was not their own, and no man could be certain it was theirs. Heres had no interest in keeping the child, either — he wanted only a productive thrall, which meant that the baby would be killed upon birth.

If the whole affair left a sour taste in our mouths, it rekindled the black disease in Egil's soul. He spoke even less than before and spent his days alone, mumbling words to himself. When the winter weather prevented us from going out, he sat by himself in a corner or lay on his back on his mattress, simply staring upward. Those of us who tried to draw him out with a word or a conversation received a blank gaze in reply. Eventually we stopped trying, though I remained concerned. It was bad enough that his sister had been impregnated. I could not fathom losing Egil, too. I spoke to the others of it, and we agreed to watch him, but I knew there was little we could do for him.

In the end, Eydis' pregnancy never made it to the following summer. She fell ill just after the Yule feast and died not ten days later. Her death was announced with a wail from the hall that woke us from our slumber. We had known she was sick, but none of us knew just how bad her illness was. Sensing something, Egil was the first to the door. We were not allowed out at night, but he bolted past our guards and sprinted into the frigid darkness.

Halfway to the hall, the guards caught up to him and as they wrestled his weak body to the snow-covered ground, the door to the main hall opened and the hearth fire cast its dim light over the area. More men emerged from the doorway, their hulking shadows looking like giants on the snow. They dragged between them a body, which they tossed unceremoniously into the snow near Egil. Even in the half light, I could see the protruding belly of Eydis. The shock of that vision was followed shortly by Egil's haunting scream — a scream that shattered the night as much as it shattered us. I turned my head away, for the pain of seeing the two of them like that tore me apart.

The guards pulled the struggling Egil back to our group as the rest of the household marched out into the night. Heres waddled ahead of them, with Tarmo and Reas not far behind. His wife, Rekon, and the rest of the household, including Turid and Sigdag, hung back. Like me, Turid and Sigdag could barely watch.

Heres stopped before Egil and regarded his thrall's tear-streaked face. "Your sister died of an illness. We tried to save her. She was useful in our household." He wiped his nose with the back of his hand and sniffed. "Her death is unfortunate, for now I have one less thrall to serve me. Do not let her loss affect your productivity, or I will be forced to punish you."

The insult just incensed Egil all the more. He writhed in the grip of his guards and spat in our master's face. "You heartless troll," he shouted. "I will kill you when I have the chance!"

Heres wiped the spittle from his now fierce face. "You are a dim-witted lad, Egil. Do you not see that you will never have the chance to kill me? That you are my property and I rule here?" He gestured to the guards holding Egil. "Tie up the whelp and put his sister's corpse at his feet to remind him of how powerless he is. But don't let him freeze. We need him in the bogs. Come," he said to the others. "Morning will soon be upon us. Let us try to rest a little longer before it arrives."

Egil survived the night, if just barely. And by the mercy of the gods, he did not have to witness his sister being dragged off into the darkness by wolves or some other beast. It is likely that the presence of the guards outside our pit-house kept the predators away, or mayhap it was the fire they built to keep themselves warm. Whatever the case, we were able to pry Egil's frozen tunic from the bark in the gray morning and carry his shivering body into the warmth of our house. His lips were blue and his teeth chattered, but he was alive. We piled our blankets on his body and built up the hearth fire until warmth filled the room, then we left for the bog. It was all we could do for him.

I did not expect Egil to live much longer, but slowly he regained his color and his strength. Though he would not say it, I believe that Heres was relieved to have him alive, for the loss of three thralls so quickly would have hurt his operations. Mayhap it was for that reason that he allowed us to nurse Egil back to health before returning him to the bog for work.

As you can imagine, his recovery did not cure him of his ill temper or his gloom. He worked as if he carried a boulder on his back and two on his legs. He cried at random moments. In the dead of night. In the fields as he worked. As he ate his night meal. He spoke to no one. Even so, I sensed that he would erupt, given the chance, and get himself killed in the process, so I did my best to include him in our hushed conversations, even if he did not respond. I wanted to include him in my plans as well, but I sensed he teetered on the edge of sanity, and I could not risk him mumbling some part of the plot to our guards. When the time came, though, I felt his bitterness would force him into the fray.

My other two conspirators would be Turid and Sigdag. I did not see much of them those days, but I knew with the loss of Eydis that a chance at escape would be far more attractive than a life — and a death — as concubines in Heres's hall. I would need to speak with them before I set the plans in motion. I just hoped that when I did, I would sense their passion or their reluctance prior to moving forward.

Winter melted into a rain-mired spring, which then bloomed into a humid summer marked by bouts of extreme heat and intermittent rainstorms. With summer's arrival, we began digging for peat to provide fuel for the furnaces, though the storms interfered with the smelting. Heres was beyond frustrated, for the market was coming soon and despite the bitter winter, we had discovered more iron than ever before.

To make up for lost time, Heres worked us mercilessly at the furnaces when the weather was fair. The younger children did not have the strength or stamina to work the bellows for long, nor the skill to know when to add more peat to the furnace, so most of the work fell to the older thralls. The work that early summer was so constant, we slept near the furnaces and did not waste time returning to our pit-house.

In the end, we succeeded in smelting all of the iron but paid for it with our bodies. As a reward for our work, Heres gave each thrall double rations and a day of rest, while he and his men feasted in the main hall. We saw none of that food, of course, but that suited me fine. I was happy slurping at my bowl, enjoying the unfamiliar sensation of a full belly. A bug floated in my water cup and I sucked it into my mouth, crunching delightedly on the carcass.

Beside me, Pipin laughed. "Do you remember, Torgil, when we arrived, how you would not deign to eat a bug? Things have changed."

I smiled. "I was a fool, Pipin."

Near us, Raban farted loudly and groaned with pleasure, and even Egil laughed at that. Herkus tossed a pebble at him, which Egil knocked aside. "It is good to have you with us, Egil," said Herkus. The lad blushed and looked away.

Heres approached us then with Reas by his side. Their eyes raked over us imperiously. Conversations died on our lips as we turned our faces to our master. "Enjoy your meal. Our winter and spring were wet, as you know, so rations are slim." I wanted to ask him then why he was wasting it on a feast, but held my tongue.

"It is time to choose those who will accompany us to market," he continued. "Since there is so much iron to move, I have decided to take the older, stronger men, Herkus and Raban. Reas," he motioned to his son, "will stay here in my stead. We will leave in five days. There is much to do until then, so I hope you keep your strength."

I watched them disappear into the hall before glancing at Pipin. It was as we hoped it would be. I nodded to him ever so slightly.

Yet another storm blew over the settlement in the following days and so Heres's departure was delayed by a day. When the clouds dispersed, we gathered on the muddy strand with the crisp, post-storm air in our noses and helped Heres load his tent, food, ale, iron billets, axe-heads, and other supplies into his knarr. Heres said his farewells to his household, then climbed aboard the vessel and cast off.

I waved to Herkus and Raban and edged myself closer to Turid and Sigdag in the process. "Do not walk away," I said in our Norse tongue to Turid. They both glanced at me, then turned back to the ship, lest the guards get suspicious. "I have a plan to free us from this place," I whispered near Turid's ear, "but I need the help of the both of you. It is dangerous and I will require you to explain it to Sigdag. If you wish to be part of it, nod once."

She nodded instantly and so I explained the plan to her.

Chapter 23

The first part of the plan was to wait until three days after Heres was gone. Three days would give Heres enough time to get to market and set up his stall. If he had not returned by then, then his journey had gone well, and he would be occupied with buyers for his iron. And I would set my plan in motion.

The day after Heres's departure, I made sure everything was in place. It was not a complicated plan, but it did require a few instruments, and it was these I focused on placing where my cohorts and I could easily find them. To say I was nervous would not be true. I was excited, not only to be free of the living Hel I had experienced for the past seven summers, but to exact my vengeance on those who had taken such pleasure in their cruelty.

My plan, I thought, was well-conceived, but the world is not perfect and rarely complies with the whims of man. On the second day after Heres's departure, Thor intervened. Despite it being early summer, He rolled across the heavens in his goat-drawn chariot, bringing rain and shaking the sky with his lightning and thunder. The foul weather did not hamper our work — we worked in most weather — but it did make me worry whether the market would continue or if we might see Heres earlier than planned.

The third day after his departure dawned overcast yet humid, the air pregnant with moisture. It had rained the night before and now threatened to rain again. In the mud outside our pit-house we supped quietly on soggy bread and watery gruel as I cast furtive glances at the beach. Heres had not yet returned, and I sent a prayer to Thor that he would stay away long enough for me to see my plan through.

"Finish the dregs!" growled Tarmo. "Time to hunt the bogs!"

I cast a lingering eye at the empty bay, then joined the others as we shuffled out into the bog with two of the younger guards, Kove and Sula, at our heels. They were not much older than me, really. They wore heavy cloaks to protect them from the impending rain which, I noticed with some satisfaction, also covered the seaxes on their belts. They would pay for that mistake.

I worked with Pipin that day, he and I side by side as we fished the wet ground with our poles. "We go today," I mumbled to him. He nodded without looking at me.

At high day, as Kove and Sula stood beside each other, their eyes only half on us as they swiped at the mosquitoes swarming about their hooded heads. Thor began to piss on us then. Steadily, the rain picked up until it fell in a steady staccato that drove off the mosquitoes but soaked us through. I glanced at Pipin through my dark, wet bangs and nodded. He nodded in return. It was time.

I bent to the earth in the spot I had mapped out for this portion of my plan and dug under the bog moss. After a moment I found what I sought — a crude shard of an iron bar not much longer than a ship nail. It had a sharp point but no handle and was easy to conceal in my sleeve. I did not even have to craft it. I had merely picked it up from the turf a scant few weeks before when we worked at the furnaces. Three similar shards waited: one beside mine for Pipin, and two more at the settlement for Turid and Sigdag. They were not swords, but they could kill if used well. As I slipped the weapon into my hand, my heart began to thunder.

"Hey!" I waved to the guards and pointed to the ground as if I needed help. Beside me, Pipin acted as if he was trying to pry a heavy clump of bog iron from the peat.

Kove said something to Sula, which made the other man smile, then walked over to our spot. The other thralls looked in our direction, then went back to their tasks. The rain fell harder, and I wiped my bangs from my eyes with my forearm.

"What is the matter?" asked Kove as he neared, and for a brief moment I thought he might stop and detect our bluff.

"Bog iron. A huge piece," I called back to him, then bent beside Pipin and made a show of pulling at something.

In my periphery, I saw Kove's boot step close to my right. I glanced up just as he craned his neck forward to see, and that is when I struck. With my left hand, I grabbed his cloak and pulled. With my right, I jabbed hard with the blade at his chest. He was falling forward, off balance, and his momentum helped drive my blade through his cloak and into his heart. He screamed as he fell to the wet turf between us, his fall tearing the blade from my hand. Before I could move to him and yank it free, Pipin pounded his blade into Kove's chest near mine. I fumbled for the dead man's seax and turned to face Sula, who had recovered from his own surprise and was coming at me with his blade drawn.

Rather than attack, he looked at Pipin and me, then at the other thralls, and decided it best to run for help. He turned, but before he could take a step, Egil swung his sack of iron into his face, sending him plummeting onto his back. Before he could rise, Egil scrambled forward, mounted his chest, and began pounding his face. Sula struggled to protect himself, but he was no match for the hate-filled barrage of punches that connected with his head. Soon, his arms lay motionless at his side. Egil spat on his victim's bloodied face, then fumbled for the man's belt, unsheathed his blade, and slashed it across Sula's neck.

The entire fight had ended quickly, leaving the six of us standing there in the rain, staring at each other. Above, the heavens thundered, bringing me to my senses. I realized that my hand stung, and I looked at it. There was a gash on my palm where my own blade had sliced me. Blood pooled around the wound. It was not deep, though I cursed myself all the same for my carelessness.

"Pipin, strip Kove and dress in his garb," I ordered. "I will do the same with Sula. Search him, too. If there is any food, distribute it."

"What about me?" asked Egil. "And them?" He pointed at the children.

"I need you to come with me," I said as I grabbed the seax from his hand and cut the leather collar from my neck.

"And where do you go?"

I knelt beside Sula to remove his belt. "Back to the hall to take my vengeance."

He nodded. "That I will gladly do."

I nodded and continued to strip the corpse. I did not need to explain the danger. He knew, as we all did, what lay in store. He grabbed the seax I had placed on the turf and made as if to cut his own collar from his neck. "No," I said. "You keep yours. At least for now. It is part of the plan." Reluctantly, he dropped his hand.

Sula's clothes were large on me, but not overly so. Dressed now, I turned to the children and explained the plan and their part in it. "I am sorry, but if we are to succeed, we need you as part of this. If we survive, you will have your freedom." They nodded, but I could see the fear and reluctance in their eyes. There was nothing I could say to soften the blow of it, and so I turned my eyes to Pipin, who had just finished disguising himself in Kove's clothes.

"By the gods, does that feel good," he said as he rubbed his collarless neck.

I ignored him. "Let us see to the bodies."

We shoved our thrall clothes into one of the iron-collecting sacks, then we dragged it and the bodies to a pond we knew to be deep. There, we tied sacks of iron to their white, cold corpses and rolled them into the muddy water. They drifted for a time beneath the rain-pocked surface, then slowly slipped away.

It was too early to return to the settlement, so I used the afternoon to clean my wound, to describe the plan in detail to the others — now that they were part of it, they had the right to know — and to rest. One of the children distributed dried venison, which both Kove and Sula had carried, and this we chewed gratefully as we rested, for it had been a long time since any of us had enjoyed the taste of good meat. As I rested, Pipin found two branches and worked the iron blades into the wood, then fastened them in place with bog grass to create two rudimentary spears. They were unbalanced, crooked, and flimsy, but better than the short shards of iron we had before.

The rain stopped as night began to darken the sky. It was time to return to the settlement. I looked at the others as I rose. "Remember what I have told you," I said. "If we stay true to the plan, we cannot fail." It was a lie, of course. I had my misgivings. But some lies are worth it.

We returned the same way we had departed that morning — with the thralls in front and the guards in the rear. I had even made sure Pipin and I carried the switches in our hands so that from a distance, we appeared as we always appeared when returning from the bog in the evenings. Only this time, when we reached the furnaces, I left Pipin and Egil there under the pretense that Egil was hurt. It was the only way I could explain the disparity in our numbers when I reached the settlement, and it gave me a good excuse to get one of the guards on his own.

Soon, I could see the lights of the main hall ahead, and my doubts returned. Were Turid and Sigdag ready? Would they follow through with the plan? Would the guard believe my voice or would he detect a ruse? The cold hand of panic clutched my chest as I checked the cord on my belt yet again to ensure I could draw my blade quickly. In the distance, beyond the children shuffling in front of me, I saw the shadow of one of the guards near the fire, preparing the night meal. He turned at our approach.

"Sula? Is that you? Where are the others?" he called to me.

"Aye. It is me. One of the thralls is injured," I responded in my best Estland accent from within the hood of my cloak. I motioned vaguely back down the trail. "They are just behind me. Coming slowly."

"Damn thralls. Always getting hurt," he grumbled as he turned back to his fire and the cauldron in which our night meal boiled. It smelled of onions.

We came closer, and the children dispersed around him. "Back, you short-wits!"

As he shooed them away from the flames, I stepped closer to my prey. He looked up at me just as I drew my blade. "You —" He started to curse, but the words died on his lips as my blade slid into his stomach and up toward his heart.

Warm blood gushed onto my hand as his fetid breath washed over me. His eyes focused on mine, then rolled upward as his body fell forward onto me. I caught him as he fell and pulled him quickly behind the flames so that he was not visible from the hall. Then I pulled my seax free and wiped it on his cloak.

Taking the man's place, I dropped the ladle into the cauldron with shaking hands and filled the first bowl of soup. I passed it to one of the children as calmly as I could. She took it quietly and, with a fearful glance at my face, retreated to the place where she normally ate her food. Two more bowls I filled, trying to act as if nothing was the matter, should someone in the main hall glance outside. It was a macabre scene, with the guard lying dead beside the fire and the children eating casually nearby, so I focused my mind on the next part of the plan.

Pipin appeared then with Egil before him. I handed Egil a bowl, then nodded to Pipin, who moved off to stand beside the doorway of the hall. My original plan had been to draw the men out by fire, but it was too risky for the women and, besides, the rains had dampened the thatch too much.

As nonchalantly as we could, Egil sat down near the children, and I went back to stirring the cauldron and stoking the fire. When everyone was in place, I called out to Tarmo. I waited, but there was no reply. I called again, my voice sounding small and shrill in my ears.

"Who calls my name?" I heard him say before his giant frame appeared at the threshold of the hall.

"It is me, Sula," I responded. "I need your help with Kove. He is ill." I pointed to the body lying on the opposite side of the fire.

Tarmo lurched outside and took a step toward me. "What is —"

It has been many winters since that night but I oft relive that moment. Oh, how I wish I could take it back. Reweave it into a thing of beauty, not the brutal mess it became.

Chapter 24

Pipin pounced as soon as Tarmo was two steps beyond the door. But Pipin was an inexperienced thrall, and unlike the others we had killed, Tarmo was a fighter. He sensed rather than saw Pipin's movement and spun just as Pipin jabbed with his seax. The blade grazed Tarmo's side. He roared and smashed his fist into Pipin's cheek before Pipin could duck. The boy staggered sideways, straining to stay upright and to keep the seax in his grip.

I was moving as soon as Tarmo spun. Egil raced beside me, our blades out. From within the hall, I heard the yell of another man — Reas — and a crash. A woman shrieked. Before us, Pipin fell to his side as Tarmo yanked his own sword free of his sheath and brought it up to strike.

"No!" I shouted as Tarmo's blade came down.

Pipin raised his own blade to block Tarmo's attack, but it was an awkward defense from an awkward position. Tarmo's power drove Pipin's arm backward so that his own seax ripped into his forehead, followed instantly by Tarmo's blade, which carved deeper into his skull.

Tarmo sensed our approach, and in one swift motion, shifted the grip on his blade, yanked it free, and stepped back with his left foot.

I recognized the move and knew instantly what to expect. I had just reached him and moved my blade to the left. At the same moment, Tarmo spun, putting his full weight behind his swing. His blade hit mine with such force that I was knocked sideways, to my right. Thankfully, Egil was two steps beyond me and free of Tarmo's blade. He hacked wildly, carving a mighty gash into that bastard's neck.

Tarmo staggered to his right, giving me enough time to recover from his previous blow. Stunned by his wound, he swung wildly at me — a swing I easily parried. Blood was now flowing freely from the big man's wound, and I could see his eyes losing focus.

"Help the girls!" I yelled at Egil just as Tarmo roared, lifted his blade, and came at me again.

I stepped into and under his swing, then drove my own blade hard into his gut. The blow drove the breath from him and rendered him helpless. He sought my face with his eyes and gazed at me with puzzlement, as if he could not understand why this was happening or why I would do such a thing to him.

"I will feed your body to the sea birds and rodents, you bastard," I hissed.

He tried to respond, but the breath had left him. I watched his lips move. Perchance a prayer? I did not know or care. Instead, I yanked my blade free and watched him crumple to the ground. Then I followed Egil into the hall.

What greeted my eyes within will stick in my mind until I breathe my last breath. I will say only that there was little left of Reas. I had placed two iron shards near the hall for Turid and Sigdag. I told them only that they were to strike Reas as soon as Tarmo stepped foot outside. Turid later told me that he had been drinking that day, and so when my call came, he rose on unsteady legs and staggered after

Tarmo. Only he never made it. Turid stabbed him in the back before he had taken two steps. As he turned to retaliate, Sigdag drove her blade into the back of his neck and killed him. I do not know if they expected him to rise or whether they had lost themselves in the moment, but they kept striking until their fury was slaked and the walls were awash in his gore.

When I found them, they seemed confused, as if they knew not what to do with him or their new freedom. I nodded at them. "You have done well," I said. "Go to the children."

They nodded and left, and I turned to Egil, who held Heres's wife Rekon by the arm, his blade at her neck. Why he had not killed her, I knew not. It was Rekon, after all, who had witnessed the treatment of the concubines in her household and done nothing to stop it or to help Eydis when she became pregnant. She was as guilty as the rest of them. "What shall we do with her?"

I was in no mood for discussing the matter. She, like the others, needed to die for her treatment of us.

"My husband will return, and he will take his vengeance on you all," she hissed at us. "He will —"

She never finished. I drove my blade into her fat belly so hard that it lifted her from the ground. Egil stepped back in shock as the breath caught in her throat. I yanked my blade free and turned to go, not bothering to watch her die.

Egil followed me into the yard, where the others waited. They studied me silently with faces aglow in the firelight. I sensed they were looking at me for direction, but I had none to give them, at least not at that moment, and I told them so.

"If we stay here, we will face Heres and his remaining men when they return. We can surprise them, but it will be a hard fight." I am certain even the children knew this, so there was no sense in telling them lies. "If we run, we will face others, for they will recognize us as runaway thralls. Still, there is a chance we can find a fishing boat and get to the mainland, which is not too distant from this island."

"And then what?" Turid asked. "We will still be runaways, only in a larger land we know nothing about."

"She is right," added Egil as he scratched at a fleck of blood on his cheek. "We need a boat that can take us where we want to go. Something that can get us away from these cursed Estlanders."

I nodded, hearing the truth in their words. "Then it is settled. We will stay. Let us bury Pipin and get rid of the other bodies. Then we will rest and plan our next steps."

We laid stones around Pipin's grave in the shape of a ship that would hasten him to the underworld. We knew not which gods Pipin worshiped and so we scratched two crude images on two of the stones — one of the Christian cross and another of Thor's hammer. We placed a crude spear in the grave with him along with some bread and cheese and dried fish from the kitchen. As we laid the last dirt over his body, I prayed he would find his way safely to his afterlife.

The other bodies we carried to the reeds that grew thickly on either side of the beach and tossed them beside each other. I wanted nothing more than to be free of their stench and to let the birds and reptiles and rodents feast on their carrion. It was all they deserved.

"Tonight," I said when we had seen to those tasks and regrouped in the main hall, "we sleep in comfort with our bellies full of Heres's food."

"And ale!" called Egil, and the others laughed.

"And ale if you wish," I conceded, though I had no intention of touching the drink. I had seen what it did to my father, and I believed it would alter my wits in similar fashion. "On the morrow, we plan and we prepare. Heres and his men will be home several days hence, so we have little time."

As much as I wanted to, I could not eat very much. None of us could. We were not accustomed to stomaching large quantities, and after forcing down some bread and cheese, I could eat no more. Nor could I fully enjoy the whiff of freedom we had achieved. I was feeling the loss of Pipin and worried, too, about Heres's impending return. And so while the others laughed and enjoyed the evening, I left the hall to sit outside near the dwindling fire, my eyes focused on the empty beach that lay an arrow's flight distant.

A footfall behind me tore my gaze from the strand. I glanced over my shoulder to see Turid standing behind me. It was evening, but the summer sun was yet bright and played on the orange in her hair. Her presence stirred so many memories and emotions in me that it rendered me speechless. Mayhap Olaf would know what to say, but my words jumbled with my emotions to produce only silence.

"May I sit?" she asked, her voice little more than a whisper.

I nodded, then tensed as she found a spot beside me. Our interactions had been so fleeting and bitter these past summers, I knew not where or how to begin with her. She must have felt the same, for she pulled her knees up to her chest and wrapped her arms tightly around them.

"I wanted to say thank you," she finally blurted.

"For what?"

"For freeing us. For fighting for us."

"I did it as much for me as for you and the others," I said. "I want to be free of this forsaken place. And besides, I did nothing to save you before, when Reas...when they took you. I do not know why you are thanking me now."

She ignored my acrimony. "You tried. Before. And were whipped because of it."

I glanced at her.

"Anyway, I also wanted to apologize. For how I...for my behavior these past winters. I was ashamed. Am ashamed."

Her comments dredged up all of those bitter memories of when I looked at her and she looked away or ignored me outright. But then, I looked away too, and so who, really, was to blame? "I should apologize, too," I admitted grudgingly.

She glanced at me with her tear-filled eyes. "You turned away every time I looked at you, and every time you did, I felt even more shame."

Her words stoked the flames of my own shame, but I did not want that. I wanted her to stay. I wanted her close. And so I sighed deeply and stared into the fire until my emotions settled.

"You are hurt," she said, indicating my hand.

I looked at her, then at it, and nodded. "A stupid mistake," I answered. "I should have been more careful."

She laughed.

"What is so funny?"

"What you did today was brave. To hear you speak of safety in the face of that is funny."

I grinned, and the fire snapped before me. "I suppose it is."

"Let me see," she ordered gently, holding her hand out for mine. I placed my injured hand in hers. She angled it toward her face and examined it more closely. "It is not deep, but it needs cleaning and dressing."

"I know," I said. "It can wait until morning."

"Do not be foolish. Wait here." She disappeared into the hall and returned with a cup, then she retook her seat. "Let me see your hand again."

I showed it to her. She dribbled water along the cut, and I hissed at the sting of it. "Hold your hand sideways to let it drain," she said, which I did. She poured more water down the channel of the cut, letting it wash away some of the blood and larger chunks of dirt. Then she dabbed at it gently with a rag she produced. I watched in silence and tried to be tough, though every part of me wanted to pull my hand away, for it stung mightily. Finally, she produced yet another rag and wrapped my hand tightly.

"There. That will keep more dirt from getting in. We will see how it looks on the morrow." She smiled, and I blushed and looked down at my newly bandaged hand.

"Thank you," I said.

We sat for a bit, side by side, in silence. The fire smoldered before us and it mesmerized my tired mind. I wanted to tell Turid that I was sorry for everything. For all of the pain and heartache she had experienced since leaving my father's hall, but I knew not where to begin or whether it would solve anything.

She spoke before my mind could settle on what to say. "I thought I would be frightened to kill Reas. That it would be hard."

I glanced at her and saw that her eyes were focused on the fire, as mine had just been. "You were not?"

She shook her head. "No. I was not. I —" She stopped, then glanced at me before returning her eyes to the flames. "I enjoyed it, Torgil. Is that wrong?"

"No. It is not wrong. He deserved every bit of your anger and then some." I suddenly grinned at a thought that popped into my mind.

"What?" she asked.

"You told me once that you had some of your father's warrior spirit in you. Tonight, you proved it."

She smiled at the memory, then yawned. "It is late. I should rest, as should you. Sigdag and I will sleep in the pit-house tonight. We cannot..." She did not finish the thought.

I nodded, knowing what memories the main hall must have held for her.

She rose and made to go, then stopped. "I am glad you were not more seriously hurt, Torgil."

"And I, you," I responded lamely.

She turned and walked away.

We spent the following days in preparation. We sharpened blades. We dug pits on the inland portion of the beach in which we planted sharp stakes and over which we laid seaweed. I taught my fellow thralls the ways of the spears and bows that we found in the main hall. There were two of each. One of the boys was adept with a sling and so I let him craft his own and practice. I did not need them to be experts. All I wanted was for them to hit their targets. Wounding our attackers was good enough.

Each day, I posted sentries out on the headlands to watch the waterways for Heres's ship. And each day, I grew more confident that we could beat Heres and his men when they returned. He only had four men with him. If we did things according to plan, then we had a chance to survive.

Each night, we practiced the plan I had in mind. It was a sound plan, but it had one shortfall: us. It was one thing to stab a man in the back, but another to have an experienced warrior charge you. Heres's men were not nearly as battle-hardened as my father had been, but they seemed tough enough. I hoped my friends would be just as stout when the time came. I hoped I would be, too.

On the sixth day after Reas's death, the sling boy, Alrek, came running into the hall from the headlands. "Heres's ship comes!"

We had been sitting at the long table in the hall and now scrambled to our feet. "It is time," I said as calmly as I could. "Remember your positions and your tasks, and we will look back on this day with a smile. Go now!"

It was time to take our vengeance.

Chapter 25

Heres's ship came into view just as we found our positions. The wind was slight, so the ship came forward under oar, dripping sea from its blades. *Like venom from a serpent's fangs*, I thought and shuddered.

For the hundredth time, I questioned our displacement and our plan. I felt the tug of doubt in my mind and glanced over at the places where I knew my friends were hiding. Sigdag was with me in the shrubs, twenty paces straight back from the beach. She had a bow, arrows, and a knife. I had a spear and my seax. Twenty paces to my right, in the stand of birch trees, hid Turid with her bow and seax. Twenty paces to my left was Egil with a spear and a seax. Alrek and his sling hid farther off to my left in the seagrass. The two other children hid farther back, behind the main hall. If things went badly for us, they at least could escape.

The ship came on, cutting through the bay's waters that glistened in the evening sun. Only the gulls protested the intrusion. Heres's rotund form stood on the aft deck, his mallet-sized hand on the ship's steer board. His four henchmen rowed steadily at the oars, their backs to us. Herkus and Raban sat at the mast. I could just see their heads above the wales.

I willed the ship closer, hoping Heres would think nothing of the silent strand that greeted him. And just as I thought that, his arm went up and he called for his men to stop. I cursed under my breath, and Sigdag cast me a frightened look.

The ship glided forward a bit, then turned slightly in the current, giving me a better look at Heres. His eyes were scanning the beach, and I knew he was wondering why no one had come to greet him. He turned and fumbled at something beside him, then raised a horn to his lips. The stentorian blast echoed across the still waters. Of course, no one came.

The ship stopped some thirty paces from the shore. So close I could see the wrinkles of consternation on Heres's pudgy face. My heartbeat hammered in my chest and at my temples, and I began to sweat. I knew my friends would be getting jumpy, but we could not yet attack. The men needed to be ashore or our chance at capturing Heres's vessel was lost.

Heres called to his men. They dropped their oars and fumbled with their sea chests. In the aft deck, Heres wiggled into his byrnie and fastened his helm on his round head. Though the others had no chain mail, they had their weapons and their shields and they put them close to hand. At the mast, Herkus and Raban looked at each other, then craned their necks to see what the commotion was about. I prayed they understood but feared that, in their confusion, they would just get in the way. My heartbeat quickened.

Heres grabbed the steer board and waved his men forward. They rowed hard until the ship's prow bit into the sand, then they grabbed their shields and weapons and leaped onto the shore, forming a rough shield wall on the beach. Heres pulled his sword, pointed it at Herkus and Raban, and ushered them onto the strand. There, he positioned them before the shield wall, intending to use them as human shields for any attack that might come.

I looked at Sigdag, who was crouched beside me. She questioned me with her eyes, and I held up my hand to tell her to wait. She nodded. As she settled, an arrow flew from the trees to my right. The missile pierced Heres's thigh, for he had exposed himself as he positioned his thralls before the shield wall. He cried out for his men to attack.

"There!" he cried. "In the trees!"

They moved to their left, toward Turid, forcing Herkus and Raban to run before them. But as they turned, they exposed their right and rear to us, and I saw our advantage. I rose and cast my spear with all my strength. It arced over the beach and glanced off the helmet of the warrior on the right flank, causing him to stumble. The others followed my lead and attacked. Sigdag's first arrow flew high. Egil's spear skittered onto the beach behind the warriors. A stone hit the back of another man, and he cursed and spun. Truth be told, it was a pathetic first round, but it was enough to confuse the men and give us the advantage.

I grabbed the bow from Sigdag's hands and tossed her my seax. The man who I had dropped with my spear was rising, and I put an arrow into his side. He dropped again with a cry of pain. Herkus and Raban scurried away from the shield wall but not fast enough. Heres's sword carved into the back of Herkus and dropped him, but as he did that, he exposed himself yet again and another arrow from Turid pierced his shoulder. He fell back into the protective circle of his men.

"To the hall!" I heard him scream.

His men formed a circle of shields around their leader and rushed for the main hall, which meant they ran straight for me and Sigdag and for our traps. I stood then so that the men could see me and know who it was that was killing them. And I stood so that their eyes would be on me and not on the ground.

When they saw me, they yelled their fury and charged. One of them stepped into our trap and screamed as the stakes pierced his foot. The others turned to help their comrade, and as they did, I sent an arrow into the back of one of the men. Turid narrowly missed with another missile, but Alrek sent a stone into the head of the man whose foot was trapped. The man ceased his screaming and collapsed.

That left three to stagger toward me and Sigdag behind their shields, but I could tell they were defeated. We sprinted to the left, away from their rush and toward Egil. They tried to follow, but an arrow from Turid cured them of that idea.

"To the hall!" Heres ordered and I almost laughed. It was as I had hoped and, yes, expected. Heres was man enough to hurt unarmed thralls, but when faced with opposition, he and his men did not have the stomach for a fight. I watched them scurry like rodents for safety, knowing that they would only find death behind those walls.

As the door shut behind them, I hooted to alert the two children hiding behind the hall. They scurried forth and barred the door with a heavy iron bar I had created just for this occasion. Egil and I ran then for the fire in the yard and pulled two iron rods from the flames. To either end of the hall we went, placing our red-tipped rods into the thatch until it smoldered. Sigdag and Turid joined us, casting burning branches and small logs onto the hall's damp thatch. They then returned to the yard and pointed their arrows at the hall's main door.

It took more time than expected for the thatch to smoke, for it had been a wet summer and the top thatch was moist. Soon, however, flames appeared, and when they did, the men inside began to panic. I heard them hacking at the door with their blades and shouting at each other. In short order, they managed to open a ragged hole the size of a fist, but it would not help them. I took the bow from Sigdag and when the hole grew, I loosed an arrow into that gap. A man shouted and fell and I hoped it was not Heres, because I had plans for him.

The hacking stopped, and the pathetic pleas of Heres began. Flames danced now on the thatch as smoke billowed thickly from the hole in the hall's door. A man coughed violently. The thralls watched me.

"Turid. Stand beside me," I ordered. "Ready your bow. Egil. Open the door."

"Let them burn," he growled.

"Open it!" I shouted.

He moved to the door and kicked the bar free, then backed away with his seax at the ready. The door flew open, and out tumbled Heres and his one remaining guard in a cloud of gray smoke and searing embers. Heres was on his hands and knees, vomiting on the ground. Egil kicked his sword from his hands. The other man staggered toward me, a sword in his hand. Turid and I sent our arrows into his chest. He was dead before he hit the ground.

"Get up!" I yelled at Heres.

He continued to cough and spit.

"Get up!"

The thrall master climbed to his feet and wobbled before us. Blood pooled on the thigh of his trousers and dripped through the chain links in the byrnie where Turid had hit him with her arrows. He coughed violently again, then lifted his face to gaze at me. "I should have killed you the day I bought you, thrall."

"Aye," I agreed. "You should have, but you did not. And now it is you who will die."

"Where are my wife and son?" he asked between more stifled coughs.

"Dead," I said simply.

Raban joined us, and I directed him and Egil to bind Heres's hands. The slave master had lost much blood and was too weak to resist. I then tied a hemp rope around his thick neck and pulled him to a birch tree that looked strong enough to hold his weight. He gawked at the tree, then back at me. "I beg of you, kill me quickly. Show mercy."

I smiled wickedly at him. "You have driven mercy from me, Heres. I have none to give you. Nor do the others." I tossed the loose end of the rope over a thick branch and yanked until it was taut. "Egil, grab the switches."

He ran to recover the twigs the guards used to whip us. I had placed them in the pit-house for safekeeping. When he returned, I addressed the other thralls. "Take the switches and repay Heres for the pain he has caused you."

"No!" The thrall owner cried. "Please. Do not!"

But it was too late. Egil tossed a twig to Raban and walked forward.

"No!" Heres cried again.

The first blow cut Heres's cheek. The next ripped his arm. Raban smacked his head and his wounded thigh. Turid attacked his face and neck. On and on it went until every thrall had slaked their thirst for vengeance and Heres had been reduced to a whimpering patchwork of bloody lines. I nodded then to Egil and Raban, who joined me at the rope. Together we pulled until Heres's kicking feet left the ground. His bound hands clawed hopelessly at the hemp that crushed his windpipe and turned his blood-streaked face blue. His body jerked like a fish on a line. And then he hung still.

I would not offer him the dignity of laying his corpse on the soft ground. I tied the rope to the trunk of a nearby tree so that his lifeless body hung there for the world to see. I hoped he would hang there for eternity, though I knew the birds and rodents would pick his bones clean soon enough.

I walked back to the group and surveyed their stony faces. Like me, they were free now, and like me, their faces displayed none of the joy I would have expected. Behind them, the hall was an inferno of flame and ash and smoke. Down near the beach, I could hear the moans of those not yet dead.

"How is Herkus?" I asked Raban.

Raban shook his head. "He is dead. Poor man."

My stomach twisted at the news. In truth, I had thought more of us would perish that day, but even still, it was hard news to hear. "I am sorry," I offered.

I walked to the beach and retrieved my spear. Then, one by one, I stabbed the bodies of the guards to make sure they were dead before taking from them their weapons, their shields, and their wealth. The booty I stacked beside the fire in the yard as the others silently looked on. They did not move to help me, and I did not want them to. This was my burden to bear, or so I felt, for I had started this and I would end it. The booty collected, I returned to the ship to inspect it. In it was silver, trade goods, food, ale, ropes, and a few tools. I called to the others to help me store it all in the pit-house.

We buried Herkus in a shallow grave next to Pipin and placed stones around his grave to form the shape of a ship. It was a pleasant spot and one we knew he would have liked. Most of the thralls cried as we whispered our prayers over his grave and said our final farewells, but I felt no such sadness. I felt only a vast emptiness that was as wide as the sea. I was still angry and not yet ready to let it go. I also felt responsible for the lives of the others, and it pressed on me like a stone.

"Tomorrow morning, we will leave," I said to them when we had finished at the graves and entered the pit-house.

"Where will we go? What will we do?" asked Raban, who then belched.

"We head to Holmgard, in the land of the Rus."

My response was met with a cackle from Raban. Sigdag frowned and shrugged her shoulders as if to say "why?" Raban then spoke. "You, Turid, and Egil are from the Northern realms. I am from Prussia, as are Sigdag and the children here," he said, using his language's word for his homeland. "It is an even split, and we have but one boat. Did you think of that, Torgil?"

Raban had always been our jester. I had never heard threat in his words, nor had I ever heard him speak his mind. It made me frown. "We go there because it is our best chance to survive," I explained with all of the patience I could muster from my weary body. "Olaf is there, as is his uncle, Sigurd, who enjoys the favor of the prince. Without their help, we are just escaped thralls. Nithings."

I did not ask Egil, but he spoke anyway. "The Estland bastards killed my family, so it matters not to me where we go, so long as it is far away from here."

"You may not have a homeland to return to, Torgil," Raban added, "but in Prussia, our homes might still exist. We could find our kinsmen there. And shelter. Instead, you would have us sail days across an unknown sea to a place we know nothing about."

I had not thought that far ahead, and his reasoning, while sound, frustrated me. I needed to find Olaf. He was my shelter and still my charge, and with him, I would exact my vengeance on those who had taken so much from us. Raban threatened to take that from me, and that thought enraged me. "You are free now because of me and the courage of those who sit around you. Unless you wish to fight me too, I ask that you accept what I am saying to you and come with us."

"So now we are your thralls?" he countered with equal force. "Beholden to you?"

"No," I spat. "You are not. You are free to walk away now and find your way home. The ship that sits in the harbor will not be taking you there. Take a weapon and some food too, if you wish. I will not stop you."

Raban snorted and eyed the others.

"Torgil," interjected Turid more calmly. "Would you really turn out Raban, Sigdag, and the children? We are few. Our chances of survival are better as a group. Besides, we know not if Olaf is even in Holmgard."

"Nor do we know if Raban's kinfolk are even alive," I barked at them. "Either direction is a risk."

Raban cursed and lay back on his mattress. The others said no more. I gazed at the unease on their faces, and my stomach twisted. With a heavy sigh, I sat back against the wall of the pit-house and ran my dirty hand through my dirty hair.

It would be a long night.

Chapter 26

I did not sleep that night. At one point, Raban woke and looked over at me, and I purposefully moved my blade so he could see it in the light of the smoldering fire. He snorted and laid his head back down.

Long before dawn broke, I sheathed my seax and wandered out into the cold morning. As I left the pit-house, I counted the bodies and made sure they were all still asleep. Outside, the air was so thick with the smell of smoke and death that it raised the bile in my throat. I glanced at the hanging body of Heres and saw that the animals had started their feast. As much as I hated the man, I could not look at that gruesome sight for long.

I visted Heres's ship resting on the beach and worried briefly whether any of us knew how to sail it. I certainly was no sailor and only slightly remembered how ships worked. But I knew also that it was too late to worry about those things now — we would have to learn.

I climbed aboard and inspected the lines, the mast, the furled sail, and the steer board. I walked the deck and studied the nails and the wood. I went below deck to inspect the water the ship had taken on and was relieved to see it mostly dry. The ship itself was large enough and sturdy enough to carry us all to Holmgard, though as I pictured the journey in my mind, Raban's words crept into my thoughts. Like all of us, he and Sigdag had experienced innumerable horrors at the hands of Heres and his men. Why were they less worthy to return home than I was to reach my destination? The simple truth was that they were not. They deserved passage to their land, just as I deserved passage to Holmgard. The difference was that I had won the ship. They had not.

Beyond the aft wale, the first light of dawn was breaking, and as it did, I beseeched my father for some guidance. As if in response, a waddling of ducks took to the air — spooked, mayhap, by some sound — and headed southwest. Toward Prussia. I smiled wryly. Whether it was a divine sign or merely coincidence, I had my answer, and it was not as I had hoped. Of course.

When the others awoke, we gathered at the fire and broke our fast on boiled oats and apple bits prepared by Turid and Sigdag. Despite the awkward silence in which we ate, I, for one, savored the meal for the taste it left in my mouth and the warmth it left in my gut. But I could only eat a little, for I was not yet used to the feeling of a full stomach — it made me nauseous.

I set my bowl aside and stood before the others. They stopped and watched me with their uncertain eyes. "Last night, I spoke of sailing to Holmgard. I have reconsidered." I did not want to tell the others of my vision, for I did not know how they would receive it. "We sail to Prussia first." My words caused a commotion, and I held up my hand to silence them. "Those of us who are left will then try to reach Holmgard and Olaf. We leave today, if the weather holds. When you have finished breaking your fast, start loading the supplies in the ship."

Raban came to me then and hugged me. There was a big, toothless grin on his thin face. "I thank you, Torgil, for this deed. It will not be forgotten." Sigdag joined us and the tears in her eyes said more to me than any words she might have spoken. I glanced over at Egil and Turid, who had not risen but who smiled all the same, and I knew I had done right by them all. I just hoped we would live to enjoy the fruits of my decision.

We left when the sun was at its zenith and pulled the boat from the bay under oar. Despite the enormity of leaving the settlement behind, or mayhap because of it, none of us spoke. We simply watched it slip away.

Beyond the bay was a narrow channel that ran northwest to southeast between Saaremaa and the island to our east, Muhu. Once in the channel, we pointed the ship's prow southeast, toward the mainland of Est. The wind was gusting and unpredictable in that waterway, and we agreed as a group that it might be wisest to keep the sail furled. Thankfully, Egil and Raban had some familiarity with rowing, as did I, so between us, we managed to get the others accustomed to the stroke.

By early afternoon, we had rounded a tree-lined point and the ocean opened up before us into a vast gulf. Far off to the south was a distant shore. Closer in, to the east, was the mainland of the Est kingdom. Yet reaching either meant sailing across an expanse of windswept sea that I was not sure our crew was ready to handle. And so I chose to hang close to the shoreline on our right, which was the southern coast of Saaremaa.

Soon the wind settled, and I ventured a go at the sail, for our crew was weary and needed a break from the oars. None of us had much experience with the rigging, but eventually we managed to hoist the heavy sail and trim it to the wind. It still flapped, but even so, the prow bit more deeply into the sea and gave us a much-needed chance to rest.

Eventually the sky dimmed, and Egil worked his way back to me. "We should find a mooring," he said. "We need some sleep. The children are already slumbering near the prow."

I was reluctant to stop, but I knew we must and so I nodded. "Lower the yard and furl the sail. Get Raban to help. Have the women row. When I find a cove that looks safe enough, I will pull in so we can sleep."

We found a cove as the blue in the sky deepened and stars began to dot the heavens. It was a shallow inlet protected on the seaboard side by a line of sand islands that curled around the cove's opening like a crooked finger. Across the cove, the beach was a confusing jumble of sand dunes and grassy wetlands and waterways that led to what appeared to be inland lakes. I saw no shelters or halls, nor did I detect the smell of smoke or livestock. Besides the smell of the sea and the sound of the waves on the seaboard side of the islands, all was quiet in that place.

We anchored the ship in the bend of that protective finger and set about preparing a cold meal for the evening. Later, we shared sentry duty or tried to sleep. It was a useless endeavor for me. My mind was awash in thoughts that I could not dispel. They were like the waves rolling onto the islands that protected our ship, each with their own size and shape and force. Could we get to Prussia? What happened if there was another summer storm? Would we be capable of navigating it? What would happen if we encountered a warship on the way? Would we fight or try to evade? Could I endure thralldom again, or would I fight to the death? The questions rolled on until I finally sat up and rubbed my face as if to wipe them away.

I rose and stepped over the sleeping forms until I reached the aft deck. There, I watched the summer night's light play on the cove's rolling waters. It was a pleasant night, calm and warm, and it set my mind at ease.

"I could not sleep either," I heard a voice confess softly. I turned to see Turid there, a blanket draped over her shoulders. She walked to my side and stared out at the cove. "It is so peaceful."

"Aye," I admitted.

"After our life with Heres, I wish to feel this peace every day."

I understood how she felt. Part of me yearned for it too. But I knew that this peace was not to be my life. I was fettered to the revenge I sought, and it would not resemble this place or this moment. If the Norns granted me my chance, it would be more like the chaos of Ragnarok.

"I could leave you in Prussia," I offered, half jokingly. "You could seek life in one of those Christian places for women." I knew not the name for nunneries then, but I had heard some talk of them.

She ribbed me with her elbow. "Mayhap I will return to the seter of Astrid's father, if it still exists. That would not be such a bad place to live."

"No," I agreed, "it would not." I wanted to add that I wished she would have stayed when she had the chance, but that felt hard and wrong at this moment, so I held my tongue. She pulled the wool blanket tighter around her shoulders, as if the very thought of peace made her cold. "If we make it through this, I will help you find such a place," I said. "Though I think you would grow bored. You have too much of your father in you." I winked at her.

She smiled. "You are a good man, Torgil. Shy, but good." I gawked at her and she giggled, then she leaned in, kissed my cheek, and walked away. My hand moved to the place her lips had just touched as my eyes followed her retreating form.

Not long after, the morning dawned blue and cloudless and warm, with a gentle onshore breeze that carried with it the smell of the sea. A fine sailing day. We broke our fast on bread and water, our conversation hushed but excited. My friends were hopeful, as was I, if mayhap a bit frightened too.

"Let us get under way," I said as soon as the meal ended, and I worked my way back to the aft deck. I had just picked up a coil of rope to move it when Egil yelled, "Ships!"

I looked in the direction he pointed and dropped the rope.

Chapter 27

Coming into the bay to our left were two sleek warships, their dragon-headed prows glistening with sunlit sea spray. They had seen us and were bearing down on us under oar.

I cursed and yelled, "Shields and weapons!" I knew there was no way to outrun them.

We scrambled for our gear, then lined the port wale. In the lead warship, helmed men filled the foredeck near the prow. Several lifted their spears to taunt us, though their cries were faint on the breeze. They did not look like Estlanders or Northmen, but what did it matter? They were coming to kill us all the same.

I knew then that I was doomed, for I had no wish to be recaptured. I called to the others, "If you do not want to die this day, hand your weapons and shield to your neighbor and run. There is no shame in it."

Alrek and his young companions dropped their weapons and scampered over the steer board wale and onto the beach. I did not look back to watch them go, nor could I blame them. Only Alrek could wield a weapon, and his sling would be no use against byrnie-clad warriors and their shields.

My mind raced back to my father and the instructions he had hammered into the young lads back on Jel so long ago. No gaps! Work together! Trust your neighbor! "Tighten up!" I shouted, and our shields moved together in the center of the knarr. I thought to employ the bows, but we had not had time to string them and now it was too late.

The warships came on, their sloping prows, half a head taller than our own, carving through the sea like blades on skin. We would be fighting upward, while their ships' warriors would need only to rain their steel down upon our unprotected heads. They would make short work of their slaughter.

The thought of it infuriated me. "Come on, you bastards!" I yelled.

Onto the prow beam of the lead ship climbed a man in a glistening byrnie. His helm was conical and worked itself into a point from which a plume of hair exploded and danced on the wind behind his head. It was not a helmet I had seen before. He held his sword aloft and pointed it in our direction, like a god commanding his minions to strike. At any moment, he would command his ship to slow and slide up next to ours so that they could fight us broadside. I tensed and gripped my blade tighter.

When the prow man did finally call out, it was not with the words I expected to hear. "Halt!" he yelled.

The oarsmen drove their sweeps into the sea and hung on tightly. In the prow, the warriors lurched, and more than a few, including the man on the prow beam, nearly pitched into the sea. The trailing ship veered off to port, its steer board oars narrowly missing the aft beam of the lead ship as it rolled sideways and away. Thinking their intention was to capture us rather than fight, I lowered my shield, brandished my seax, and yelled at them. "Fight us, you cowards!"

But they did not. The warships glided to a stop some twenty paces from our gunwale, the warriors regarding us silently.

"Is that Torgil Torolvson I see? And Turid too?" called the man from the prow of the lead ship.

I lowered my sword and glanced at Turid. The confusion on her face was as great as my own. "Who are you?" I called.

He pulled the shining helmet from his head, and there stood Olaf before us, hale and vibrant and smiling from ear to ear.

A man with straight red hair pulled into a ponytail appeared beside him. "Thor's hairy balls, Olaf. What is the meaning of this? Why did we stop? Your careless command could have been the end of both of my ships." His face was as red as his hair.

Olaf's smiled vanished. He pointed to our ship. "Those," he said loud enough for us to hear, "are my friends: Torgil —-" he pointed his sword at me, then moved it to Turid —- "and Turid. The rest are the thralls with whom I lived and worked these past summers."

The man gazed at us, and I could see a resemblance to Astrid and to his father, Erik. And for the first time in days — mayhap months — I laughed.

"These are Sigurd's ships," Olaf explained with a jerk of his chin toward the tall, red-haired man who stood surveying the gaunt, wretched thralls who had escaped with me. Olaf reclined against the aft wale with a grin on his face, looking more like a man to me with his soft whiskers and fine tunic than ever before. Behind me, the others enjoyed the food and ministrations of Olaf's crew, giving us some time to speak alone. "I convinced Sigurd to come for you," Olaf said with his eyes on his uncle, "but he does not know that. He thinks I have come for the markets hereabouts that are lucrative, yet are not paying their share in taxes to the prince in Holmgard. And he thinks there is one man who is responsible for it, as well as for the enslavement of his sister."

"Klerkon," I guessed.

His grin stretched. "Klerkon. Aye. The bastard who killed your father and raped and sold my mother. The man who threw us into the cesspit of thralldom."

"Could you not have explained all of this to Sigurd when he found you last summer?" I asked a bit too sourly. "He might have come then. It would have spared us months of misery and the deaths of Pipin and Herkus."

His expression sobered. "There is nothing in the world that would have pleased me more, Torgil, than to rescue you all from Heres last summer," he said, and I believed him. "But I simply could not have then. I was newly found and had no leverage with my uncle. You are important to me, but to speak plainly, your family is not known to him and he is oath-sworn to a leader who has far greater issues to contend with. It took many conversations to convince him of the wealth of these markets and the guilt of Klerkon." He smoothed an errant strand of hair behind his ear, and for the first time, I noticed the gold ring that hung from his lobe.

"What's that?"

Olaf fingered the earring. "It is nothing. Just a little trinket I purchased in Holmgard."

"A gold ring is not nothing, nor is it a little trinket," I remarked suspiciously. I thought Olaf might tell me it was a gift from his uncle, or that he had earned it doing some great deed. I did not expect the answer he gave.

"Every Viking who comes to Holmgard wears one. It is to pay for my burial, should something befall me. Sigurd loaned me the coins to purchase it."

"Oh," I said, taken aback at first by the unexpected response, though I quickly recovered. "I hope you can repay it before you fall."

Olaf frowned. "I do not plan to fall," he responded haughtily.

I grinned. "No one plans to fall. Anyway," I switched the subject, "how long have you been in Estland?"

Olaf's brows furrowed. "We arrived half a moon ago. Our original plan was to come for you, then to sail for the market at Saaremaa and find Klerkon there. But weather delayed us. So instead, we headed for the market and struck." He grinned wolfishly. "Sigurd was well pleased with the booty and the information we gathered. Sadly, we missed Heres. It would have been a pleasure to kill that fat bastard. But it turns out that he did not escape danger. You left little of him or his family to find."

"They deserved it," I spat.

"They did," observed Olaf. He leaned closer. "I hope you took some of his wealth before you razed his place."

"We have some," I answered cagily, then switched the subject. "Have you found Klerkon?" I asked. "And what of your mother? Have you heard of her whereabouts?"

"We have not seen Klerkon, but we know where he lives. It took a little doing, but we eventually found a few Estlanders who were willing to tell us of his whereabouts." His eyes shifted to his leg. "Of my mother we have heard nothing."

I could hear the sadness in his voice. I was sad, too. She, like Olaf, had been my charge and as close as family. It pained me greatly to think she might still be alive somewhere, serving some master, yet I could not afford to dwell on it. Not until Klerkon was in his grave. I forced my thoughts back to the present. "Where is Klerkon?" I asked.

"Close," Olaf confirmed, then held up his hand. "But we will talk of it later with Sigurd. Tell me how you came to be here. Part of it, I can guess. But why here?"

I told him my horrid tale, starting with the plan that formed in my mind and ending with our escape. When it was told, Olaf clapped his hands together and hooted. "It is a remarkable story. I am proud of you, Torgil. I just wish I could have been there to see those swine breathe their last breaths. So where were you headed when we found you?"

"To Prussia," I mumbled, though I knew not why. Mayhap because I was afraid of the reaction I knew would come, and come it did.

Olaf laughed. "Prussia? Why?"

The heat rose in my cheeks, but it was not due to embarrassment. I was angry that Olaf would so callously disregard my words without understanding my reasons. "To return Raban, Sigdag, and the children to their homes," I said a bit too bitterly. "Would you not have done the same?"

He snorted and scrunched his face as if I were addle-brained. "No. I would not have. I would have sailed straight to Holmgard, with or without them." He relaxed back against the aft wale. It seemed he had grown in Sigurd's court, both in his body and his maturity. He was no longer a boy; he was a young man trying to make his way in the world. And he, like me, had been honed and whittled down by his thralldom. It remained to be seen what sort of man he had become, though I knew even then that I would need to readjust my thinking toward him.

"I gave Raban, Sigdag, and the children my word," I explained.

Olaf shrugged. "Your word no longer counts. The way I see it, these are Sigurd's ships, and he makes the call now. Which puts you in a predicament, Torgil. You can join Sigurd in our hunt for Klerkon, or you can refuse and sail with your crew to Prussia."

The smile on his face tore open every wound from our childhood. I wanted nothing more in that instant than to rip that smug expression from his face and for him to know that he was not as powerful as he thought he was, even with the backing of his uncle. Yet I also knew he was right — sailing to Prussia was folly and this hunt for Klerkon was the perfect excuse to rid myself of my promise. Stronger still was my hunger to kill Klerkon for the death of my father and all that had come after. And so, with those thoughts clawing at my mind, I acquiesced. "I will need you or Sigurd to explain the new plan."

Olaf smiled. "I am glad you have found your way to reason."

A short time later, Sigurd gathered together the ex-thralls, including the children, who had come back aboard when they saw no fighting. Olaf stood by his uncle's side, helping him translate into the Estland tongue. The other crewmembers hung off to the side. Anyone of them looked armed enough and capable enough to kill us all.

"My nephew," he began, motioning to Olaf, "has told me of your plight. It is good luck that we have found you. Our plan here in Estland is simple. We are here to take what riches are due to Grand Prince Sviatoslav in Novgorod —- the place we Northmen call Holmgard. And we are here to kill a slave trader named Klerkon, whom I believe you all know. When that is done, we will sail home. You may join us or you may go. If you go, you go by foot from here. We can provide weapons and food, but that is all. The knarr comes with us."

As Olaf translated, storm clouds broke on the faces of Raban and Sigdag, who looked at me. "I suppose you will be sailing with Olaf and his lord?" Though Sigurd did not understand the Est language, he heard the accusation in Raban's question and frowned.

I nodded. "I made an oath long ago to Olaf's father that I must keep. And I have vowed to avenge the death of my father, who died by Klerkon's blade. Did Klerkon not catch you, too? And you, Sigdag?"

This caught Raban off guard, and he shut his mouth. He looked at Sigdag and the three children who stood nearby. Finally, he nodded, as if confirming my question and coming to some sort of an agreement with himself all at once. "I will go with you," he said to Lord Sigurd in the Est tongue. "But in Holmgard, I will seek passage home."

When Olaf translated, Sigurd turned his gaze to Sigdag and Egil. They nodded in turn.

"So be it," replied Sigurd.

"So where do we find Klerkon?" I asked Sigurd. "Where is he hiding?"

Olaf indicated to an older man I had not seen before. He was standing among the Rus warriors, his hands bound before him. His straight silver hair fell to his back and partially covered his thin face, which showed several cuts and bruises. It was a familiar face, though I could not place it exactly. "We have found someone who knows. Juhan, here, used to fight for Klerkon. You might remember him? In any case, Juhan tells us that Klerkon lives just inland from a place called Viltina, which is southwest of here along the coast."

"Can we trust him?" Egil asked.

"No," answered Olaf, "but we have some insurance against his lies. His family sits in the other ship."

"We rest here today and plan," Lord Sigurd concluded firmly. "Tomorrow, we hunt."

Chapter 28

It was late morning by the time we angled into the bay. The weather had turned during the night and the clouds hung low and heavy over the rolling sea, partially shrouding the hill that climbed from the water on the far side of the deep inlet — a hill our captor, Juhan, identified as Viltina. Our destination.

I could see torches flickering on the crest of that place and felt my stomach tighten. According to Juhan, Viltina was a sacred meeting place and a burial ground, where for generations the Estlanders in this region had buried their chieftains. On the far side of the hill, beyond our sight, was a small harbor, and beyond that, inland, was a place known as Linnamae pold, which in the Est tongue meant hill-fort field. It was there, in a circle fort on a hill, that Klerkon housed his warriors and their families. Our mission was to draw Klerkon from his lair, if he was there at all.

The plan was simple. We were to approach Viltina in the knarr, disguised as traders, and take the sacred hill. On our signal, Sigurd's longships would then come behind us and find anchorages on the bay side of Viltina, out of sight of the fort. If we managed to draw Klerkon out, it would then be a race to our ships with the hope that Klerkon would follow.

"Why do we not just take and hold the hill and let Klerkon come to us?" I asked.

Sigurd frowned at me. "And give Klerkon time to plan and gather support from his neighbors? We have not the men to last in a battle of that sort, even if we stand on a hill. We need to provoke him so that he comes quickly. And we need to make him believe he can capture us."

Olaf stood near the prow of the knarr, Lord Sigurd at the steer board. At the oars rowed twelve of Sigurd's trusted Rus, six to a side. They were dressed as simple traders, though they carried swords and axes and seaxes on their belts. Raban, Sigdag, Turid, Egil, and I sat in the middle of the ship dressed as thralls, though each of us kept a weapon close to hand. It was not hard for us to look the part. We were the bait — the items to be traded. From my spot at the mast, I looked at Olaf, who must have felt my gaze upon his back because he turned and smiled his mischievous smile at me. It was meant to reassure me, but it twisted my stomach even more. I had seen that grin too many times to believe something good might come of it.

As our knarr drew closer to Viltina, warriors gathered on the hilltop, their spears and cloaks silhouetted by the flames. Below them, the sea rumbled and exploded as it crashed on a line of jagged rocks. Sigurd adjusted our approach, angling around the hill toward the place where we knew the harbor to lay.

The warriors trailed us as we rowed along their shore. One ran off, and I knew he headed to Klerkon's fort to alert the bastard of our presence. Several others marched down a narrow trail in the direction of a jetty that, like the hilltop, danced eerily in the glow of firelight. As we passed the jetty, a small dock with room enough for two ships came into view.

"Portside oars!" Olaf called, and the men on that side of the ship dug their oar blades into the sea as Sigurd pulled on the steer board. The ship pitched to port and glided toward the old dock, where four warriors now waited. Each carried a sword as well as a spear, but wore no armor or helm. They would regret that, I thought. Behind them, farther up the hill, stood two more warriors.

Olaf raised his hand, and the oarsmen back-rowed the knarr to a halt ten paces from the end of the dock.

"Greetings!" called Olaf in the Est tongue.

"Who are you?" called a dark-haired man from the head of the small group. "What is your business here?"

"We have heard that there is a renowned slaver in this area and we have wares for sale," Olaf called back, motioning toward us "thralls" as he did so.

"You are familiar. Have we met before?"

"It is possible," replied Olaf casually. "We are Estlanders, like you, and come from the mainland. We do not often trade in the islands but do so from time to time when we have goods to sell." Olaf shrugged. "May we dock? It has been a long journey, and I, for one, yearn for the feel of land beneath my feet."

The Estland leader studied Olaf, mayhap detecting a small accent in his speech, then raked his gaze over us until his eyes found Sigurd. Finally, he turned his attention back to Olaf. "I find it strange for a man so young to command a ship and crew."

I held my breath, but swift-minded Olaf did not hesitate. "Oh, I do not command here. My father does," he said, indicating Sigurd. "Long ago, the Rus took his tongue. I merely do the speaking for him."

The man hesitated for a long moment, then, finally, nodded. "Come ashore. We have sent for our lord. He shall be here soon."

"That is music to my ears," called Olaf. "We hope to make short business of this and be on our way." He motioned to the crew. "To the dock." He waved us forward.

The crew tossed our lines to the Estland warriors, who moved to tie them off on the pilings. It was then that our men struck. Olaf leaped from the foredeck, his sword hacking into the back of one of the men attending the lines. As he swung around to face another of the Estland spearmen, one of the Rus warriors sliced through the leg of the leader, who had come to peer over the gunwale into our ship. The leader fell screaming to the dock, where a sword thrust finished him. Another of the Rus hacked into the stomach of a third warrior before he could drop the line in his hand and parry with his spear. The fourth man, standing nearest Olaf, reacted quickly to the threat. He jabbed his spear at Olaf's chest, but Olaf thwarted it with his sword. Before the man could strike again, another of the Rus stabbed the Estlander in the back.

It was over before the Estlanders had time to scream their warning, but it mattered little — the two men on the hill had seen the skirmish and were now sprinting for the safety of the fort.

"Olaf! Go!" called Sigurd.

"Torgil! Turid! Come!" Olaf waved to us, and we scrambled up onto the gore-slickened deck and over the Estland corpses. I felt my legs wobble as we reached land but pushed through the sudden vertigo as I followed Olaf up the trail to the hilltop. I could hear Turid's footfalls and breathing behind me, but dared not look for fear of tripping on one of the many stones that dotted the path.

Cresting the hill, I gazed quickly around me. Hissing torches encircled the entire hilltop and the myriad grave mounds that lay upon it. I put the graves from my mind and cast my gaze about the place, looking for defenders but finding none. We sprinted to the far side of the hill, where we could look out upon the bay and the sea beyond. Though the clouds still hung low, I could just see the dragon ships near the bay's entrance. I hoped that they could see us too.

Olaf grabbed one of the torches and waved it side to side above his head. I, on the other hand, tossed one the torches down the hill toward the sea in the hopes that the men aboard the dragon ships would see the streaking flame and understand its meaning. A long blast on a battle horn carried to us from across the waves, and I hollered with delight. They had seen our signal.

"Torgil," Olaf commanded, "get to the other side of the hill and watch for Klerkon. Call to me when you see him coming. Take Turid with you."

The two of us sprinted to the inland side of the hill, dodging gravestones and leaping grave mounds as we went. Once there, we peered inland, spotting the fort in an instant. It was some three long arrow flights from our position —- closer than I expected.

The circle fort sat on the flat crest of another hill. Within its circular palisade huddled dozens of thatched rooftops. Below it, to the west and south, the landscape was lined with fields and dotted with dwellings of various sizes. To the east, the bay on which we had sailed narrowed into a finger of water that snaked around the hill fort and disappeared inland. Two large ships lay on the beach beside the waterway, and it was there that a throng of men had begun to gather. More men streamed from the dwellings and fort, called to service by the repeated blast of another horn. Even from this distance, I could see their weapons and shields and knew this would be no easy battle.

"There!" Turid said between heavy breaths, pointing to a large man near the ships around which others gathered.

I, too, was panting. "Aye," I confirmed. "There's the bastard himself."

"Should we call to Olaf?" she asked.

"Not yet. Let us see them move the ships into the water, and make sure that Klerkon is with them."

In the end, we need not have waited, for they did what Sigurd had expected them to do and pushed one of the large ships into the water. As the men clambered aboard behind their leader, I nudged Turid. "Time to go." Raising my voice, I called to Olaf. "Klerkon comes! Back to the ship! Make haste!"

He waved at me in confirmation, yet I still watched until I saw him move back down the trail. I knew him too well and did not believe he would stick to the plan. It was only when I saw him gain the dock that I raced after them. Turid had reached the dock as well and she called for me to hurry.

I ran as quickly as my feet could carry me. With myriad protruding stones and roots, it was not an easy path to run, made all the more difficult by Klerkon's ship, which I saw off to my left, coming toward us. On the dock, the crew had untied the knarr and were yelling for me to hurry. I pounded onto the dock, my breath heavy in my ear.

"Come on!" cried Olaf from his post in the knarr's prow.

I was five strides from the knar when crew pulled the ropes into the ship and pushed off. I leaped as it glided from its berth and landed hard on the packed deck, crashing into an oarsman as I landed. With a bellowed curse, he tumbled from the sea chest that served as his bench and collided with the steer board gunwale.

"Get him up and rowing!" Sigurd bellowed from the steer board.

Raban grabbed the oar from the man's hands and righted the sea chest while Egil yanked the man back into his place by his collar. I hauled myself over to the mast, doing my best to get out of the way as the oarsmen pulled our knarr about and pointed it in the direction of the sea.

"Pull, you louts! Pull!" roared Sigurd.

The oarsmen heaved on their oars, and we gained speed, albeit slowly, for the wind and tides were against us and knarrs are wider and slower than their sleek fighting sisters, the dragon ships. I stood and ventured a glance past Sigurd, back toward Klerkon's ship. To my alarm, his vessel had gained distance and was no more than two arrow flights from us. I looked in the opposite direction and saw our own dragon ships carving the sea under sail, coming fast, but still some distance off.

And in that instant, I knew that Klerkon would reach us first.

Chapter 29

We did not make it much farther.

In thirty strokes, Klerkon's ship had closed the distance, its prow beast now only a stone's throw from our small knarr. Our own dragon ships were still some distance off but coming fast. Estland warriors had gathered in the foredeck, yelling their jeers and curses so that the air reverberated with their calls. A few had bows, and they loosed their missiles at us as we rowed, though the rolling seas threw off their aim so that only a few came close to a victim.

Lord Sigurd made up his mind quickly. He raised the horn at his neck and blew a long blast into it, then he called out to us, "Let us give these ass-lickers something to remember! Hold tight!"

Olaf shouted the command for the benefit of those who did not speak the Northern tongue, but I was already on the move, clutching the mast with one arm and Turid with the other. Egil, Raban, and Sigdag gripped whatever stationary thing they could find.

Sigurd did not wait to see to our safety. "On my command!" he shouted, then waited for the dragon to close on us. He was waiting for the warship to commit to a side, for it would attack broadside either on our port or steer board wale. As soon as he saw its prow move to our steer board, he roared, "Steer board, dig in! Port side, oars up!" He waited for a heartbeat. "Now!" he bellowed.

Our knarr pitched dangerously as our oarsmen followed their leader's command and strained against the whirling momentum of the ship. Loose items skittered across the deck, some flipping over the wale and splashing into the cold sea, which lay not a hand's width from our steer board wale. The oarsmen on the port side held fast to the port wale, their oars momentarily forgotten and clattering in their oarlocks. A collective howl rolled from our lips as our knarr careened almost fully, then suddenly righted itself, landing broadside to Klerkon's approach.

On the aft deck, Sigurd held fast to a line with one hand and to the steer board with the other. "Shields!" he thundered, and those crewmen on the steer board side pulled their shields from the shield rack.

If there had been time, I would have muttered a prayer or scampered from the mast, but there was not. Klerkon's ship was no more than two ships' lengths distant, its prow beast towering above our craft and coming fast. Had Klerkon not veered right or left, his ship would have sliced our knarr in two, but in the slicing, the timber of his own ship would have crumbled. He must have known the danger, for he frantically waved his vessel off so that it passed not an oar's length from our stern. The Estlanders in the prow of his ship grabbed hastily for the wale or else stumbled backward with the force of the sudden change. Those oarsmen not quick enough to hold fast to something slid from their sea chests and rolled across the deck. Like Sigurd, Klerkon eventually righted his dragon, but not before it had sailed several lengths past us.

"Port side —- row! Steer board —- back row! Come about. Quick now," called Sigurd. For all of its clumsiness, a knarr is smaller than a large dragon, and this Sigurd used to our advantage. He brought the vessel around so that we now followed in Klerkon's wake.

"Row, men! Row!" Sigurd urged. "After them!"

Ahead of Klerkon's ship, our two dragons came quickly. I smiled at Klerkon's predicament, for our ships would press him from fore and aft, and he would be forced to fight on two fronts. But the wily bastard did not panic. He shouted a command that was lost in the breeze. His men drove their oar blades into the sea, then rowed in the opposite direction. Back toward us. My smile evaporated, for it was clear what Klerkon intended. He had seen the two dragons and knew this was a trap. His best hope was to return to his fort.

"Port oars, pull! Steer board oars, back row," Sigurd called.

Slowly, our knarr turned broadside to the oncoming prow of Klerkon's ship and blocked its path. I looked at Sigurd, wondering what he intended, but his stony gaze told me all I needed to know: he would not let Klerkon escape.

Klerkon's ship had picked up speed, and now he was left with a choice: ram our knarr, and possibly sink his own ship in the process, or try to evade once again. His portside oars lifted from the sea and his dragon ship tilted and turned in an attempt to skirt astern of us.

"Back row!" roared Sigurd.

The Rus crewmen dug their oars into the waves and pulled.

"Brace yourselves!"

With the sickening crunch of splintering wood, our knarr crashed into the hull of Klerkon's dragon as it tried to slip past our stern. The force of the collision spun our vessel broadside into the port wale of the warship, smashing oars and throwing men from their sea chests on both ships. Klerkon's ship tilted violently, then rolled back to port. Our own ship listed to port, and a wave of seawater splashed across our deck. We "thralls" clung to anything we could find, though still Sigdag and Egil slid across the deck into the port wale of our knarr, tangling with two Rus warriors there. At the stern, Sigurd hugged the steer board to keep from losing his feet.

"To arms!" he shouted into the chaos.

With surprising speed, the Rus hauled themselves to their feet, yanked shields from the racks, and slid blades from scabbards. Sigurd joined their ranks as they gathered amidships. I drew my own sword, hefted my shield, and formed up with my fellows behind the Rus. I would have liked to have looked into their faces and offered a last word of encouragement, but things were happening too quickly and my thoughts were too scattered.

Before us, Klerkon's men had recovered from the shock of the collision and were gathering themselves. Several of them hastily tossed their spears, but the weapons either sailed overhead or missed their targets. Up in the foredeck, Olaf hollered curses at them and brandished his blade. A few of Klerkon's men aimed their bows at him and loosed their arrows. Two missiles thudded into Olaf's raised shield. Two more streaked by his body. Another slammed into the prow near his head. "Your men are blind, Klerkon!" Olaf crowed. "My dead father can shoot better than that!"

I would have liked to haul my foolish charge from the foredeck, but I knew I could not reach him and so I left him to his fate. "Stay together!" I called to my friends. "Do not let them separate us."

"Back to your oars!" Klerkon called to his men. "Back, you louts!" He knew he could not engage, that doing so would expose him to our oncoming warships. But his men did not listen. Their arrows pounded into our shields, followed closely by their spears and their cries for blood. Something whizzed by my ear, and I ducked involuntarily.

Something else slammed into my shield. I thought it was a spear until I saw one of Sigurd's warriors fall at my feet, an arrow protruding from his forehead.

Klerkon's men poured over his gunwale, leaping the distance between our decks and slamming into our meager group of defenders. Some of the Rus caught the attackers mid-leap on their spear points. Others, they hacked as soon as they landed. I saw Sigurd sidestep a spear thrust, then spin and slice his blade across the spearman's face.

The sheer mass of warriors coming against us drove our men backward. Order evaporated. Over the chaos floated Klerkon's futile orders to return to the ship. Before me, a Rus warrior stumbled backward as an axe smashed his shield rim. The axe wielder was a giant of a man, but I did not hesitate. As he lifted his blade to strike again, I thrust my sword into the man's exposed armpit, then yanked it free. He turned to me — surprised, I suppose, to find me there — then died as the Rus warrior took his head.

To my left, I heard Turid shriek. She had fallen to the deck and lay on her back. As an Estlander stepped forward to finish her with his hand axe, I hacked into the man's spine. So deep did my blade bite that it would not dislodge. To my right, another warrior lunged. I had time only to raise my shield as his blade flashed. The force of his blow knocked me sidelong. He pursued me as I staggered but made it only a step before Turid hacked into his leg from her place on the deck. I smashed my shield rim into his nose as he bawled his pain, then fumbled for the axe that Turid's attacker had dropped. I turned to finish him, but there was no one to attack. Klerkon had managed to get his crew to return to his ship, and the surviving Estlanders were now scrambling to their sea chests and oars.

Without thinking, I tossed my axe at the slaver as he called to his men. It spun over the heads of the Rus and thudded, blade first, into Klerkon's armored chest. He staggered backward, shocked at the blow. But then the blade dislodged and fell to the deck. His armor had saved him, though I am certain my axe had pierced his skin. It certainly got his attention. His eyes found me standing on the knarr. No recognition crossed his face, but he raised his blade and pointed it at me in challenge as his men pushed their injured vessel from our ship and pulled away.

The fighting had ended on our ship, leaving in its wake a sickening weave of carnage. At least ten of Klerkon's men lay in warped postures of death, their limbs at strange angles or strangely absent. Intertwined in those corpses lay six of Sigurd's men. Raban lay near them in a puddle of blood, an Estland warrior across his legs. There was a puncture hole in his chest and a deep gash across his forehead. Crumpled beside him was Sigdag, her arm across his chest. Egil sat against the mast, his arm half-severed and bleeding profusely. Sigurd and six of his Rus warriors stood in the human wreckage with hands on knees, gasping for breath but alive.

"Turid. See to Egil!" I yelled as I scanned the deck for Olaf.

My eyes found him up near the foredeck. He lay face down, unmoving. I ran to him and knelt by his side, the hand of panic gripping my heart, a lump of grief in my throat. I rolled him over and searched his gore-slimed body for a wound but could find none. All I could see was a deep dent on his helmet. "Olaf!" I called.

Nothing.

Across from us, Klerkon and his men started to row, their oars smacking our hull as they clumsily pulled their listing craft against the current. I hesitated, caught between my desire to exact my revenge and my fear of losing Olaf. I turned back to my charge and shook his shoulders. "Olaf!" I yelled at him. "Get up!"

The port wale of Klerkon's ship crashed hard into our stern, throwing our vessel off-kilter yet again. Several of the crewmen stumbled backward, as did I. It was only when I recovered that I realized that one of our own dragon ships had arrived, cracking oars and timber as it scraped along the steer board length of Klerkon's vessel and drove it back into our knarr.

Lines flew from the Rus ship onto Klerkon's deck. Rus warriors streamed over the gunwales and onto the enemy vessel. The Estlanders grabbed their own weapons and flew from their sea chests. Seeing my chance, I quickly found my feet and rushed toward the prow, sword and shield in hand. I hauled myself up and onto the aft deck of Klerkon's ship and yelled at my prey.

"Klerkon!"

He spun and studied me with those calculating blue eyes, a hand axe in each hand, no shield in sight. He wore his byrnie and a helm, but it was those eyes that held my attention. They brought me back to the day that my father fell and we were enslaved. I could tell that the bastard had no clue who I was. It pained me to realize that, for I had dreamed of this moment for so long and yet I was no one to him — just one of hundreds whose lives he had destroyed.

"You do not remember me," I spat at him.

"No," he sneered, "though I will enjoy capturing you and selling you."

"You already did, you bastard. And for that, you will die!"

If he was intimidated by my words, he did not show it. He came at me with his hand axes swinging. He was lower than me and swung at my legs. I blocked the hack low to my left, then shifted my shield to the right, barely catching his second swipe with the rim of my shield. As his left arm came back, I swung down with my sword at his left shoulder, but he must have known the swing was coming, for he sidestepped right to avoid my blade, then slammed his axe down onto my blade. The blow was meant to knock the blade from my hand, and it nearly did, reverberating up my arm to my shoulder. I hung tight and moved right, jumping from the aft deck to give myself some space.

It was the wrong move.

Rather than stepping back and making him climb up to me, which would have proved difficult with my long sword and his hand axes, he was now on the same level and coming fast. As soon as my feet hit the deck, I spun and raised my shield to block his right axe, then jumped back to barely miss the swing from his left. But as I leaped, my feet landed against a sea chest and I fell backward over it. He came down hard with his right axe, barely missing my left leg, which lay awkwardly across the sea chest.

I now lay between two sea chests, my head propped against one and my legs draped across another. Klerkon yanked his axe from the chest near my leg and readied himself to finish me. And I knew that if I moved — if I removed my eyes from him even for a moment — he would kill me. And so I waited.

He smiled then, for he knew I was a dead man. To my right, I was vaguely aware of the fighting on the ship as his arm rose, then came down. I jerked to my right, just enough for his blade to find the wood of the sea chest instead of my skin. At the same time, I swung my blade across the deck and into Klerkon's ankle. It was not a hard blow, but he hollered nevertheless and leaped back, favoring the fresh wound.

I took that instant to roll over my right shoulder and come to my feet. Only it did not happen as I envisioned. My shield impeded my roll, as did my sword, so that I came to my feet awkwardly and much slower than I'd expected. Knowing Klerkon would be coming, I lifted my shield even before I stood. His blow struck so hard, it ripped through the wood planking and bit into my forearm and in the process, knocked me back once again. And once again, I found myself on my ass and looking up at my executioner.

"Rot in Hel!" he bellowed as he lifted his axe to strike.

But the blow never came.

Chapter 30

Before he could bring his blade down, Klerkon suddenly lurched forward.

I did not know what happened, but I did not hesitate. I drove my sword up into that bastard's stomach with all my might, a scream of fury on my lips as I felt his chainmail give way to my thrust and my sword slip into his body.

He looked down at the sword, at his blood seeping from his gut, then at me, those calculating blue eyes now squinting in outrage. He tried to swing his blades at me, but his arms would not obey his mind, and I grinned at his helplessness.

"Long ago, you killed my father and enslaved me and my friends. I claim your death in the name of my sire, Toralv Loose-beard, and my foster sister, Astrid Eriksdottir. May the fish feast on your corpse."

I yanked my sword from his belly and watched him stagger toward me, his hand axes still in his grip. He took a feeble step in my direction, then crumpled to the deck of his ship. With a roar that embodied every injustice, every pain, every loss that the Norns had woven for my life, I hacked my blade into that sorry creature's skull and finished him.

It was only after I ended his life that I saw the axe protruding from his back. There, on the aft deck, stood Olaf, wobbling on his feet but alive, an awkward grin on his face. "You are welcome," he called, then he, too, crumbled to the deck. Klerkon forgotten, I rushed to Olaf's side. His eyes were open, and his face stretched in a wide grin. "My head hurts," he mumbled.

"Better that than split by a blade," I countered, remembering the deep dent in his helmet. He was helmetless now but there was a mighty purple knot where the blow had struck and where a shallow crease in his skin seeped a dark rivulet of blood. He was lucky.

On Klerkon's ship, the fighting had stopped with the appearance of our second vessel and the death of Klerkon. Seeing their peril, the Estlanders had tossed their weapons to the deck and surrendered. Lord Sigurd climbed to the aft deck and studied the remaining Estlanders. He then looked down at me. "Tell them what I say."

I nodded.

"Which of you is Klerkon?" he called.

At the mention of their leader's name, the Estlanders looked at each other. I understood their confusion and pointed my sword at the corpse. "He is there, lord."

Lord Sigurd looked at me, then at the dead man on the deck. He stared at Klerkon for a long time, until finally he spat and turned back to the Estlanders. "We were here to kill this man, who enslaved my sister and my nephew. It is done now, and he has paid for his crime." He nodded to me and I translated. When I finished, he raised his index finger and continued, "But you lot have not paid. You have aided in his slaving and so you are partly to blame. And so, I will give you the choices you gave my sister and my nephew: death or thralldom. Which will it be?"

As soon as the Rus heard their leader's words, they stiffened between their shields, for they knew what his words meant. When the

Estlanders finally heard my translation, they raced for their weapons. None made it. Two of the Estlanders turned and dove into the sea, choosing a watery grave. I stood watching from the aft deck, too tired and too blood-sick to join the slaughter.

"Search the dead for wealth," Lord Sigurd commanded as he gazed upon the deck of the ship and the carpet of corpses that now covered it. "Then toss the Estlanders into the sea. Igor," he called to one of his men, "Inspect Klerkon's ship. If it is seaworthy, we will take it. If not, we will use it for kindling and to burn our own dead."

"What of their fort, lord?" asked another of his men.

Sigurd gazed at it and at the men gathered around the second ship that had not yet set sail, then shook his head. "We have not come to take the fort. We have come to kill Klerkon, and that we have done. I want us gone soon. Let us not give those Estlanders a reason to come for us again."

We left on the slack tide, leaving the badly damaged knarr to sink in the channel and dragging Klerkon's dragon behind us. On it lay our own dead, waiting until we could find a suitable place to burn them. Turid, Olaf, and I offered to ride on Klerkon's ship to keep the swooping gulls from the corpses. I did not like riding with the dead, for it was common knowledge that their restless souls could wander. But I liked less watching the birds pick the skin from their bones, especially the bones of our friends. Their deaths seemed punishment enough. I just prayed we would reach a suitable mooring before dark and give our friends and comrades the burial they deserved.

At that thought, my eyes fell on Raban and Sigdag, who lay next to each other. And Egil, whose bleeding had not stopped and who had died despite Turid's efforts to save him. I had thought myself incapable of grief after my treatment as a thrall, but there it was, rising from some unexpected well with such force that I was unable to control the tears that filled my eyes and bathed my cheeks. I gazed at my lap, ashamed of my weakness but incapable of suppressing it. Turid placed a gentle hand on my arm, which only made matters worse.

"They fought bravely, you know," she said, meaning our friends. "The gods will be kind to them."

I looked up at her and blinked away my tears. "I hope so. This was not their fight, and I feel the weight of their deaths on me."

"It was so their fight," Turid responded. "Klerkon enslaved them too. You must not carry the burden of their deaths."

I did not feel as resolute as Turid in that thinking. Still, I forced my mind to another thought that had been troubling me. "Where are the children?"

"They are safe on one of the ships," said Turid.

I sighed with relief, for I had forgotten about them. At least they still lived.

My eyes turned to Olaf, who stood amid the corpses, staring down at them with a strange detachment, as if they were dead bugs he had just discovered on the ground. It made me uncomfortable.

"Do you ever wonder why the Norns cut one man's life-thread and not another's?" He rolled a dead man over with his boot and stared into the man's white face.

"Aye, sometimes," I offered hesitantly.

"I do also," he admitted as he came over to us and sat. "I wonder, too, if they know their life-string is shorter than most. If they feel it, in here." He tapped his chest.

I did not know what Olaf was trying to say, nor did I want to be discussing some strange philosophy at that moment and so I held my tongue.

Turid broke the uneasy silence. "Do you feel it?"

"Aye. Only I do not feel the weight of doom. I feel something different. I cannot explain it, but the Norns have great things planned for me. They always have. My father used to tell me such things when I was little, but it is only now that I understand his words and feel that calling in my bones. And here." He patted his chest. "It is as if the Norns have woven a better path for my life."

I snorted. "The Norns have a funny way of showing their favor. They clip your father's threads. Enslave you. And knock you senseless in your first real battle. Had it not been for your helmet, you would be lying over there among the corpses." I motioned to the deck with my whiskered chin. "If you ask me, you wear the mark of a man who is lucky, not the mark of one chosen by the Norns for better things."

Turid laughed. "I agree with Torgil, Olaf. Besides, it is not wise to tempt the gods with all of this bluster about great things."

Olaf frowned and looked away. "You do not understand, but you will see."

I did not know how to respond to that, so I let the silence stretch and my memories waft back over the days and months and seasons I had spent with my friends in the bogs. They had been so close to freedom. So close.

"So we sail to Holmgard?" Turid asked, interrupting my sad reverie.

"Aye," Olaf responded, suddenly excited. "You will like it there. It is very cold in the winter, but the summer is beautiful. Uncle Sigurd has a large estate near the town. There is plenty of room and comfortable beds. No more sleeping on the ground in the cold."

I smiled at the thought.

"That does sound nice," whispered Turid.

"Uncle Sigurd is a good man. He lives well and treats his people fairly. It will be the same for you both. I am certain of it."

"What will we do there?" I wondered aloud.

"I suppose you will fight beside me, in Sigurd's guard. After his losses here, he will need more men." He nudged me with his elbow and grinned, seemingly unaware of the callousness in his words.

"What makes you think I would want to fight beside you?"

Now it was Olaf's turn to snort. "Because you made an oath to your father to protect me and you cannot break that oath."

I grunted, remembering my father's words about oaths and how they were like the strongest iron. "I have an oath to your mother, too. We should look for her."

Olaf nodded. "Sigurd has expressed no interest in it, so it will be up to us. And now is not the time."

I nodded. "We will go together to find her," I offered, then added, "When it is time."

"And me?" asked Turid. "What will I do on Sigurd's estate?"

Olaf shrugged. "I am certain you can find work. It is large and there is plenty to do. You will see."

"What if I do not wish to milk cows or serve ale to drunken warriors?"

Olaf and I looked at Turid. She returned our gaze but spoke no words, leaving the two of us to wonder at her meaning.

"We will discuss it with Sigurd," Olaf finally suggested.

And so we sailed for a mooring to bury our friends, and then to Holmgard, which the Rus called Novgorod, where I would join Sigurd's guard and Turid would find something to do besides milking cows or serving drunk warriors. And where Olaf would seek greatness, as the Norns had preordained.

Dear reader,

We hope you enjoyed reading *Forged By Iron*. Please take a moment to leave a review in Amazon, even if it's a short one. Your opinion is important to us.

Discover more books by Eric Schumacher at https://www.nextchapter.pub/authors/eric-schumacher-historical-fiction-author.

Want to know when one of our books is free or discounted for Kindle? Join the newsletter at http://eepurl.com/bqqB3H.

Best regards,
Eric Schumacher and the Next Chapter Team

You might also like:

God's Hammer by Eric Schumacher

To read the first chapter for free, head to:

https://www.nextchapter.pub/books/gods-hammer-historical-viking-adventure

Historical Notes

There were several historical tales written of Olaf's birth and flight from Norway, though all of them paint a slightly different picture. Nevertheless, through them runs a common storyline to which I tried to adhere. Olaf's father, Trygvi, died at the hands of Erik's sons. Olaf fled Norway, heading east with his mother and her foster father. The foster father's son, Torgil, was with them. During that flight, they were captured and enslaved by the Estlanders and eventually saved by Olaf's uncle on his mother's side, a man named Sigurd.

First, to those who know this saga, you will recognize that I altered the age of Olaf. While the sagas aren't clear on Torgil's age, they do state that Olaf was born while fleeing the agents of Harald Eriksson. I chose to make Olaf older at the start of the book. The boys will go through life together, and I wanted their interactions to start early on in this first book. In addition, if I adhered to the sagas, King Trygvi would have been rather old by the time he had Olaf, and it seemed just as plausible to make him slightly younger at the birth of his first child.

About Vingulmark. The name is believed to mean "impenetrable forest" on account of the forests that covered the area at that time. According to the sagas, the district, or fylke, of Vingulmark was given to King Trygvi by King Hakon Haraldsson (aka Hakon the Good) to rule. On Jel Island (or Jeløya), there are signs of inhabitants going back to the Iron Age, especially in the area around Thordruga, which is to-day called Torderød Gård, or Torderød Estate. There is no record of a borg on the hill where I placed Torolv's hall, but Jel Island was known as a stronghold in Vingulmark and so it seemed plausible enough to put something there.

Erik Bjodaskalli from Oprostadir is purported to be the father of Queen Astrid. It is believed his nickname means the "bald-head of Bjo-dar." The footnote about this in the Finlay and Faulkes translation of *Heimskringla* is "The nickname Bjodaskalli may refer to a farm called Bjodar, and this place is recorded in Hordaland." Hordaland is far to the west in Norway. Yet, the sagas also state that he is from Oprostadir, which is the name of a farm in Agder in southern Norway. All of this would suggest Astrid's father lived in western or southern Norway.

When Trygvi is killed in eastern Norway, the sagas state that Astrid fled to her father. It would make little sense for Astrid to flee west or south to her father's lands in Hordaland or Agder, respectively, and then flee again east to Sweden. Hence, I have made Oprostadir a place called Oppegard in eastern Norway, close to the path that Astrid takes to escape through Sweden. There is another reason, too, that I have changed Oprostadir to Oppegard in east Norway. Erik Bjodaskalli is said to have had sons with "estates in the east of the land," while Astrid had brothers who "dwelt east in the Vik." Since Erik Bjodaskalli's sons all seemed to have lived in the east of Norway, it is hard for me to imagine that Erik Bjodaskalli would live in the west or south, i.e., Hordaland or Agder.

My characters flee east from Norway into Sweden, pursued by an agent of Gunnhild. The pursuer in the sagas is named Hakon. Given the number of Hakons in my stories, I changed his name to Holger.

The fleeing group travels past Lake Vanern and through a small town called Ormsbro. Today, the town is called Örebro. There is no indication that it was once named after a fictitious founder, Orm, or even existed during this time period. The earliest we know of it is from roughly the thirteenth century, when it was called Örebro.

I also have my characters pass a tar production area in their flight to Sweden. Recent excavations have unearthed large-scale tar manufacturing areas in Sweden that seemed to have appeared in the eighth century. With the Viking maritime activities, tar production increased and tar became an important trade commodity. I added that historical nugget, not just to add a little spice to the story but also to point out that the Vikings may have been more advanced or industrialized in their pursuits than originally thought.

Regarding Olaf's capture by the Estlanders. *Heimskringla* mentions that Olaf was sold by Klerkon to a man named Klerk, and then to a churl named Reas for a cloak. In that account, Reas has a wife named Rekon and a son named Rekoni. The names are different in Oddr Snorrason's account, which is written earlier than *Heimskringla*. In his tale, the churl's name is Heres. His wife's name is Rekon. His son's name is Reas. I chose to use the names from Oddr's account since they were less similar and hopefully, less confusing. I also omitted Klerk from the story since nothing is known of him and he could very well have been the same person as Klerkon.

Furthermore, in *Heimskringla* it is stated of Olaf's time on Reas's (or Heres's) farm: "There tarried Olaf long and it fared well with him, and always was he mightily beloved by the churl." He may have been beloved by the churl, but I have a hard time believing that the son of a nobleman would have been overly excited to be the thrall of a churl, so I took creative license with that portion of the story.

About bog iron there has been much research. Most domestically produced iron in the Viking era was produced from bogs. There were usually two ways for people to find iron in bogs. In streams and bog pools, bog iron leaves an iridescent oily film on the surface of the water indicating that bog iron lies in the muddy depths somewhere nearby. Bog iron could also lie beneath peat in bogs. Using poles and turf knives, people located the small nodules of bog iron beneath the surface and harvested them for smelting. It was a painstaking, backbreaking process.

The harvested bog iron was smelted in carefully constructed furnaces to produce what is called the bloom, a mixture of low-carbon iron, slag, and charcoal. Repeated folding of the bloom drove out the impurities to create the final result: a billet or bar of malleable low-carbon iron, ready to be forged into tools and weapons. Because of the time-consuming processes used to create it, smelted iron was valuable. Rough iron bars were used as trade goods and even currency, and from them, weapons and other tools were created.

A study written by historian Andres Tvauri titled "The Migration Period, Pre-Viking Age, and Viking Age in Estonia" indicates that, since the Viking Age, the most "definite article of export" from Estonia was iron — a raw material that was in short supply all over Europe in the Iron and the Middle Ages. Iron from Saaremaa had low phosphor content, making it "especially high quality," and thus "a highly appreciated raw material." That historical tidbit became the basis for the thrall experience of Olaf and Torgil on Saaremaa.

According to the sagas, Olaf happened upon Klerkon in a marketplace in Holmgard (Novgorod) and drove a hand axe into the man's head to exact his vengeance for Torolv's death and his mother's enslavement. I wanted Torgil to be part of the action and I didn't want the encounter to be something that happened by chance. Hence, I kept the axe but changed the setting and action surrounding the encounter.

Which brings me to Klerkon's lair. Research unearthed a place called Linnamae pold, which in the Est tongue meant hill-fort field and was located just inland from an ancient burial ground on Saaremaa. There is no record as to who ruled in the fort, but excavations have discovered some riches there, suggesting it was a seat of power through the earlier days of Saaremaa. I chose that "hidden" fort to be Klerkon's seat of power.

Olaf and Torgil have now escaped the clutches of their masters and are headed to Holmgard (aka Novgorod), where more adventures await.

Other Books by Eric Schumacher

Eric Schumacher has also written a trilogy about Hakon Haraldsson (also known as Hakon the Good), which is available on Amazon, Audible, and other bookstores worldwide.

Hakon's Saga
Book 1 – *God's Hammer*
Book 2 – *Raven's Feast*
Book 3 – *War King*
Novella – *Mollebakken: The Rise of Bloodaxe*

About the Author

Eric Schumacher was born in Los Angeles in 1968. In addition to *Forged by Iron*, Schumacher is the author of three other historical fiction novels — *God's Hammer, Raven's Feast,* and *War King* — and one novella titled *Mollebakken: The Rise of Bloodaxe.* The trilogy and novella tell the story of the first Christian king of Viking Norway, Hakon Haraldsson, and his struggles to gain and hold the High Seat of his realm.

Schumacher's fascination with Vikings and medieval history began at a young age, though exactly why is not clear. While Los Angeles has its own unique history, there are no ancient monasteries or Viking burial sites or hidden hoards buried in fields. Still, from the earliest age, he was drawn to books about medieval kings and warlords and was fascinated by their stories and the turbulent times in which they lived. He is also certain that Tolkien helped feed his imagination with his Norse-infused stories of Middle Earth.

Schumacher now resides in Santa Barbara with his wife and two children and is busy working on his next book.

He can be found here:
Website: ericschumacher.net
Facebook: www.facebook.com/EricSchumacherAuthor
Twitter: @DarkAgeScribe

Printed in Great Britain
by Amazon

56094023R00177